In
a Midnight
Wood

ALSO BY ELLEN HART

In
a Midnight
Wood

ELLEN HART

MINOTAUR
BOOKS
NEW YORK

First published in the United States by Minotaur Books, an imprint of St. Martin's Publishing Group

www.minotaurbooks.com

Library of Congress Cataloging-in-Publication Data

Names: Hart, Ellen, author.
Title: In a midnight wood / Ellen Hart.
Description: First edition. | New York : Minotaur Books, 2020. |
    Series: Jane Lawless mysteries ; 27
Identifiers: LCCN 2020012779 | ISBN 9781250308443 (hardcover) |
    ISBN 9781250308450 (ebook)
Subjects: LCSH: Lawless, Jane (Fictitious character)—Fiction. |
    Women detectives—Minnesota—Minneapolis—Fiction. | Murder—
    Investigation—Fiction. | Lesbians—Fiction. | GSAFD: Mystery fiction.
Classification: LCC PS3558.A6775 I5 2020 | DDC 813/.54—dc23
LC record available at https://lccn.loc.gov/2020012779

Our books may be purchased in bulk for promotional, educational, or business use. Please contact your local bookseller or the Macmillan Corporate and Premium Sales Department at 1-800-221-7945, extension 5442, or by email at MacmillanSpecialMarkets@macmillan.com.

First Edition: 2020

10   9   8   7   6   5   4   3   2   1

For my grandchildren,
Avery Kruger-Williams, Mirabel Gibson,
Isaac Kruger-Reeh, Dylan Gibson and Teddy Damm.

And finally, at the beginning and at the end,
for my beloved Kathy.

Cast of Characters

Jane Lawless: Owner of the Lyme House restaurant. Podcast researcher/investigator.

Cordelia Thorn: Theatre director. Jane's best friend. Hattie's aunt.

Emma Granholm Anguelo: Friend of Jane and Cordelia. Small business owner. Owns home on Ice Lake. High school student in 1999.

Dave Tamborsky: Police officer/detective in Castle Lake. Longtime resident. High school student in 1999.

Mitch Tamborsky: Dave's father. Onetime chief of police in Castle Lake.

Monty Mickler: Manager of the Avalon Motor Inn. Dave's best friend. High school student in 1999. Longtime Castle Lake resident.

Kurt Steiner:	Butcher. Poet. Longtime Castle Lake resident. High school student in 1999.
Danny Steiner:	Kurt's son. Recently graduated from high school.
Sam Romilly:	Wendell's son. Scott's older brother. High school student in 1999.
Wendell Romilly:	Bank president. Sam and Scott's father.
Scott Romilly:	Banker. Sam's brother. Wendell's son. One year behind Sam in high school.
Leslie Harrow:	Mayor of Castle Lake.
Darius Pollard:	Mechanic. Friend of Sam's. High school student in 1999. Longtime Castle Lake resident.
Ty Niska:	High school student in 1999. Notorious bad boy.
Jim Hughes:	Real estate agent. High school student in 1999.
Wilburn Lowery:	Prospector. Former mail carrier in Castle Lake. Owner of antique store.
Ted Hammond:	Owns construction company. Senior Class President in 1999.

Carli Gilbert: Bank teller. Wife of Aaron. Friend of
                        Leslie Harrow.

Bobby Saltus: Police officer/detective in Castle Lake.

He was born in a midnight wood,
flesh of pine, of loam and mud.
He lived as a man and not a man,
with visions of a gaudy hope, till
tendrils of earth welcomed him
home to that place where sunlight
searches for that lost and lonely
child of midnight, who hungers still.

KURT JACOB STEINER
In a Midnight Wood

In
a Midnight
Wood

SAM

Saturday, October 9, 1999
Castle Lake, Minnesota

On the last day of Sam Romilly's life, he rose before daybreak and sat at the edge of his bed staring at the red numbers on the digital clock on the nightstand next to him. He spent a few moments struggling to fight off all the second thoughts trying to undermine his decision, but eventually gave up and simply started moving. He'd already prepped his backpack, which rested on a chair by the open window. A chilly breeze came in through the screen, ruffling the curtains. He hated sleeping in a warm room. Even in winter, he kept that window cracked at night. If his dad happened to notice, he'd come in and slam it shut, and then deliver a lecture. "We don't need to heat the entire outdoors, you know. You're wasting my money. One day you'll find out how hard it is to make a buck." And blah, blah, blah.

After yanking on his jeans, a sweatshirt, and hiking boots, Sam ran a hand through his hair. He needed to brush his teeth but was afraid that might wake his dad, so instead he unwrapped a stick of peppermint gum. His mom was dead to the world. These days, she drank in the evenings. At the kitchen table. And smoked. His dad had given up trying to control her drinking. She was apparently, like Sam, a lost cause.

After creeping past his brother's room, Sam turned and made his way down the stairs into the living room. In the darkness and the early morning quiet, every piece of furniture, every surface, spoke to him. There was the time his dad had rammed Sam's head into the wall next to the fireplace. The time he'd grabbed Sam's hair and pulled him over the back of the couch, dragging him upstairs to his bedroom and locking him in.

The worst beating Sam ever got was when he came home—way after curfew one weekend night during his sophomore year—and found his father sitting on the front porch waiting for him. The old man demanded to know where Sam had been. It was two freakin' a.m., he'd all but screamed.

Sam explained that he and a couple of his buddies had gone to see the *Rocky Horror Picture Show* in Fergus. He hadn't mentioned it because he knew he wouldn't be allowed to go. That was bad enough, but when his dad grabbed the front of Sam's shirt, pulling him close, Sam knew he was in for it. It took a moment for his dad's eyes to narrow, for his jaw to clench. He demanded to know what was on Sam's face. Sam stammered that it was eye makeup, which he'd forgotten to remove. He tried to explain that it was all part of the schtick. Everyone wore makeup to the movie, even the guys. As his dad hurled him off the porch, Sam heard him mutter that he would rather have a dead son than a gay one. "Is that what you think I am?" Sam demanded. The only answer he got was a vicious kick to his ribs.

In the last few months, much to Sam's amazement, a shift had begun to occur. The one part of the parental equation neither of them had foreseen was that Sam would one day grow up to be bigger, taller, and stronger than his dad. At seventeen, Sam was an athletic six foot one. He might still be scared of his old man, but the size thing was beginning to change the dynamics.

When his dad had come at him for some perceived infraction a few days before, fist clenched, Sam, almost as a reflex, had backed him up against the kitchen wall with a hand to his throat. The sheer surprise had been enough to disconnect his father's rage. He'd even noticed a small flicker of fear in his dad's eyes. But what Sam knew all too well was that it wouldn't end there. At times he felt the only way the war between them would ever end was if he killed his dad—or his dad killed him.

Sam stood by the front window for a few seconds, looking up at the sky, seeing the first rays of morning light. He had to get going. But as he was about to open the front door, he stopped and turned back to the stairs, sure that he'd heard the floor creak. He gave it a full minute before he slipped out and ran across the street. Hiding behind a tree, he watched the window shade on the second-floor landing slowly rise. He couldn't make out the dark silhouette behind it, but it had to be his father. And that pissed him off. On this day of all days, when his life was at a crossroads, his father wasn't going to dictate what he could and couldn't do. Hoisting up his backpack, Sam took off at a dead run toward Victory Park and the woods beyond.

1

Present Day, Castle Lake, Minnesota

Sgt. Dave Tamborsky, one of Castle Lake's finest, pulled his black-and-white police cruiser into a parking space in front of Rowdy's Hamburger Shack. It was eleven in the morning, and the temperature was already in the mid-nineties, a ridiculously hot day for late September. It might be kind of early for lunch, but Dave hadn't eaten any breakfast because he'd been called in early to work. He often stopped by Rowdy's because the couple who owned the place never charged him. Several years ago, he'd been the one to find their missing dog, Buttercup. He'd discovered the little Bichon by the side of the highway and rushed her to a local vet, thus saving her life. He'd just been doing his job, of course, but wasn't about to turn down free food.

Ordering a bacon cheeseburger, fries, and an ice-cold root beer, his usual, he climbed back into the front seat and drove slowly through town. His chief, Grady Larson, made it clear that none of his officers were supposed to eat while behind the wheel, but since Dave was a detective sergeant, one of only two on the police force, and a man with a love-hate relationship with rules, he sometimes ignored the instruction.

As he drove down Main, he nodded to the people he knew,

which was just about everyone. Dave had grown up in Castle Lake. His father, Mitch Tamborsky, had served as the town's police chief for sixteen years. From the time he was a little kid, Dave knew he wanted to be a cop. For one thing, he idolized his dad, thought he was the coolest, bravest, most honorable guy on earth. Beyond that, he liked being an authority figure. He also liked, much to the surprise of his younger self, helping people.

After high school, Dave was accepted into the law enforcement program at Hibbing Community College. His aunt lived in Hibbing, so he'd stayed with her while he was in school. After graduation, he'd taken a position with the Fergus Falls PD and was finally hired by the police department in Castle Lake three years later. The best part for Dave was the sense that he'd made his dad proud.

Turning off Main, Dave polished off the last of the fries as he drove past Grace Lutheran. It was a newer church, mostly one story except for the sanctuary part. It was nothing like Holy Trinity, the Catholic church two blocks farther east, with its red-and-tan patterned brick, clock tower, and gothic spires. In Dave's opinion, a church should be both beautiful and imposing. It shouldn't look like a bank.

Castle Lake, with a population of some forty-two hundred mainly upstanding souls, had seventeen churches of various denominations. While Dave's father was a firm believer in God, he'd never been interested in organized religion. He'd passed his distaste on to his children. Dave was a nominal member of Mount Olive Presbyterian. In a small town like Castle Lake, churchgoing, for anyone in the public eye, was more or less expected. If Dave had a weakness, it was his image. He wanted to be seen as a decent, fair, honest guy. So he went to church—not with any regularity, but he did show up for Sunday services every now and then, enough to look the part of the God-fearing citizen.

Driving past Holy Trinity a few minutes later, Dave pulled

into the rear parking lot to take a look at the graveyard, which stretched all the way to the wooded area south of town. It was the largest and oldest graveyard in Castle Lake, a place where teenagers, much to the displeasure of the priests, liked to hang out. Dave had busted a couple of kids for smoking dope there just last week. He'd taken the blunt away, given them a stern talking-to, and sent them packing, saying that if he saw them with any more weed, he'd arrest them. He'd taken the blunt home that night and smoked it in the privacy of his basement. Hypocrisy was also part of public life—not a lesson he'd learned from his father, but an important one nonetheless.

Seeing a knot of people standing around a backhoe a good thirty yards away, Dave parked his cruiser and got out. As he made his way across the grass, he noted that two priests were also in attendance, though it clearly wasn't a burial. "What's going on?" he called, seeing that a gravestone had been removed and set askew in the grass behind a freshly dug hole. A workman was standing in front of it, so Dave couldn't see the name on the stone. When the man moved and Dave saw it, his curiosity turned to concern. "Ida Beddemeyer?"

"Ah, Sergeant," said one of the priests, the ever-smiling Father Malcolm. "We're doing an exhumation."

Scowling, Dave demanded to see the documentation.

"It's all in order," said the priest, handing over several folded pages. "Although, I do agree, this is a rare situation for us."

"Al Beddemeyer, her husband, ordered it?" asked Dave, scanning the form

"That's right." Father Malcolm pulled on his earlobe. "Do you know Mr. Beddemeyer?"

"He was the principal at the high school when I went there."

"Then perhaps you've heard he's in hospice. The thing is—" Another pull on the earlobe. "It seems his wife always slept on the right side of the bed. He slept on the left."

"So?"

"It was that way in life. He wants it the same way in death."

"Are you serious?"

"Yes, I'm afraid I am."

"But Ida's been dead for—"

"Twenty years. She died a few months after I came to Holy Trinity. Al bought two plots right together, so I didn't see it as an insurmountable problem. We've already dug the new grave, as you can see. Once we're done, we'll exhume Ida's coffin and move it over, thus making room for Mr. Beddemeyer on his preferred side."

It was the most idiotic thing Dave had ever heard.

"We like to accommodate our parishioners whenever we can," continued the priest.

One of the workmen lowered himself into the newly dug hole and started sawing off tree roots left by the backhoe.

"We were hoping Mr. Beddemeyer could be with us today," added Father Malcolm, folding his hands in front of him, "but, sadly, that wasn't possible."

Dave moved to the edge of the pit and watched as the workman struggled with a particularly difficult root. As the man tugged at it, pulling it this way and that, a large chunk of dirt from the sidewall facing Ida's still-intact grave fell away, revealing something bright red behind it.

"What's that?" asked the priest.

"No idea," said the man in the hole.

"Dig it out."

Glancing over his shoulder, Dave saw that everyone had come to watch.

The workman removed a trowel from his back pocket and began working the red fabric free. "It's a backpack," he said after a few seconds. After brushing it off, he tossed it up to the man who, up until then, had been operating the backhoe.

7

"How'd it get under Mrs. Beddemeyer's grave?" asked the backhoe driver.

"Why don't we take a look inside?" said Father Malcolm.

"Give it here," ordered Dave. Amazingly, the nylon fabric was still in pretty good shape, and the zipper still worked. Crouching down, he placed it on the ground, then opened it, gazing at the contents. He removed a billfold and flipped it open, seeing a familiar name on the driver's license.

"What's it say?" asked the backhoe driver.

Clearing his throat, Dave looked up. "Sam Romilly."

Father Malcolm gave an audible gasp. "Wasn't he the young man who went missing?"

"I heard his dad did it," said one of the workmen.

"I heard that, too," muttered the guy in the pit.

Rising from his crouch, Dave said, "I've got to call this in. We need the crime-scene people out here. Nobody touch anything, hear me? You," he said, motioning to the man in the hole, "get out of there." To the priest, he said, "Don't leave. Don't touch the backpack. Don't touch anything. You're in charge until I get back."

Dave knew he should stay at the scene, but at the moment, he didn't care. There was a phone call he had to make ASAP. And for that, he needed privacy.

2

"When was the last time you had a long talk with Emma?" asked Cordelia, playing a game of solitaire on her phone as the trees and cornfields whizzed past.

"Oh, gosh," said Jane, slowing her truck so the man in the muscle car behind them could pass. Not that she needed to slow down. The guy had been going at least ninety when he'd roared up mere inches from the Ridgeline's bumper.

"Jeez," said Cordelia, sitting up straight. "That jerk's an accident waiting to happen. But back to my question."

"I suppose it was when we drove up for the funerals. Must be three years." Both of Emma's parents had died in a small-plane crash. Leo had been a licensed pilot since his mid-forties. He owned his own Cessna and flew it often, mostly back and forth to the cities. "Like you, we keep in touch mostly through emails."

"And now Emma's back home for another sad reason. But this time, it will be Cordelia and Jane to the rescue."

"How do you figure that?"

"We'll cheer her up. And then we'll provide her with lots of sage advice."

Jane wasn't so sure Emma wanted advice.

Jane Lawless and Cordelia Thorn were best friends—had been

ever since high school. While Jane had gone on to become a restaurateur, developing The Lyme House on Lake Harriet in Minneapolis, Cordelia had been working as a creative director, first at the Blackburn Playhouse in Shoreview, and later at the AGRT in St. Paul. She and her generally missing-in-action sister, Octavia, had opened the new Thorn Lester Playhouse in downtown Minneapolis in 2012.

Jane had first met the Granholms when they'd rented the house next to her family home in St. Paul. After a lengthy stint in the military, Leo was finally finishing his law degree at William Mitchell and at the time, his wife, Audrey, was a stay-at-home mom. Jane's dad and Leo became fast friends, bonding over the law and their love of fishing. After the Granholms moved back to Castle Lake, where Leo and Audrey had grown up, they'd invite Jane's family, often including Cordelia, up for a long weekend every summer. It all seemed like such ancient history now.

"Hattie and I drove up two summers ago, when Emma and her daughter had flown back from California for the dedication of that bronze plaque in honor of her mom and dad." Cordelia searched her purse, probably looking for something to eat. "Remember? If it hadn't been for Audrey and Leo, there wouldn't be an art center."

"Did Hattie have a good time?"

Hattie Thorn Lester was Cordelia's thirteen-year-old niece. She'd lived with Cordelia since she was a little girl, mainly because her mother, Cordelia's sister, was usually on the hunt somewhere in the known universe for her next husband.

"She loved it. So many new bugs to examine and categorize. She's moved on since then. Did I tell you she's into Carlo Rovelli now?"

"Who's he?"

"A theoretical physicist. She has one of his books with her at all times. In fact—" Cordelia looked over both shoulders and then lowered her voice. "I squirreled one of them out of the house before I left."

"Why?"

"I need to figure out why she finds his ideas so compelling."

"I'm sure she'd tell you if you asked."

"Oh, she reads me passages all the time. Things about gravity. Electromagnetism. The space-time continuum—things I already know everything about. No, there has to be more. Did I mention what she wants next?"

"Let me guess. A mass spectrometer?"

"A private math tutor. Get this: She said the entire cosmos can be understood in terms of math. Math! Nothing about theater or music or literature. It boggles the mind."

"She's every bit as intense as you are, Cordelia, she just has a different approach."

"Yes, but this science thing gets kind of old. I mean, offer her a book on art deco and one on metallurgy and which do you think she'd pick?"

"I see your point."

"To have a titan of the arts for an auntie seems like such a waste."

"But you adore her."

"Well, there's that."

They were driving up on Saturday so they could both relax for a few days before the annual Castle Lake Arts Festival began. Emma had convinced Jane to offer a gourmet dinner, prepared by her, as a way to make money for the silent auction benefiting the center. Cordelia had agreed to do several meetings and speeches and a visit to the local high school.

Emma lived in California these days, but because her marriage was in trouble, she'd come home to Castle Lake for the summer to get away and try to figure out what to do next. She'd confided to Jane that she was glad now she'd been unable to sell her parents' house. It was a place where she felt comfortable and safe, a retreat from her chaotic life in Mountain View. She wanted Jane and Cordelia to stay with her while they were in town.

"Does it make you feel old that you used to babysit Emma?" asked Cordelia.

"No. Yes. I don't know." Emma was forty, Jane thirteen years older.

"Take Ewing Road to the lake," said Cordelia. "It's faster."

"I know how to get to the house," said Jane.

"Consider me a GPS with opinions."

It was just after three when they pulled into the driveway next to the Granholm house. The stone-and-timber structure was the largest and grandest property on Ice Lake, having been built in the early nineteen hundreds by the son of L. R. Granholm, the patriarch of the family. According to what Jane had learned from Leo, L.R. was a dairy and wheat farmer who was responsible for the development of the Farmer's Grange Association in Castle Lake, Clarksville, and Fergus Falls. His son, Edward, worked as a land developer. He was the one who had amassed the family fortune, such as it was. He was also one of Castle Lake's longest-serving mayors.

As soon as Jane eased the truck to a stop on the cobblestone drive, Cordelia was out the door. Jane spent a few minutes removing luggage from the backseat of the cab, waiting for Cordelia to return with Emma. When she did come back, she was alone.

"Nobody's home."

"Really?" said Jane. "I texted her when we'd be arriving."

"Well, she's not here."

As they dithered about what to do, a white convertible came sailing around a curve in the Granholm's private access road, one that connected the house to the highway.

"Ah, our landlord," said Cordelia.

Emma pulled up next to them and cut the engine. Her long brown hair was tangled by the wind, held away from her face by a pair of sunglasses. She pulled the glasses down over her eyes before she spoke. "Sorry to be late."

"What's wrong?" asked Cordelia. "Have you been crying?"

"I just got some bad news. It's about my old boyfriend, Sam Romilly."

Emma had talked about him many times over the years, telling Jane that he'd gone missing at the beginning of their senior year. Nobody had ever seen or heard from him again.

"What about him?" asked Jane.

"I just talked to Dave Tamborsky, this idiot football jock I went to high school with. He's a cop now. Still a jerk. Seems Holy Trinity was excavating a grave this morning, and a workman found Sam's backpack underneath the coffin."

"His backpack?" repeated Jane.

Emma looked from face to face. "There were bones, too. This is so unbelievable. I can't get my head around it. After all these years, to find him like that. I mean, why on earth would someone bury him under Ida Beddemeyer?"

Cordelia did a double take. "Who's Ida Beddemeyer?"

"She was the wife of our old high school principal."

"Heavens," said Cordelia, waving air into her face.

"Are they sure the remains belong to Sam?" asked Jane.

"Dave said they'd need to send everything to the Bureau of Criminal Apprehension in St. Paul for testing, but yeah, he was pretty sure."

"Let's go inside, out of this heat," said Cordelia, slipping her arm around Emma. "I'll get you something cold to drink. Then we can all sit down together and talk."

Emma nodded, allowing herself to be guided toward the front door.

Jane was left to schlep the luggage inside by herself.

3

Steiner's Meats had been a fixture in Castle Lake since 1947, when Kurt Steiner's grandfather had opened the doors for the first time. Kurt had learned the butchering trade from his dad. He loved the shop and enjoyed working with local farmers to find the best, the most humanely raised animals. Unlike big cities, which were only now catching on to the notion that buying local was a good idea, small town folks had known that forever.

Kurt usually spent his afternoon break sitting on a bench outside the storefront on Main Street. He liked to get a little fresh air when he could, though today the heat and humidity didn't offer any great pleasure. Still, he needed a breather, and this was all he'd get until the store closed at six.

Several years ago, Kurt's dad, Otto, had been thinking about adding a few shelves of groceries and produce, but Kurt had argued against it. Grocery stores in rural Minnesota were hard to come by and sustain. Castle Lake was lucky enough to have one that was prospering, and Kurt saw no reason to compete with it. On the other hand, he'd been aching to buy a used commercial rotisserie from a store over in St. Cloud that was going out of business. Along with rotisserie chickens, he wanted to offer a few sides. Nothing weird. Mostly, he'd chosen things he'd loved all his life, such as cornbread, baked beans, potato salad, and coleslaw. His father had eventually agreed to buy the rotisserie and slowly, their little mini-deli had begun to bring in new customers.

At seventy-two, Kurt's dad still worked a couple days a week. His mom pitched in most Saturdays. At the moment, they were in Florida on vacation, which meant that their only employee, a local woman, Judy Nygaard, was putting in extra hours.

Returning to the shop, Kurt took a few seconds to check out the meat counter and the deli case from his customer's-eye view. Everything looked good. Judy had worked from ten to two and always left the displays looking clean and neat.

This was the slowest part of the day. Kurt did most of the butchering in the early morning hours, when the market was closed. Today, before he left to go home, he needed to finish making one of the store's bestsellers, a Rostbratwurst flavored with caraway and marjoram. People in town usually bought it and served it with sauerkraut and potatoes and a side of horseradish cream. As he swung around the side of the counter and headed into the workroom, he heard the bell over the front door ding.

"Hey, Steiner," came a male voice. "You got a sec?"

When Kurt turned around and found Monty Mickler leaning his arms over the top of the counter, his mood instantly soured. Kurt thought of himself as a generally easygoing guy. He liked most people, but Mickler was someone he loathed. He hadn't spoken to him in years and saw no reason to change that now.

"What do you want?" demanded Kurt.

Lowering his voice, Mickler said, "Got a call from Tamborsky a while ago. Seems they were exhuming a coffin this morning in the graveyard behind Holy Trinity. They found Sam's backpack and a bunch of bones."

Kurt felt as if he'd been hit in the head with a baseball bat. "How—"

"Don't ask me anything else because that's all I know."

Images came flooding back, mental snapshots he thought he'd buried long ago.

"You okay, man?" asked Mickler. "You've gone totally white."

Kurt raced for the back door to the alley. He reached a rusted metal drum just seconds before he threw up. Wiping a hand across his mouth, he saw that Mickler had followed him outside.

"Hey, keep it together, bro. Dave's gonna handle it."

"How?"

"He's a cop. Everything's cool."

Still leaning over the metal drum, Kurt said, "Get out of here."

"What?"

Turning to face him, he yelled. "Get the hell out of here before I beat the living crap out of you." He went at him with his fist clenched.

"Jeez," said Mickler, backing up. "Don't shoot the freakin' messenger."

"Leave," screamed Kurt, feeling blood rush to his face.

Mickler barely missed a stack of packing crates as he scrambled out of the alley.

4

When Dave was finally done at the graveyard, he drove over to the home of Wendell Romilly, Sam's father. It wasn't the same house where Sam had lived during his high school years. This one was newer, bigger, with a view of the river.

Romilly, dressed in white slacks and a blue golf polo, ushered him into an expansive living room. Going from the outside heat into the refrigerator-like cold inside the house made him shiver. From Romilly's annoyed demeanor, Dave assumed he hadn't heard the news. Sam's mother had died long ago, so at least she would be spared learning the truth about what had happened to her son.

Dave figured that most people in town saw Wendell Romilly as a pillar of the community. He was president of one of the local banks, active at his church, served on several boards. But Dave viewed him differently. To him, Romilly was an entitled asshole, unimpressed by any authority other than his own. Police officers simply didn't show up unannounced at his front door. This was the one part of his job Dave really liked. He enjoyed seeing people like Romilly thrown off balance.

Romilly was a slight man in his late sixties. His skin was so dark from hours spent on the golf course that he looked like a wizened nut. Dave remembered when he hadn't been quite so wrinkly, back when his hair was dark and his glasses were larger, hiding his owlish glare.

"I'm afraid I've got some bad news," said Dave.

"Oh?"

"I think we should sit down."

Romilly lowered himself hesitantly onto a chair. Dave sat on the couch. He explained about the backpack found under Ida Beddemeyer's grave, the billfold found inside. Through it all, Romilly remained silent and stoic. At the very least, Dave thought, he could have squeezed out a little surprise. "I'll need to take a sample of your DNA."

"To prove the remains belong to my son."

"It's not painful."

"I know that, Dave."

Dave's jaw tightened. "Thank you, Wendell. 'Course, I could ask Scott if you'd prefer." Scott was Wendell's younger son.

"No, I'll do it. Just let me know where and when."

"Will do." As Dave rose, Romilly did, too.

"That's it?" asked Romilly.

"For now."

"So, you're saying Sam was the victim of a homicide?"

"We're treating it as a suspicious death, but yes, I don't think Sam buried himself under that coffin. Would you like me to give Scott the news?"

"No, I'll do it." He paused. "You may think my reaction is somewhat less than it should be. All I can say is, I gave up believing I'd ever see my son again a long time ago."

"Uh-huh."

"Any idea who might have done it?"

"Not yet."

"I hope you do a better job with your investigation than your father did."

Dave stiffened but refused to take the bait. His dad's investigation had been the best it could be, under the circumstances. He turned and started for the door.

"I suppose this will stir everything up again," continued Romilly. "People will come out of the woodwork with all their ridiculous theories. I seem to be an easy target. You know, of course, that your father cleared me of any wrongdoing."

"Did he?"

"Talk to him. He'll give you the details."

"I'll do that." Walking out on the front step, Dave touched the brim of his hat. "Thanks for your time." Asshole.

Dave's dad's house was only a few blocks away from the public safety building, where the police station was located. He found him wearing nothing but swim trunks and a pair of old running shoes, in the alley, halfway to the end of the block. "Hey," he shouted.

His dad turned, looking confused.

"Hey, Pop, I need to talk to you."

"Now?"

The garden hose was lying in the grass in the backyard, belching water. Dave wondered if his father had hosed himself down to cool off in the afternoon heat and forgotten to turn it off. "Where were you going?" he asked as his dad tramped back into the yard.

"I was . . . looking for something."

"Like what?"

"My lost youth. What do you want?"

Dave turned off the hose on his way to the house. "Where's that big fan?" he asked, coming into the living room. "You told me you were going to bring it up from the basement."

"I forgot. Besides, we're supposed to have a storm tonight. That should blow in cooler temperatures."

"But until it does, you need some air movement in here." Dave headed into the front hall and opened the door to the basement.

Once downstairs, he quickly found the fan pushed behind a bunch of clutter in the laundry room. He dug it out and returned upstairs, plugging it into an electric socket next to the TV. "There," he said, hands on his hips. It didn't seem right that a creep like Wendell Romilly lived in a refrigerator when his dad, who'd spent his entire life serving the community instead of making money off it, had to live inside an oven. "I got you something."

"What?" asked his father, stretching his hands toward the breeze.

Dave went back out to the squad car, lifted a box out of the backseat, and carried it into the house. "I got this for you at the hardware store yesterday. The air conditioners were all marked down for an end-of-summer sale. Won't take but a few minutes to install it in your bedroom window. At least then you can sleep tonight."

"I can put it in," said his father, getting up to take a closer look at what was written on the outside of the box.

"You sure?"

"I'm not an invalid, although I'm not sure I can afford it."

"Consider it an early Christmas present."

His father looked up at him. "You're a good son."

"Whatever. Look, there's something I need to talk to you about."

"Go get us a couple of cold ones and then I'll be happy to talk about anything."

Crossing into the kitchen, Dave saw that the sink was full of dishes. His father might be spit-and-polish when it came to his uniform, back when he was still wearing one, but he'd never taken much interest in housework. When Dave opened the refrigerator, he found his dad's billfold next to the mayonnaise. Dave had noticed other instances of his dad's forgetfulness in the last couple of months, but wasn't sure how much he should worry about them.

Returning to the living room, he sat down on the couch next to his father. "Were you looking for this?" He held up the billfold.

21

"Not that I remember."

"It was in the refrigerator."

"Probably wanted to cool off. Only one beer?"

Dave handed it to him. "It's a little early for me. Besides, I've got to write up a report."

"Too bad for you." He twisted off the cap and tossed it into an ashtray already filled with caps.

"Listen," said Dave, watching his dad down half the beer, "we found Sam Romilly's remains today."

"That kid in your class who went missing? Where?"

"In Holy Trinity cemetery."

"My God. You're sure?"

"Besides the bones, which, by the way, we found under a coffin that was being exhumed, we also found his backpack and billfold."

"Wow," said his dad, leaning back against the couch cushions. His gaze locked on Dave.

"What?"

"Nothing."

"No, tell me."

"It's nothing, son. Why are you so jumpy?"

"You handled the original investigation."

"Right." He took another swallow of beer.

"What do you remember about it?"

"Well," he said, resting the beer bottle on his thigh. "As I recall, we didn't have many leads. I followed up on what I could, but it never went anywhere."

Dave waited, but when his dad said nothing more, he continued, "I just talked to Wendell Romilly. You remember him?"

"The father."

"He said you'd cleared him of any connection to Sam's disappearance."

"Nah, that's not right. Since we couldn't prove a crime, I could hardly clear anyone. Check my report. I probably filed more than one."

Dave had already looked at them. Right after he joined the force, it was the first thing he'd done—privately, of course. He also knew that a police officer didn't always put everything he'd learned or suspected in an official report. That's what he was after—that and one last confirmation that his father really didn't know anything. "Okay, but what about your field notes?"

"There was a box in the basement with some of my notebooks in it. Your mom would get sick of looking at them and toss them in it to get rid of them. If you can't find the box, go ask her if she knows where it went."

Dave's mom and dad had divorced many years ago. Theirs had not been a match made in heaven. Then again, living with a cop wasn't easy. It was one reason Dave had remained single. These days, his mom lived in Hackett with her two Westies, which was fine with him. They'd never gotten along.

"I'll take a look in the basement," said Dave. "Except I can't do it now." He was disappointed that his dad didn't have more to offer. "Think about your investigation, okay? Maybe when we talk next, you can go into more detail."

"I'll try," said his father. "Hey, before you go, get me another beer."

Dave studied him a moment, seeing nothing but the ever calm, always forthright older version of the man he'd always been so proud to call his father. "Sure thing. One beer coming right up."

5

Emma had planned to make her mother's famous fried chicken for dinner, but because she was so unhinged by the news about Sam Romilly, Jane took a look in the refrigerator and offered to do it herself. She'd found one of Audrey's old recipe books and, while Cordelia and Emma talked out on the patio, Jane got to work.

By six, they were seated at the dining room table, enjoying the chicken, some roasted potatoes and carrots with fresh rosemary, and thick slices of homegrown tomatoes. After a few glasses of wine, Emma seemed to be in a better mood, so the conversation drifted to less fraught topics.

"How goes the candy store?" asked Cordelia, reaching for the corkscrew to open a second bottle of wine.

Emma had received her bachelor's degree in psychology from Stanford. While there, she'd met a young man, Philip Anguelo, a computer whiz who had just partnered with a couple of friends to build a tech start-up. The start-up took off like a rocket, and Philip and Emma married the following year. Their daughter, Verity, came along soon thereafter.

Emma was home with Verity during her early years, but when her daughter was diagnosed with childhood diabetes, Emma turned her energy to creating sweets that her daughter could actually eat.

That led to other parents wanting the sweet treats, and eventually Emma set up a website and began to offer her wares online. She'd apparently never wanted to be a stay-at-home mom, so she was more than willing to ride the wave.

"I'm selling the company," she said, pressing a napkin to her lips.

"Selling?" said Jane.

"But what about our annual Christmas box of chocolates?" asked Cordelia.

"You'll get one this year, but after that, you're on your own."

"What happened?" asked Jane.

"I got this incredible offer last spring, and I couldn't turn it down. I had to think about it for a while, which is why I never talked about it." She held her wineglass as Cordelia refilled it. "I might as well tell you right up front: I've asked Philip for a divorce."

"Oh, Emma," said Jane. It wasn't unexpected, but she was still sad that it had come to that.

Emma held up her hand. "But turns out, it's not that simple. Philip is Catholic. Or, I should say, his parents are Catholic. As long as they're alive, he says he's stuck with me and I'm apparently stuck with him. Even so, however it turns out, I'm done forever with the marriage thing. The good part is, asking for a divorce has given me some unexpected leverage. I promised him I wouldn't file if he signed a document stating that he had no claim to my business."

"Before he knew about the sale?" asked Jane.

"Exactly."

"Was it a lot of money?" asked Cordelia, never one to be compelled by social niceties when she wanted information.

"Yes, it was more than generous."

"Will you move out of your home in Mountain View?"

"I can't. We have to keep up appearances. And I need to be quiet about the split, or any men I choose to date."

"What about Verity?" asked Jane. "Does she know about the marital problems?"

"We haven't talked about it, but . . . probably." She ran a hand through her hair. "My daughter is fifteen going on thirty. She doesn't miss much. When I decided to come back here for the summer, I asked her to come along. I saw right away that it wasn't going to happen. She's too involved with her friends to want to spend three months in a small town in the middle of nowhere. And she's a real daddy's girl. I don't blame her. Her father is exciting. I sell candy. Big whoop."

Cordelia dropped her napkin next to her plate. "What's it like being back?"

Emma laughed. "As soon as I set foot in town, I got nailed to head up a committee for our twentieth class reunion. It's next weekend, by the way. The woman who had been heading the committee had to bow out for health reasons. Believe me, there's way too much to do. I'm working with Kurt Steiner. Have you heard of him?"

"The name sounds familiar," said Jane.

"Coleridge Street Press published his first book of poetry, oh, maybe eight years ago. *In a Midnight Wood*."

"Oh, sure. A friend gave me a copy. He's a farmer or a baker or something, right?"

"Butcher," said Emma. "His family owns the only butcher shop in town. We've become really great friends over the summer. He's even taken me fishing a couple of times, just like my dad used to do. And he's easy to look at."

"Oh?" said Cordelia.

"I'm not interested, if that's what you're suggesting. You can call me shallow if you want, but I like being around beautiful men. I mean, he's got this cute, toothy smile. Telling a guy he's cute is never a good thing, but he is. And he's got a great mustache that turns down around the edges of his mouth. There are so many tragically ugly mustaches these days, don't you agree?"

26

"I do," said Cordelia, offering a deeply sympathetic nod.

"As a friend, he's been a real gift." Looking away, Emma added, "Sam will need to be included in the class memorial. Kurt and I are organizing that."

It was the topic Jane had been wanting to talk about. But as soon as Emma said Sam's name, her eyes began to tear.

"Will you excuse me?" she said, getting up. "I just need a moment." She walked stiffly out of the dining room.

Jane and Cordelia exchanged glances.

"We should probably clear the table and clean up the kitchen," said Jane.

"I suppose," agreed Cordelia, though with little enthusiasm.

As Jane busied herself putting the leftovers into containers, Cordelia's phone rang.

Fishing it out of her back pocket and checking to see who it was, her expression brightened. "Oh, it's Hattie. Do you mind?"

Whether Cordelia's change in mood was because Hattie was on the line or because she had found an excuse to get out cleaning up—or both—Jane couldn't tell. Not that it mattered. She was hardly a stranger to dishes.

After turning on the dishwasher a little while later, she grabbed a glass of iced tea and went outside. The heat of the day still lingered in the air as she made her way down the broad front lawn to a strip of beach. She set her glass on one of the Adirondack chairs, then kicked off her sandals, rolled up her jeans, and waded into the water, feeling the fine sand squish between her toes.

Besides wanting to spend time with Emma, Jane had another reason for wanting to get away. She'd had an off again, on again relationship with a woman, Julia Martinsen, for many years. During the final year and a half of Julia's life, Jane had taken her into her home and cared for her until her death last February. Everyone assumed Jane was reeling from the loss of Julia, and that it was why she appeared so weighed down, yet that was only part of it. She'd taken a week off from work in March to grieve and try to gain some perspective. The only conclusion she'd come to was that she was a fool. She'd told no one, not even Cordelia, what had happened after Julia's funeral, and perhaps that was a mistake. Cordelia had always warned her about Julia's malign influence, but Jane felt she knew better.

Hearing a noise, she turned to find Emma, wine bottle in hand, coming—or perhaps more accurately, weaving—down the grassy hill from the house.

"Sorry I left so abruptly," she said, making herself comfortable on one of the chairs.

"Are you feeling any better?" asked Jane, picking up a stone and skipping it across the water.

"I need to talk. About Sam."

Jane returned to her chair and sat down.

"Can I bend your ear?"

"Of course. Well, except, here's the thing. You know that, for the last six months, I've been working part-time for a podcast in Minneapolis."

"I've listened to a few," said Emma. "They're good. Minnesota cold cases. I like true crime."

Besides owning a restaurant, Jane had been a licensed P.I. for many years. People who didn't know her thought restaurateur and investigator were an odd combination, but for Jane, they represented two of her biggest passions. When she came on board as a producer for Minnesota (N)ice last April, with a significant investment of both time and money, she stepped back from doing any P.I work. Initially she'd only been involved in research for the podcast, but when one of her interview segments was included on air, the reaction to her voice, her interview style, and her analysis was so positive, she was now being encouraged to think about becoming one of the hosts. In the last few months, she'd been tasked with developing new leads for upcoming programs. And it seemed as if one had just dropped in her lap. Sam's disappearance now qualified as a legitimate cold case. Jane hadn't been all that close to Emma when Emma was in high school. That connection had come later, after Emma's marriage. Emma had mentioned Sam a few times over the years, of course, and Jane remembered commiserating about his loss, but now that it was being looked at as a potential homicide, she wanted to ask Emma more questions. "I might want to look into his death a little more closely."

"For the podcast?"

"Would you have a problem with that? I mean, I'd like to talk to you about it, about him. I wouldn't use what you tell me unless you gave me permission."

"There's no problem. I want answers. Who knows? Maybe you can help." She held the wine bottle up to the fading light to see how much was left. "Fire away."

"Okay. You dated Sam. When was that?"

"We'd been friends since ninth grade. It turned into something more during our junior year. We dated for ten months, until he disappeared in early October of our senior year."

"Refresh my memory. What did you think happened to him?"

Emma took several swallows of wine directly from the bottle. "At first I thought he'd run away."

"Why?"

"Because his father is a sadist."

Jane was a bit taken aback.

"You want to know why I think Wendell Romilly is a sadist?" She waited for a rumble of thunder to pass. Above the distant tree line, dark clouds had begun to erase the sunset.

"Where do I start? Okay, so there was this one time. Sam's dad had been given a bunch of old religious pamphlets published by a fundamentalist religion—The Worldwide Church of God. One of them said that doctors might be okay for setting bones and delivering babies, but for everything else, it was best to rely on God.

I guess there's a Bible verse that says something about anointing the sick with oil, laying your hands on the person, and asking God to heal them. Right around that time, Sam got this terrible pain in his stomach. His mom wanted to take him to the hospital, but Wendell wouldn't hear it. He found some peanut oil in the kitchen and poured it on Sam's head, did the hand ritual, and waited for God to do His job. By midnight, Sam was writhing in pain. By then his mom had had enough, so she took him to the emergency room. It was his appendix. It was so inflamed that a doctor ended up taking out part of his intestine."

"Did his father learn his lesson?"

"Sam told me his dad thought he'd done the ritual wrong. He was hoping for a do-over. But nobody in the family was ever that sick again, and I guess Wendell eventually lost interest. They joined the Methodist church in town a few months later."

A gust of wind hit them as lightning lit up the sky. Jane wondered if they shouldn't head in, but she didn't want to interrupt Emma. "Anything else?" she asked.

"Oh, it's endless." She leaned her head back. "Wendell liked to gaslight Sam. He'd get all red in the face and demand to know why Sam hadn't cut the grass or washed the car or swept the garage. The problem was, he'd never *asked* Sam to do it. Once a transgression was established, the physical abuse would start. Wendell would slap him. Throw him against a wall. Once he grabbed Sam's hair, hauled him up to his room, and locked the door. Yes, there was a lock on the *outside* of the door, installed by Wendell himself."

"Was Sam an only child?"

"No, there's a younger brother—Scott. They were fourteen months apart. When Sam took off—" She stopped herself. "I mean . . . died, Scott was just starting his junior year."

"Did Scott get the same treatment from his dad?"

"Amazingly, no. Sam was happy for him, but I could tell it bothered him."

"Was Sam close to his brother?"

"Not really. Scott was sort of quiet, hard to read. I never really knew him. Sam was a free spirit, gregarious. He was smart, but he hated school, saw it mostly as a social occasion. He had tons of friends, and believe me, there were lots of girls who wanted him to ditch me and date them. He was pretty hunky. Strawberry blond hair and these amazing light gray eyes."

"If he didn't like school, what did he like?"

"Me. His motorcycle. Kurt Cobain. Grunge rock. Weed and Chips Ahoy cookies. And he loved taking chances—stupid, pointless risks. There were times when I wondered if he had a death wish. The other thing that always stood out was . . . if someone crossed him, he would figure out a way to get back at them. He put a different spin on it. He called it justice, said that's what he was after, but it seemed more like revenge to me."

Shining a light on the life of the victim was often a good way to help figure out why the individual had died. Jane had so many more questions, but the storm was moving in. "I think we better go inside."

"Before we blow away," said Emma.

"To be continued?" asked Jane.

"Absolutely. I'll do anything I can to help you figure out what happened to Sam."

6

The following morning, while Cordelia and Emma were still asleep, Jane drove into town to find a place to eat breakfast. Thankfully, last night's storm had blown in cooler, more seasonable weather.

After a quick look around town, Jane parked on Main, across the street from the White Star Cafe. Carrying an iPad, she entered and stood at the front, searching for an empty table. She vaguely remembered the place, thinking she must have eaten here at some point, though she had no memory of just when.

The interior felt like something out of *American Graffiti*. Formica-covered tables. Chrome stools with red Naugahyde seats at a long lunch counter. It wasn't that the place had been renovated to look retro, it *was* retro. No sooner had she slid into a booth than a middle-aged waitress in a white blouse, black jeans, and a MAGA hat arrived with a mug and a pot of coffee. Glancing around, Jane noticed quite a few other MAGA hats.

"Cream?" asked the waitress. Her name tag announced that she was Brenda.

"Black is fine," said Jane.

"You look familiar. Didn't I see your photo on a poster in the window at the art center?"

Jane had no idea a poster had been created. She quickly explained that she was a restaurateur in Minneapolis and that she was in town to participate in the center's silent auction.

"Oh, right, the arts festival. I remember now. You're the one who's offering to cook that gourmet dinner-for-four next Saturday night. Goes to the highest bidder."

"That's me," said Jane.

"I suppose it will get pretty pricey. I was thinking I'd put in a bid myself, but I doubt I'd win. Anyway, menu's behind the napkin holder. I'll be back in a jiff, unless you know what you want."

"I need a minute," said Jane.

"Sure thing, hon. FYI, the griddle cakes might not be gourmet, but they're fabulous. So are the hash browns. And our cook makes real hollandaise, if you're up for a Benedict."

As the woman walked back behind the lunch counter, Jane opened the plastic-covered menu. She settled on orange juice, two eggs over medium, sausage, and a short stack. She also ordered half a dozen caramel rolls to take back to the house.

"You're lucky you're here early," said Brenda when she came back to take the order. "We run outta those rolls pretty fast on Sunday mornings. If I don't bring at least one home for my husband every weekend, he gets downright snippy."

Jane smiled as Brenda wrote her order on the guest check. After she moved on to the next table, Jane turned on her iPad, waiting for it to boot up. Before bed last night, she'd called the executive producer of her podcast, Will Gulmain, and explained about Sam's remains being discovered. She said she'd followed the disappearance at the time, though most of it was lost in the mists of memory. Will wasn't familiar with the case, but said he'd get some information together for her and send it ASAP. It arrived in her Dropbox just after seven. She figured this would be a perfect time to take a look at it.

The twenty-year-old police report didn't contain all that much information. The investigating officer, Sgt. Mitch Tamborsky, stated in a short, typed paragraph that a call had come into the dispatcher at 11:14 p.m. on Saturday, October 9, 1999, from Diane Romilly. "Dispatcher said Mrs. Romilly's son Sam had been missing all day. None of the friends she'd contacted had seen or heard from him. She was upset and said she thought something bad had happened. Drove to the Romilly home on Goodson Avenue and spoke with both parents. Wendell Romilly, Sam's father, dismissed his wife's concerns, saying that his son was willful and erratic, that he would turn up eventually. Left assurances with the family that I would look into it."

A second report was filed three days later by the same person. "Conducted interviews with Sam Romilly's brother, Scott, and six friends—Taylor Olsen, Jim Hughes, Laura Vogel, Pete Schemmelmeyer, Emma Granholm, Todd Ott. None knew anything about his disappearance, and none could think of a reason why he might want to run away. I also interviewed two of Sam's teachers—Marion Collier and Burt Riley. They said that Sam was an indifferent student, though extremely well-liked. Neither had any reason to believe that someone meant him any harm. Patrolman Overstad and Patrolman Brand searched fields and woods around Castle Lake. Nothing was found. Mrs. Romilly continues to call every day for updates."

A final report was dated one week later. "Diane Romilly hired a local man, Tom Judson, who owns a bloodhound (cadaver dog. We've used him a couple of times). After a thorough search of the area, he informed her that the dog had alerted on a spot in a clearing near the Mill ruins and east of the river. I was called in. With the chief accompanying me, we did a careful inspection of the area and found no evidence that the ground had been disturbed. Patrolmen were ordered to dig down six feet where the dog alerted. Again, nothing was found. Mrs. Romilly remains adamant that the dog did, in fact, locate the crime scene where her son had been murdered. I assured her that I was still working the case."

Under the police reports, Jane found a short biography of Wendell Romilly.

"Wendell Clark Romilly was born in Mandan, North Dakota, and attended North Dakota State, earning a BA in business. He moved to the Twin Cities and was offered a job at Twin City Federal in Minneapolis. He worked his way from an entry position to branch manager and eventually took a pay cut so he could accept the job of vice president at Lakeside Community Bank in Castle Lake. He married Diane Ann Harrison the year after he moved to Minneapolis, and later had two sons with Diane, Sam and Scott."

Jane sat back, sipped her coffee. She remembered a couple of TV interviews Sam's mother had given.

Diane Romilly was an exceptionally photogenic, well-spoken woman, one with a tragic story to tell. By stoking the fires of public awareness through interviews on radio and TV, she kept the story of her son's disappearance in the news. In the material her producer had sent, Jane found a page stating that Diane's church had offered her a room in the basement to use as a gathering place and command post. She set up a couple dedicated phone lines, organized a citizen's group to make a more thorough search of the area. She also flooded the area with flyers offering a $5,000 reward for information leading to her son's recovery.

In every interview, Diane stressed that if Sam had decided to run away for some unknown reason, he would never have left his motorcycle behind. She said he loved the thing so much he would have slept with it if she'd let him. She also stressed a second point: Sam would never willingly cause her so much pain. He was a good son. A thoughtful young man. Diane had apparently mastered the art of the interview. She became a fierce advocate for Sam, a grieving mother defying what she considered official police apathy and ineptitude. She made it hard for anyone to look away.

Jane was about to start jotting down some notes when her food arrived. A moment later, so did Cordelia. With her height and girth, and wearing a NEVERTHELESS SHE PERSISTED T-shirt and red cap that simply said NO in big block letters, she breezed down the aisle and slipped onto the bench across from Jane. Heads turned to watch.

The waitress came over almost immediately. "Would you like to order?"

Cordelia nodded to Jane's plate. "I'll have what she's having, except I want a full stack, and I don't want orange juice. I'll have a big glass of grapefruit juice with lots of ice. I like crushed ice, not the big cubes. And I want cream for my coffee. And extra syrup."

The woman eyed Cordelia's cap, then dropped her eyes to the T-shirt. "I'll . . . ah, put your order in."

Cordelia straightened her silverware. "Why didn't you wake me?"

"How did you find me?"

"Duh. Your truck's right outside."

"Did you hitchhike?"

"Emma offered me her car keys. Go ahead and eat. I'll just sit here and try not to look faint with hunger."

"It's kind of early for you to be up," said Jane, tucking into her food.

Cordelia shrugged, removing her hat and fluffing her Medusa-like auburn curls.

"How was your bed?"

"Adequate."

Cordelia had a thing about any bed other than her own. It often devolved into a *Princess and the Pea* scenario.

"How's Hattie? We never got a chance to talk about your conversation with her."

"Oh, it's the usual adolescent drama. She doesn't like one of her new teachers. Thinks he's a moron. She's not happy with what Bolger's been cooking for dinner. She wants a new phone." As Cordelia ticked off more complaints, the waitress arrived with coffee, cream, and the large glass of grapefruit juice. Cordelia glanced at it and said, "Perfect. My compliments to the chef." While stirring cream into her coffee, she yawned. "Remember, Janey, we have that party tonight."

"What party?"

"The one Emma is throwing at the house to introduce us to the movers and shakers in Castle Lake."

Jane had forgotten about it.

"Did you bring a fancy frock?" asked Cordelia, examining her pale lavender nails for imperfections.

"I don't own a fancy frock."

"When it comes to your clothing, Janey, all I can say is, I do my best to keep hope alive."

When Brenda finally returned with Cordelia's food order, she also brought the sack of caramel rolls with her, which she set on the table.

Cordelia peeked inside. "Ah. Dinner."

As Jane surveyed the restaurant, she noticed a guy at the lunch counter watching her. He was an older man with fleecy mutton-chops and generally grizzled facial hair.

"What are you looking at?" asked Cordelia, glancing over her shoulder.

"Nothing."

"Oh my stars and garters. Two more MAGA hats just walked in. We're not in Kansas anymore. Or . . . maybe we are." She stabbed a sausage. "Anyhoo, you gonna let me read what Will sent you?"

37

Cordelia had been in Jane's bedroom, lying on the bed, when Jane had called her producer last night. "Have at it," said Jane, pushing the iPad across the table. When she looked up, she saw Mr. Muttonchops was staring at her again, pushing a pair of wire-rims back up his short, stubby nose. After tossing some cash on the counter, he picked up his newspaper. As he passed the booth, he stopped. Leaning a meaty hand on the table, he looked Jane straight in the eye and said, "You like history?"

"Excuse me?"

Cordelia bristled. "Feel free to move on."

"Ever wondered why this cafe is called the White Star?"

"Can't say that I have," said Jane.

"The couple who opened it back in the day, Ole and Bertha Johansen, came over from England on the RMS *Oceanic* in 1905. They were poor, so they traveled steerage. The *Oceanic* was the pride of the White Star Line, the largest ocean liner in the world until 1901. Interesting, huh?"

"Fascinating little tidbit," said Cordelia, stabbing another sausage.

Still concentrating on Jane, the man said, "You're Jane Lawless, right?"

Another person who'd seen her picture in the window of the art center. "That's right."

"The podcaster."

She cocked her head. "You know about that?"

"I listened to one of them last night. It was pretty good."

Not a ringing endorsement, but she'd take it.

"Gonna listen to the rest tonight. If I like what I hear, I'll see you around." He glanced back at Cordelia, then lifted his hand off the table, revealing a business card.

Jane waited until he'd gone outside before picking it up. "Wilburn Lowry. Prospector," she read out loud. "There's a phone number but no address." Turning to the window, she watched him walk across the street to a white van, one that was covered in red stars.

"Nice wheels," said Cordelia. "Odd guy. Then again, I like odd. Now, let's get back to the matter at hand: Sam Romilly. My little gray cells are entirely at your disposal."

7

Ever since Monty Mickler had stopped by the previous afternoon, Kurt had thought of little other than Sam. Sitting at his desk in the small office next to the butcher shop's workroom, he stared at Sam's photo in the yearbook.

Things had always come so easily for Kurt. Part of it was his ability to ignore issues that confused him, and part of it was his nature. Once upon a time he'd been an optimist, a basically happy, live-and-let-live kind of kid, blessed with a close and caring family. His childhood included the usual rough patches, but mostly his memories were good. Only later did he realize that he'd been breezing along, living entirely on the surface of things. Maybe that's what kids did. He'd had no real need to go deeper. Nobody in his young life had ever died, or even become seriously ill.

Kurt earned reasonable grades without having to study too hard. He wasn't a social butterfly, but he did have a few good friends. He loved to go fishing with his father and talk books and movies with his mom. He couldn't remember exactly, but he must have spun a life scenario something like this: He would graduate from high school, get married, have a couple of kids, and work for his dad at the butcher shop. He'd never really wanted to go to college. He loved to read so figured that was the way he'd continue his education. The problem was, as Socrates pointed out, the unexamined life wasn't worth living. Even more than that, the unexamined life was full of pitfalls and roadblocks, problems he'd never expected because all he ever looked at was what was right in front of him. All that changed on a hot August evening a month before the start of his senior year. He'd been out on a swimming raft with a few guys from the school swim team. That night the sky had fallen in on his predictable, secure little world, and nothing had been the same since.

"Hey, Kurt," came a familiar voice.

Feeling his mood lift, he got up and walked into the workroom. Ted Hammond stood next to the screen door that led to the alley. "When did you get in?" Kurt asked, walking over to give him a quick hug.

"Last night. Late. I think I woke my mom up."

"I'm sure she didn't mind," said Kurt. "Come back to the office."

They sat down on metal folding chairs.

"Judy here?" asked Ted.

"Yup."

"Okay, well, I won't stay. I thought I'd stop by to see if we could grab a beer later."

"I'd like that. Earl's Tap?" It was his favorite dive bar.

"Sure. Six? I've got plans with my mom tonight. I'm taking her to a movie. But I do want to talk to you."

"About something in particular?"

"Let's not get into it now." He nodded to the yearbook. "You all ready for the reunion?"

"Yeah, sort of." Ted had been the senior-class president. He'd also been voted "most likely to succeed." Not that anyone in high school knew what success meant back then.

"Oh, hey," said Ted, his expression sobering. "I heard about Sam. How crazy is that? I'm so sorry, man."

"Thanks."

"I know you two were close. You been thinking about him?"

"Yeah." Kurt pulled the yearbook closer. Sam's handsome face stared back at him. His hair looked ridiculously shaggy. Sam hated getting his hair cut, as if the barber was hell bent on removing some vital piece of him.

"You okay?" asked Ted.

It was a simple enough question, and yet the only way Kurt could answer it was to lie. "Yeah, I'm good."

"Okay. Well, I better shove off."

They said their goodbyes at the screened door.

Kurt spent the next few minutes conferring with a customer about a special order. He took down the information, then returned to his office to enter it into the computer. As he came back out, he found his son, Danny, standing in the workroom, removing his sport coat, tie, and dress shirt. Once he was down to his T-shirt, he seemed relieved.

"Did you drive to Fergus to see your mom?" asked Kurt.

"Just got back." Looking a little worried, he added, "I sent you a text."

"I left the house this morning without my phone."

Kurt wanted to hear about it, but first things first. Danny had graduated from high school last spring. He was currently working a part-time job, which caused him to be scrupulous about spending money on anything he could get at home. "Are you hungry?"

"When am I not hungry?"

Kurt smiled. "What do you want?"

"A couple pieces of cornbread, some beans, and potato salad. Don't pull a rotisserie chicken just for me."

"I've got half a chicken in the cooler. Go get it, and I'll dish up the rest."

For the last year, Danny would often drive his old Mazda over to Fergus Falls on Sundays to take his mother to mass. She lived in a group home for people with psychiatric problems. While Kurt was happy to see them forging a relationship, he had certain misgivings about his ex-wife's influence.

Danny had recently begun to talk more seriously about his future. He was a solid kid—hardworking, decent, good-hearted—and he was searching for his place in the world. His employer, Toller Aviation, one of the better places for a kid to land in Castle Lake, trained him for the specific job they needed, but also wouldn't give him more than thirty hours a week. Because he wasn't full time, they didn't have to provide vacation pay or benefits. It was the way of the economic world these days. Kurt was happy that Danny still lived at home. He was still on Kurt's insurance, too. It wasn't particularly good insurance, though it was better than nothing. Danny had pretty much dismissed the idea of college, and to be honest, Kurt was relieved. He didn't have the money to help him with tuition, and he didn't want his son saddled with a huge debt just when he was starting out in life.

Pulling up a chair next to his son in the workroom, Kurt had to stifle a laugh as Danny devoured the food; he loved watching the kid eat because he always did it with such gusto. "How's your mom doing?" asked Kurt. He hadn't seen her in years. He and Vicki had divorced quietly when Danny was nine.

"Not as good as last time," said Danny. "I took her out for a walk after mass. When we got back, we sat around the common room for a while. She kept stealing glances at the TV and kind of zoning out. At one point, she pointed to the guy who was being interviewed on some news program and said, 'Did you hear him? Did you *hear* what he said to me?'"

Vicki had been diagnosed with schizophrenia when Danny was three. Even before that, Kurt could tell something wasn't right. After the diagnosis, she'd gone on to spend her life in and out of mental health facilities, but had never returned to her home with Kurt and Danny. The group facility in Fergus Falls, which she'd moved into four years ago, was a big step for her. Danny had always had a lot of questions about his mother. The fact that she finally wanted to see him was huge.

"She still after you to join the Catholic church?" asked Kurt.

"Oh, yeah. She talks about it all the time."

Vicki hadn't been like that when Kurt had known her. In fact, she'd never said anything about her religious views.

"She gave me a bunch of stuff to read."

"Did she. Are you going to?"

"Maybe. I mean, I don't want to hurt her feelings, but religion isn't really my thing, you know?"

Kurt wasn't surprised.

"Say," said Danny, dropping a chicken bone on his plate. "I heard about that guy, Sam—the one who went missing your senior year. I was totally stunned to learn he'd been buried in Holy Trinity cemetery all this time. That is so wrong. Who would do something like that?"

Kurt shook his head.

"I mean, you were friends, right?"

"Yeah."

"So you have any idea what happened to him?"

The question caused the ground beneath Kurt to tilt sideways and then disappear. He was standing at the edge of a dark chasm while his son finished his potato salad.

"I've heard gossip around town that his father did it. Do you know his dad?"

"Not really," said Kurt, hearing the bell over the front door ring.

"Really sad shit." Danny pushed his plate away.

Emma appeared in the workroom doorway.

"Oh hi, Mrs. Anguelo," said Danny, wiping his mouth on a napkin.

"Remember, you were going to call me Emma," she said, smiling.

He nodded, returning her smile. "Hey, um, I should probably get going. I promised I'd meet up with Tanya when I got back. She's home for the weekend."

Tanya was Danny's girlfriend, someone Kurt liked a lot. She'd moved to the Cities in July to live with her aunt. He could tell the long-distance romance was proving more difficult than they'd expected.

"So catch you both later." Danny grabbed his coat, shirt, and tie and, with a wave, took off out the back door.

"He is one really cute kid," said Emma after he'd gone.

"Yeah," said Kurt, tossing Danny's plate in the trash. "I'm pretty proud of him."

"He looks a lot like you did when you were his age. Broad shoulders. Same height."

"He's actually two inches taller."

"Really." She took a few steps into the room. "You got a minute?"

"Sure."

Lowering her voice, she said, "I assume you've heard about Sam."

"Monty Mickler came by with the news."

"Isn't it awful?"

He put his arms around her. He knew so much that she didn't, things he hoped she would never find out.

"Anyway," she said, wiping a tear off her cheek, "we need to write something, so he's included in the class memorial. I've got some old photos we can put up on the photo wall. We don't have to talk about it now, but we should get going on it. I thought we could each write a few notes, and then we could combine them."

"Sounds good."

"Listen," she said, looking up into his eyes. "I know this comes out of the blue, but I'm giving a cocktail party at the house tonight to introduce my houseguests to some of the people on the town council and the art board. A friend will cater it, so there will be lots of food. I thought you might want to join us."

"Me?"

"You're a business owner. You never know who you might meet or what opportunities might arise."

Emma was a lot more ambitious than he was. He doubted a bigger, better, slicker butcher shop was in his future. "I don't know."

"Think about it. These people, they're mostly old and boring. It would be nice to have someone there I could talk to. We could sneak out for a while. Go sit by the lake. It's supposed to be a beautiful night."

"It's sounding better. Am I your only personal guest?"

She hesitated. "There is someone I'd like to invite, but I can't."

"Because?"

"Multiple reasons, none of which I want to get into."

He'd already concluded that she'd been seeing someone while she'd been in town. Since he wasn't interested in her romantically, it meant that he was entirely free to be her friend. "Come on, Emma. Do I know the guy?"

She smiled. "Probably. No more questions. So what do you say?"

"Do I have to get dressed up?"

"You have a tux, right?" His surprised look caused her to laugh. "I'm kidding, silly. It's completely casual, although I wouldn't wear jeans. You do own something other than jeans?"

"Cargo shorts and black socks?"

"Perfect, as long as the socks match."

He accompanied her to the front door. "What time is this shindig?"

"Starts at seven." Turning to him, she said, "Oh, please come."

"You're good at twisting arms."

"I'll take that as a yes." She stood on her tiptoes and kissed him on the cheek. "You're saving my sanity."

KURT

August 20, 1999

Just before sunset, Kurt hoisted himself up the ladder on the pontoon raft, the one that floated about thirty yards out from the shoreline of Elbow Lake. The old planked-wood base had given him more than one painful sliver over the years, so he was careful moving across it. Lying down between Jim Hughes and Todd Ott, both friends from the high school swim team, he looked up at the puffy clouds drifting by.

"You done with work for the day?" asked Todd.

"Yup," said Kurt. "You guys been doing laps?"

"Nah," said Jim lazily. "I had kind of a late night last night."

"I did a bunch," said Todd, playing with the five hairs on his chest. "My timing's shit. I'll probably end up on the bench most of the year."

"No you won't," said Jim. "If I have anything to say about it, you'll be under the bench."

Kurt raised his head as Sam Romilly climbed up the ladder and sat down cross-legged next to Jim.

"Hey, dawgs," said Sam, whipping his wet hair away from his face. "What's happening?"

"Nada," said Todd. "Crap, anybody know what time it is?"

48

"I'd say around eight-thirty," said Kurt.

"Shit. I promised Krista I'd take her to the nine-fifteen movie over in Clarksville."

"Can't disappoint a good woman," said Sam.

"What's showing?" asked Jim.

"*Mercury Rising*. It's a Bruce Willis flick, so it should be okay." Scrambling to his feet, Todd cannonballed into the lake, sending a spray of water over the raft.

"Asshole," yelled Kurt.

"He's never gonna make it in time," muttered Sam.

"I should head in, too," said Jim with a sigh.

"You guys are no fun," said Sam. "You leaving, too, Steiner?"

"Nah, just got here."

When Jim jumped in, his cannonball was a dud.

"Head down," called Sam, mimicking the nasal voice of their coach. "Dig! Dig!"

Jim stuck his hand out of the water and gave Sam the finger.

Sam stretched out next to Kurt. They spent the next few minutes arguing about *The Blair Witch Project*, which Sam had hated, calling it Mickey Mouse and totally lame. Kurt loved being scared, and on that, the movie had delivered. Eventually, they moved on to baseball and other pressing matters.

During a lull in the conversation, Sam asked, "How're things at the butcher mart? You still get your rocks off cutting up dead carcasses?"

"I live for it."

Sam grinned. "God, can you believe we're about to start our senior year?"

"Can't wait. You?"

"I'll be glad when it's over." He pointed to a flock of geese flying low over the water. "You hunt?"

"I used to go with my dad."

"Why'd you stop?"

"I didn't, my dad did. How about you?"

"I might *hunt* my dad, but I'd never go hunting *with* him."

Kurt wasn't sure what he meant.

"I see you with Vicki Nestor a lot," said Sam. "You two getting it on?"

"Yeah. She's nice. You still with Emma?"

"Attached at the hip."

"You're lucky. She's really pretty."

The orange orb in the sky had sunk to the level of the treetops.

"You interest me, Steiner," said Sam, running a hand through his wet hair.

"That makes me feel like a bug under a microscope."

He shrugged. "You're not shy, but you're quiet. I like that. You're not always pointing at yourself and yelling 'Look at me!' And I see you watching people, standing back and, like, you know, observing."

Kurt had never thought of himself that way, though now that Sam pointed it out, he supposed it was true.

"I think a guy learns a lot by keeping his mouth shut and listening," said Sam. "I wish I did more of it."

"Yeah?"

"Yeah."

They sat in companionable silence as light around them faded.

Out of the blue, Sam stood. "Let's race to the beach. First one there has to buy the other a cheeseburger. Not tonight. I'm busy. But . . . sometime."

"Deal," said Kurt, pushing to his feet.

Sam counted to ten, and they both dove in.

Kurt got off to a slow start, but he was the stronger swimmer and made it to the shore first. He dropped down on the sand, breathing hard.

Sam joined him a few seconds later. "Screw that," he yelled, gulping air. "You're a speedy SOB. But then, I already knew that."

They flopped on their backs and watched as the stars began to appear. Kurt felt tired and loose and happy, like he could stay on the beach forever. "This is nice."

"It is," said Sam, his face suddenly looming over Kurt.

Kurt felt his body rise as Sam kissed him. It was only an instant, though it felt much longer, and then Sam got up and ran off. Nothing was said. Kurt turned around and watched him hop on his cycle and roar off. Touching his lips, he listened to the sound of the engine fading into the distance.

8

Jane and Cordelia stood under the dining room arch, watching people line up at the buffet table. Jane hadn't eaten anything since breakfast, so the chafing dishes beckoned. The downstairs looked lovely, with evening light streaming in through the multipaned windows overlooking the lake. Most of the house looked the way it had when Emma's parents were still alive, though she'd removed the oriental carpet in the dining room as well as some of her parents' knickknacks, favoring a more minimalist vibe.

Cordelia was all set to make her usual splash, dressed in a white Roman toga trimmed in gold, one shoulder bare. She had a theatrical love of costume—and of the outrageous.

"The combat boots are a nice touch," said Jane.

"I thought so." She touched a pinky to her bright red lips. "And you've outdone yourself, as predicted." She looked away, but Jane could hear the dismissive sniff.

Jane had brought along a fitted black velvet jacket and black jeans, thinking it would be okay for a dressy occasion. "I think I look great."

"Of course you do. By the way, if you're hungry before bed, I've got that sack of caramel rolls up in my bedroom."

"I thought we'd decided to share them for breakfast tomorrow."

"Assuming any are left, I'm happy to share."

"There were half a dozen rolls in that bag."

"Your point is?" Bending close to Jane, Cordelia whispered, "I saw you talking to Emma out on the patio when we got back. Did you learn anything I should know about?"

Cordelia always inserted herself into Jane's investigations. According to Cordelia, she was the one who solved most of the cases by dint of her phenomenal gut instinct. To be fair, she did have good instincts, though with Cordelia, people usually had only once chance to make an impression—for good or ill.

"I wanted to get the names of a few of Sam Romilly's closest friends back in high school," said Jane. "I'm hoping to talk to them, get a feeling for what Sam's last few weeks were like. Emma said that over half the senior class left the area after graduation."

"How big was the graduating class?"

"Sixty-eight."

"How many are attending the reunion?"

"Maybe sixty-five, if you consider significant others. They scheduled it the same weekend as homecoming, hoping to fatten the attendance. Most will be going to the game on Friday night. I imagine many of the attendees will have known Sam."

"Good timing for us."

"We'll see."

When Emma came over, Jane saw that she'd changed from her afternoon sundress into a black satin plunge-neck blouse and skinny black-leather slacks. Definitely not a look that was likely to be popular in Castle Lake. "There are so many people who want to meet you two."

"Great," said Jane, stealing a sideways glance at the food.

In reasonably quick succession, they were introduced to the fire chief—a meaty middle-aged guy with a broad smile and a scar on his right cheek—three members of the art board, and two women who sat on the town council. Everyone was friendly and asked lots of questions. Jane was happy to let Cordelia do most of the talking. She was, after all, the one they were most interested in. However, when they were introduced to Grady Larson, Emma's uncle and the chief of police, Jane had a few questions of her own. As Emma and Cordelia were pulled away into another conversation, she stayed put. "Have you made any progress on the death of Sam Romilly?"

Grady was gray-haired and portly. "It's a terrible thing. I'm sorry your visit to our town coincided with that revelation. All I can say is, we're going to treat it the same way we treat any other homicide. I'll admit that we don't get many of those, but we will pursue the case aggressively."

"You'll be putting out a statement, I assume." She was surprised that they hadn't already issued one.

"I'm leaving that to my detective, Sgt. Dave Tamborsky."

"I'm told he was a friend of the victim."

"He was?"

"You don't think that might be a conflict?"

"No, not at all."

Jane could tell he wanted to move on to another topic, but she wasn't done. "I believe Sgt. Tamborsky's father did the original investigation back when Sam first went missing."

"You're remarkably knowledgeable."

"I work for a true-crime podcast in Minneapolis."

She could tell by his expression that he had no idea what she was talking about. "Can you share any details? How he died? What your evidence is that it was a homicide?"

"I'm afraid I can't comment on an open investigation."

"But do you have any suspects?"

"Again, no comment. Now, if you'll excuse me—"

"I've read the police reports that were written in 1999."

"Have you now." His expression grew stony. "Well then you know we did everything we could at the time. It wasn't viable to search all the wooded areas around Castle Lake or interview everyone who knew Sam Romilly. We did our best then, and we'll do our best now." With that, he caught the eye of the fire chief and walked over to talk to him.

Jane took the opportunity to find herself something to eat. The food on offer at the buffet table was definitely old school. Spinach dip in a bread bowl surrounded by celery and carrot sticks. A pasta salad, heavy on the mayonnaise. A fruit salad, which appeared to be mostly watermelon. Deviled eggs. Tater Tot hot dish, a Minnesota specialty. Cocktail weenies in barbecue sauce. Cheese, crackers, and cold cuts. Most of the platters and chafing dishes were pretty picked over. Jane found a clean plate and helped herself to a couple of weenies, a deviled egg, slathered a few crackers with Brie, and finished with fruit. As she was dithering over a tray of lemon bars, an attractive woman in a white linen suit and gray silk blouse walked up. Jane had noticed Cordelia talking to her while she was having her conversation with the police chief. Her one thought at the time was, leave it to Cordelia to attract the best-looking woman in the room.

"I've been reading about you," said the woman, fingering a silver necklace. "You and Cordelia were featured in today's paper."

"We were?" Jane licked some Brie off her finger.

"I'm Leslie Harrow, the mayor of Castle Lake."

"Nice to meet you."

Her voice took on a mock serious tone. "I have some questions about your offering for the silent auction, the gourmet dinner for four."

"Are you interested?"

"Very much. Can I ask what's on the menu?"

"Well," said Jane, "it depends. I want to prepare something that the winner will enjoy."

Close up, she could see that the woman was older than she'd appeared from across the room. Like Jane, she was probably in her early fifties. She wore her dark blond hair short and feathered over her ears, with side-swept bangs.

"But how does it work? Would you come to my house to cook the meal? Would we do it somewhere else?"

"Again, that depends," said Jane.

"On?"

"Your kitchen."

"Ah." Another smile. "I have a wonderful kitchen."

"So you plan to put in a bid?"

"If I do, I intend to win."

Before Jane could respond, Emma strolled up with a man in tow.

"Mr. Kurt Steiner," said Harrow, turning to him and extending her hand. "And Emma. I hope you're having as much fun tonight as I am."

Emma seemed annoyed and Kurt appeared to be the cause.

"I'm a little late," he said, looking sheepish. "I'm not much of a partygoer these days."

He was good looking but also seemed terribly shy. Jane found it an interesting combination.

"Jane is the one who's offering the gourmet dinner for the silent auction," said Emma.

"Oh, sure," said Kurt, smoothing his mustache and looking around nervously. "I thought that was a great idea."

"I may need to come to your shop and look around," she said. "Depending on the tastes of the person who wins the meal—"

"That will likely be me," said Harrow, raising a finger.

"We have the finest meat in town. And we have lots of local, wild-caught fish. Seafood is another matter. It's hard to get fresh seafood in a place like Castle Lake."

As the French doors leading to the patio were opened to let in some fresh air, Jane felt a sudden urge to ditch the party and find somewhere private and quiet. While she'd never been shy, she was an introvert, and like Kurt, parties such as this one weren't high on her list of ways to spend an evening.

"Would you like something to eat, Kurt?" asked Emma, nodding to the buffet table.

"Um, no thanks."

"Kurt wants to go sit down by the lake. I thought I'd join him. I think I can leave for a few minutes without anyone missing me, right?"

"Go for it," said Jane. As the two of them made their way outside, Jane turned back to Harrow. They'd no sooner resumed their conversation when a man in a plaid sport coat ambled up. He held a martini glass and seemed impatient when the mayor didn't immediately acknowledge him. "I was looking all over for you."

"I wasn't hiding, Don."

When he raised the glass to his lips, Jane noticed a wedding ring. Putting two and two together, she assumed the guy was Harrow's husband.

"There's someone here I want you to meet," he said, draining his glass.

"Not now."

"But they're leaving soon."

"I'm not working tonight."

"Come on, Leslie. The mayor is always working."

She regarded him a moment, then finally relented. "I'm sorry, Jane. I was hoping we'd have a bit longer to talk. Are you going to stick around a while longer?"

"I'm not sure," said Jane. "Probably not."

"Okay, well, then I'll see you around town."

"Don't forget to put in a bid for the dinner."

"Oh, no worries on that score." She touched Jane's elbow before walking away.

9

Kurt waited for Emma to sit down on the end of the dock before he joined her. It was a beautiful evening, cool and clear, with a nearly full September moon creating ribbons of light across the water.

"Why were you so late?" asked Emma.

"Oh, you know. I lead a very complex social life. At least give me credit for ditching my jeans."

"You do clean up well."

"Thank you." He glanced back at the house. "You know, this is the first time I've been here."

"No," said Emma. "That can't be right. You must have been to a few of my summer parties on the beach back in the day."

"Nope," said Kurt. "Never. I didn't run with the upper crust in high school."

She turned to look at him. "Is that a joke?"

"Only slightly. Come on, you have to know we have a class system in this town. In high school, lawyers' and doctors' kids were friends with bankers' kids. Blue-collar kids hung out with other blue-collar kids. It wasn't completely hard and fast, but it was real. Think about it. Who were your friends?"

"Well, I mean—"

"Be honest."

She blinked a couple times. "Of course—"

"Yes?"

Looking away, she said, "I never thought about it that way. But, I mean, it's not like you were poor."

"No, we weren't. As a kid, I had everything I needed. But there were kids, friends of mine, who didn't. Some who had it really hard."

Emma seemed uncomfortable with the topic. Kurt knew her well enough now to believe she'd think about what he'd said. It wasn't meant as a criticism of her personally, though it was a criticism of the system. When you were inside a box, it was hard to see what the world looked outside. He decided to change the subject. "Would you mind if we talked a little more personally? About you and Sam? We've never really talked about that."

"I guess."

"I remember you two were pretty serious. Did you think you'd marry him one day?"

After thinking about it for a few seconds she said, "I don't know. I just knew I loved him."

"Was he your first?"

"Boyfriend?"

"Well, you know—the first guy you . . . were with?"

"I'm not sure that's any of your business."

"Oh, crap, Emma. I've offended you. I'm so sorry. Forget I asked." A glow over the distant treetops caught his eye.

"What about you and Vicki Nestor? Was she your first girlfriend?"

"Yeah."

"Did you think you'd marry her?"

"I rarely thought about the future back then, I just went with the flow. Vicki was pregnant when I married her. Actually, she was pregnant when I took her to the senior prom, only I didn't know about it until after graduation."

"Wow. Did you feel trapped?"

"Yeah, I suppose."

"Did you love her?"

"This may seem strange . . . What I loved was the idea of having a child. And then, you know, you get all caught up in the wedding stuff. It's like a speeding train that's impossible to get off."

"I know." She twisted the ring on her finger. "But you're right. Danny's pretty special." She paused. "Don't you ever wonder what Sam would think of us now, twenty years on? What we've done with our lives?"

Kurt thought about that a lot. "He'd be disappointed in me."

"Yeah, in me, too."

"I assume the police are going to begin an investigation of his death," he continued, trying to cover his uneasiness with a casual tone. "We'll probably get asked a bunch of questions."

"Bring it on. I'm happy to tell them everything I know—which, sadly, isn't much."

"Hey, are you cold?" he asked, turning to face her. "You can have my jacket."

"You're a lot like Sam, you know that? He was such a kind person. I don't think he showed that side of himself to many people, but he did to me. Since we're talking about him—" She paused before continuing, "Was it my imagination or did he have this weird kind of energy before he died? There were times when he couldn't sit still. Once he jumped up in the middle of a conversation and raced off."

Kurt wasn't sure how to answer.

"Am I off base?"

"I know he was angry at someone."

"About what?"

"I hate to dredge up stuff I don't know that much about."

"But if it had something to do with his death—"

"I seriously doubt that it did."

"Did it have anything to do with that party at the beginning of our senior year? Maybe I'm wrong, but things changed after that. I could feel it. There was something in the air at school. Did you feel it, too?"

"A bunch of bad stuff was going on around that time, Emma."

"Like what?"

"Were you at the party?"

"For a while. I'd been feeling crummy all day, but in the evening, I spiked a fever. My throat was like sandpaper. Sam and I weren't there for more than an hour when I told him I wanted to leave. He said he'd take me home, but then one of my girlfriends was leaving, so I caught a ride back to town with her. Did something bad happen after I left? Come on, Kurt. If you know, you've got to tell me. Sam was super silent the next day. What was going on?"

He had to give her something. "Sam was really pissed at his brother."

The comment seemed to startle her. "Scott? Why? Was *he* there that night?"

"If he was, I never saw him. All I can say is, Sam and Scott were both hot about something. World War II–level hot."

Emma's gaze traveled to the glow in the sky. "I wonder what that is over there? A late summer bonfire?"

"It seems too big."

"A house? Oh, Lord, I hope not. Maybe we better tell the fire chief."

Before they were halfway up the lawn, Kurt picked up the sound of sirens in the distance. At the same time, a dozen or so party guests began streaming out onto the patio, all pointing to the tree line.

"Anybody know what it is?" he called.

"A house fire," one of the men called back.

"Crap," said Kurt. "I've got to get back to town. If it's my place or my parents' house—"

61

"You go," said Emma. "Call me when you know something."

He rushed around the side of the house. As he reached the parking area, he saw that he wasn't the only one leaving. He checked his phone for messages. Seeing none, he jumped into front seat of his van and edged into line behind the other cars as the slow procession made its way out to Ewing Road.

Cordelia wasn't about to stick around while a real-life drama was unfolding. As the party broke up, she sidled up to Jane and proposed that they see what was going on for themselves. On their way to the door, Emma caught them and asked if she could grab a ride into town. By the time they were cruising down Grant Street, one block north of Main, the glow from the fire seemed to light up the night sky. They dropped Emma off in front of an old brick building that had once been the only large hotel in Castle Lake. The last time Jane had been past it, it had looked like a ruin.

"This used to be the Griswold Inn," said Jane as Emma slid out of the cab's backseat. "Did they restore it?" The bottom floor had been turned into an upscale-looking bar called The Outpost, which appeared to be Emma's destination.

"No, it's been turned into condos."

"Do you want us to pick you up when we're done?"

"Not necessary. I'll catch a ride back with one of my friends."

Main Street became county Highway 8 when it hit Castle Lake and turned south. Jane followed a line of cars as they made their way out of town. They passed several motels, a hamburger stand, a feed store, and half a dozen other small businesses, eventually leaving the city limits behind. Another mile, and Jane pulled up behind a flatbed truck parked on the side of the road.

Cordelia was out the door in a flash. Jane followed, feeling the heat of the fire before she saw it. They walked along the shoulder, mostly gravel and weeds, until they reached several dozen bystanders clumped together behind a squad car.

Cordelia's toga seemed to cause a moment of group confusion, though everyone's attention snapped right back to the blaze.

"It's Carli Gilbert's place," said the man standing closest to Jane. "God, I hope she's not inside."

The woman next to him said, "If they could just open up the garage, they'd know if her car was there."

"You want those boys fried to a crisp, huh Karen?" asked the guy. "They can't get near that garage."

"I'm just saying if they could."

"I know what you're saying." With a disgusted look he turned to Jane, though his gaze seemed drawn to Cordelia. "You're not from around here, are you?"

"No, just visiting," said Jane.

"Well, an FYI, we got a volunteer fire department in this town. Those guys are brave as hell, but they're getting old. Hard to find younger guys these days willing to do the job. No money in it. Just a lot of risk. Hell if I know what's going to happen when we can't find volunteers and we can't afford to pay full-timers. Maybe we should all move to the big cities and take our chances with the rapists, murderers, and drug dealers."

"Stop with the den of iniquity crap," said Karen. "Nobody wants to hear it."

"Can you leave your door unlocked in those inner-city hell holes?" he demanded. "*Can* you?"

"You shouldn't leave doors unlocked anywhere," said Cordelia offhandedly.

"Bullshit. My parents never locked their doors. Neither do I."

"Then you're a silly man."

"What the hell did you just call me?"

"Thank you," said Karen. "You see, Jack? I'm not alone."

Jane doubted that inserting the results of an academic study, one that said living in rural areas was now considered more dangerous than city living, would be well-received. Interestingly, limited access to emergency services was considered one of the main problems. Also, drug use, once considered the scourge of the inner city, was now rampant in small-town America, with far fewer resources to help with the problem. But why bother anyone with facts, thought Jane, especially in a country where facts were considered nothing but fake news.

Taking one last disapproving look at Cordelia and her outfit, the man grabbed his wife's arm and tugged her on down the road.

"Pleasant fellow," said Cordelia, waving a hand in front of her face. "That fire is giving off so much heat, I think I may be melting."

"Like the Wicked Witch of the West."

"*Context*, Janey. That was a water situation, and she was evil. This is fire situation, and I'm good. Too bad I left my magic wand back at the house."

Another woman, this one wearing slippers and a blue velour robe, walked up and planted herself next to Jane. "I shouldn't be out here dressed like this, but . . . I'm so scared for Carli. I live back there in one of those trailer homes," she said, jabbing her thumb over her shoulder. "Behind those tall pines. I can't believe this is happening." She tugged nervously at the back of her gray hair.

"So you know the woman who owns the house?"

"Sure do. She's a lovely person."

"Does she work in town?"

"She works a couple of jobs. She's the town recorder—posts updates and events to the town website. It's only a few hours a week. She's a good friend of the mayor, which is how she said she got the job. Her main work is at Lakeside Community Bank. She's a teller."

"She live alone?"

"Since her husband moved out, yeah. They're separated. It's so sad. Last time we talked, she said she was filing for divorce." Nodding to Cordelia, she added, "My granddaughter wore something like that for show-and-tell last year."

"Really," said Cordelia, brightening. "What grade is she in?"

"Kindergarten. I wonder," the woman continued, "what will happen now."

"In what way?" asked Jane.

"With . . . you know." She nodded to the burning building. "I don't like to gossip."

"Of course you don't," said Cordelia. "But sometimes it's just too hard to stay silent."

"That's true. I love Carli and Aaron. They're wonderful people. But—"

"But?" said Cordelia

"I've heard both of them like to cat around. Hard to build a marriage on such shaky ground."

"The husband," said Cordelia. "He the vengeful sort?"

The woman seemed taken aback by the question. "Are you suggesting—"

Cordelia raised her eyebrows.

"No, no. He's not like that. He's a hard worker. Has his own handyman business."

The woman quickly excused herself and moved on up the road, where she began talking to a man she appeared to know.

Out of the side of her mouth, Cordelia said, "Randy handymen never commit crimes."

If it turned out to be arson, her point was well-taken. Even so, Jane felt it was important to examine the potential motive from a different angle. The police would undoubtedly look at the estranged husband, which was to be expected. But after the discovery of Sam Romilly's remains, a young man so many assumed had run away, anything odd or irregular—or violent—that happened in Castle Lake needed to be scrutinized in the light of that. Murder had a particular impact on those who knew the victim, some of whom might know a lot more than they'd ever said, and some of whom might want to cover their tracks, even twenty years later. She might be way off base, but if it did end up being ruled an arson, it was that aspect of the burning house Jane felt should be looked into. If she had the time, she'd do it herself.

10

Emma skirted the edges of The Outpost bar, head down, hoping nobody she knew was around. She made it to the back hallway and took the elevator up to the third floor. Before she knocked on the door, she ran a hand through her hair. She was still dressed for the party. She looked hot and knew it. Damn Philip and his trophy girlfriends. What was good for the gander, in this case, was good for the goose.

When Scott opened the door, he pulled her inside, his mouth on hers, his arms holding her tightly against him. "I needed to see you tonight so bad," he said coming up for air briefly. He tugged her toward the couch, undressing her as they went.

"Me, too," she tried to say, though it came out more, "Mmm ooh."

She wanted to talk first, to tell him in person how sorry she was about his brother, but he had other ideas. The faster her clothes came off, the more his idea became hers. After they were done— if she'd clocked it, it was probably less than five minutes—he sat up, zipped up his pants, and buttoned his shirt. She grabbed her clothes and headed into the bathroom to get cleaned up. When she returned to the living room a few minutes later, he'd poured each of them an inch or so of bourbon—his preference. Also clearly not his first of the night. She preferred wine, but what the hell.

Even though the sex had been the equivalent of wham, bam, thank you ma'am, she appreciated his passion, something Philip had lacked for years. She scolded herself for being so hard on Scott. Even though the sex was quick, she was sure he cared about her in his own way, that he wasn't just using her, any more than she was using him.

"How are you doing?" she asked, sitting down on the couch opposite him. She'd texted him last night about his brother's remains being found, feeling bad that she couldn't come over. He'd texted back that his dad had called. Emma was appalled that his father hadn't come by to tell him face-to-face. It further cemented her view of his old man as mean and thoughtless.

"I'm okay," he said, tossing back half his drink.

She couldn't let it go. "Why didn't your father come tell you in person?"

"Oh, who knows?"

"How can you work with that awful man every day?" Scott had been the senior loan officer at Lakeside Community Bank for many years. His father had hired him right out of college and helped him climb the ladder, so there was that. But Scott had good skills and was a reasonably affable human being. He could go anywhere with his experience and find a job.

"I'm paid well at LCB. I love my condo. One town or city is a lot like the next. And I'm settled. I know what each day will be like, and I want that."

What he really liked was that he could keep his head down, do his job, come home, and forget about work. He spent his evenings and weekends watching TV, playing video games, cooking for his many friends, or meeting someone at a restaurant for dinner. He coached soccer for local kids during the summer months, and was passionate about running, something Emma admired and hoped to start doing herself when she got back to California. He liked to have a good time, which generally included food and alcohol, and that was fine by her.

Emma hadn't been in town long when a girlfriend invited her for happy hour at The Outpost. They sat at one of the long tables. Two more old friends from high school drifted over to join them. At some point, a pizza was ordered, followed by a pitcher of margaritas.

At first when Scott sat down next to her, Emma hadn't recognized him. Gone were the grunge clothes and curtained hair of his youth. In the years since she'd last seen him, he'd filled out and grown up. Sam had been blond, like his mother. Scott was dark haired and had his dad's long, narrow face and closely set eyes.

That first night she'd wondered if he was trendy enough to maintain a permanent scruff. Turned out his beard was so heavy that by evening, if he didn't shave a second time, that was the way it looked. He wasn't handsome, and yet the more they talked, the more she began to recognize that the tenor of his voice and the way he expressed himself was a lot like Sam. Maybe it was nostalgia, or maybe she was lonely, having just left her home in California. Whatever it was, she began to warm to him. Scott was a living, breathing connection to the young man she'd once loved so deeply.

"Don't bitch about my dad," said Scott, knocking back the other half of his bourbon. "He's okay."

"I doubt Sam would have seen it that way."

"It wasn't all Dad's fault." He rose from the couch and walked over to his sound system, on a shelf by the TV. After turning on some Coltrane, he returned to the couch. "You weren't there. Sam was always pushing boundaries, doing the exact opposite of what Dad asked him to do. When he got caught, he'd respond with his usual load of snark."

"Your dad is a bully."

"Yeah, okay, but so was Sam."

"What are you saying? That he bullied you?"

"Sure. All the time."

She remembered what Kurt had said, that Scott and Sam had been fighting about something before Sam died. "Anything specific?"

"Meaning what?"

"I've heard rumors that you and Sam were pretty angry at each other before he died."

His reaction was swift. "That's total bullshit."

"So, it's not true?"

"We argued all the time. Meant nothing." He slipped his arm around her and leaned in for a kiss. "Let's talk about something else."

Even though he wanted to change the subject, she could tell his mood had darkened. She supposed that everyone dealt with grief differently. "You want to talk about what happened to him?"

"I want to talk about you."

"Me?" She cocked her head. "Not that much to say. I'll be heading home this time next week, but you already know that. I guess we better make the best of the time we have left."

He pulled away. "You mean you're still planning to go back?"

"Of course."

"But I thought . . . what about us?"

She touched his face. "It's been wonderful being with you this summer. You've single-handedly restored my faith in men. But I can't stay away from home forever."

"But you said your marriage was over, that you and your husband had separated."

"We have."

"So? I'm here and I love you."

"You what?" He'd never used that particular word before.

"We could have a great life together."

"Scott, come on. I thought we understood each other." This was a conversation she'd never thought she'd need to have with him. She assumed they saw their relationship the same way, nothing but a delicious summer fling. Sure, she'd come to care about him, but the last thing she wanted was another marriage. "I have a daughter, Scott. She's fifteen. I can't just leave her to be with you."

"Why can't she come here and live with us?"

Was he totally clueless? She tried to be patient. "Verity's whole life is in Mountain View. Her school. Her friends. I can't just uproot her. That would be cruel."

"Kids are pliable. They can roll with the punches."

"Really? And you know this how? Do you have a kid hidden around here I've never met?"

His eyes showed a flicker of anger, something Emma had never seen in him before. "No, no children. It doesn't disqualify me from having a valid opinion." He poured himself another bourbon. "Okay, so how about this: She lives with Philip during the school year and comes to stay with us during the summer."

"You're not hearing me."

"I could say the same for you."

She tried to get up, but he put his hand on her arm and gripped her hard. "You're hurting me."

"Don't leave. Stay the night. We need to talk this through."

She yanked her arm away. "I can't."

"Why?"

"You know why. I have houseguests. And I'm still a married woman."

"Didn't stop you before."

This was getting plain weird. For just an instant, she had the sense that he might physically prevent her from going. "I can't." She swerved around the coffee table and reached down for her scarf. Once out in the hall on the way to the elevator, her heart still hammering, she tried to make sense of what had just happened.

Maybe it was the booze. That had to be it. He was drunk. He'd never behaved like that before.

As she left the building, she realized she had another problem. How was she going to get home? She'd assumed Scott would drive her, as he had before. That wasn't going to happen. She'd need to figure out another way.

Crossing into the alley next to the bar, Emma walked quickly through one of the rougher areas of town to Mill Avenue, where tiny houses lined both sides of the street. It wasn't an area she was familiar with. She walked along, looking behind her as she went, until she came to a white house. The light next to the front door was on, revealing the number 617. It was narrower than some of the other houses, but it was a two-story, or maybe one and a half, and it had a cozy-looking front porch. When the bell didn't seem to work, she pounded on the door. A moment later, Danny appeared.

"Oh, Mrs. Anguelo," he said, looking surprised. "Um, I mean, Emma."

She smiled uneasily. "Can I come in?"

"I guess." He backed up.

As she entered, she saw that the interior of the house was larger than it had looked from the outside. The walls were painted the color of a paper bag. The trim was white. Large framed art posters made the space seem both dramatic and funky. Danny had been sitting on the couch in the living room with a bowl of popcorn. The TV was on. "I'm sorry to interrupt—"

Danny reached for the remote and stopped the movie.

"Is your father here?"

"He's out in the backyard. It's right through there." He pointed to a room that wasn't much bigger than her closet at home in California. A table pushed up to the window was filled with books, papers, stacks of file folders, and a laptop. Since Danny wasn't in school anymore, she assumed this was where Kurt worked. When

72

she passed through the kitchen, she found a row of homegrown tomatoes in varying degrees of ripeness resting on the windowsill, and a freestanding butcher block table with a small bouquet of summer flowers—zinnias, snapdragons, and a few wispy cosmos—under the window.

Coming down the back steps, she heard Kurt's voice. She found him by a picnic table talking on his phone, facing away. He was still wearing the clothes he'd worn to the cocktail party, though he'd taken off his suede jacket. His body language suggested he was upset.

"Yeah, it sure as hell *was* out of the blue." He turned slightly, pinched the bridge of his nose. "It's a lot to drop on a guy." He listened again, longer this time. "Fine. I told you I'd think about it and I will. But right now, I gotta go." He clicked the phone off and stuffed it back into his pocket. "Screw it," he muttered, grabbing a bottle of vodka off the picnic table and taking a swig.

It must be the night for the men in Emma's life to get drunk.

Kurt weaved away from the table and hefted a log onto a chopping block. Emma noticed a stack of cut firewood next to the house. Pressing a splitting wedge into the center of the log, Kurt backed up, wiping a hand across his mouth.

"I'm not sure you should use your lumberjack skills when you've been drinking," she said.

He whirled around. "How long have you been standing there?"

"Long enough to know you should leave that ax where it is." She nodded to one resting against the concrete steps.

His phone rang.

"Go ahead and answer it."

"Not interested," he said, removing the phone from his pocket and slapping it on the picnic table. "What are you doing here?"

She sat down at the table, reached for the vodka, and took a sip. "The party ended right after you left. You want to talk about . . . whatever it is that's got you so upset?" She nodded to his phone.

He dropped down on the other side of the table. "No."

"You've listened to me bitch about Philip all summer. Listening to your romantic travails is the least I can do."

"Why do you assume my problem is romantic?"

"Isn't it?"

He didn't reply.

She shrugged. "You're too nice a guy not to have someone important in your life. I realize you like your privacy, but expressing your feelings doesn't make a man weak."

"You're saying everyone has to pair up, otherwise life is meaningless?"

She laughed. "Hardly."

"I have no problem expressing my feelings, Emma."

"Really?"

"You're mixing me up with Sam. I'm not as complicated as he was."

She didn't believe any of it, but let it pass. She gazed up at the house, a bit surprised that she'd never considered what kind of place he lived in before. She knew he owned a home because he'd given her the address, but that was all.

"Not exactly a palace, is it?" he said, grabbing the vodka back. "But it's more than I ever thought I'd have. I love the place."

"What's the square footage?"

"Maybe nine hundred."

"Seems bigger."

"That's for the first and second floors. The basement is dry and clean, but we don't use it for much other than storage. I hate basements."

"How long have you lived here?"

"Since Danny turned four. My dad helped me with the down payment. It was a dilapidated wreck, so I got it cheap. Danny and I were living with my parents at the time—after Vickie left. Mom babysat every evening for almost a year while Dad and I made it livable."

"It's wonderful."

"How diplomatic."

"No, I mean it."

"What are you doing in town?"

"I was still in a party mood, so I thought I'd have a drink with some friends at The Outpost. Jane and Cordelia dropped me off on their way to go take a look at the fire. I don't suppose you've heard anything more about that?"

He shrugged. "No. Why would I?"

He seemed unusually defensive, which she put down to the phone call. "I thought maybe a neighbor had said something, or that you'd heard about it on the news."

"Nope."

"Look, Kurt, the reason I'm here is because none of my friends showed up at the bar, so I need a ride home."

"Oh." He started to get up.

"No, no. You're not taking me anywhere in the condition you're in."

"Suppose you have a point. Danny can do it." He headed for the back door.

"Are you sure?"

"Emma, I'm in no mood to argue. Let him drive you or don't. It's up to you." He disappeared inside the house, letting the screen door slam behind him.

KURT

August 28, 1999

He finished his apple as he undressed. He'd spent the afternoon at the butcher shop working the counter and later helping his mom clean the walk-in refrigerator. His parents had come home briefly to shower and change and had left almost immediately for a church supper. Kurt was left to make his own. The apple was easy, so he'd grabbed that, thinking he'd heat up some frozen pizza rolls later.

As he was coming out of the shower, the telephone rang. Standing in the hallway, a towel around his waist, he answered it. He assumed it would be Vicki. Instead, Todd Ott's voice came over the line.

"Hey man, I scored two six-packs of Grain Belt. Come over and help me drink it."

"How'd you manage that?"

"Simple. Theft. Old man Hanson left them in a cooler on his back porch."

"What about your parents?"

"They're playing board games at a friend's house."

"Who else is coming?"

"The usuals, depending on who's around. So stop with the

twenty questions and come. I'm in the basement. I'll leave the back door unlocked."

Todd's place was a couple miles away. After pulling on some clean jeans and a T-shirt, Kurt jumped on his old Murray Cruiser and pedaled over to the house. When he sailed into the drive at the back of the property, he saw that Sam's motorcycle was parked next to Todd's junkyard heap, a Ford Taurus. He hadn't seen or heard from Sam all week, which was good, because he had no idea what to say. As he headed up the walk, he found Sam standing by the side of the house, smoking a cigarette.

"Hey, man," said Kurt, feeling his stomach twist.

"Hey," repeated Sam. With his eyes fixed on the tip of the cigarette, he said, "You gonna hit me?"

"Hit you? Why would I do that?"

Sam's sullen look instantly changed to a smile. "Absolutely no reason I can think of." Flipping the cigarette into a flower bed, he entered the back door, with Kurt following behind. They trotted down the basement steps and found Todd and Jim already ensconced in two of the four ancient recliners. Kurt figured this basement was where recliners went to die.

Jim spent the next few minutes ragging on one of their classmates. Kurt didn't know the guy all that well, so he just sat back and sipped his beer. He was glad when Sam weighed in on something because he could watch him without feeling weird. He realized that he'd never really looked at Sam before, not carefully and certainly not curiously. Kurt didn't consider himself an expert when it came to beauty, but thought Sam was definitely good-looking.

As Todd passed around a fresh set of beers, Kurt glanced at Sam out of the corner of his eye and saw him looking back. The look felt like a jolt of electricity and almost made him jump.

"So, here's the good news," said Jim, pulling the tab off his beer. "Corey Lang's throwing a party on Saturday night, two weeks from now. You all know him, right? Graduated last year?"

Everyone nodded.

"His parents will be away the entire weekend, so when the cat's away the rats, that's us—and whoever else wants to come—will play. He said he's getting a keg and a couple of his buddies will have the harder stuff. You know where the Lang farm is, right?"

"I don't," said Kurt.

"It's up Lawson Road, maybe five miles out of town. I'll draw you a map. So who's in?"

"Can we bring our girlfriends?" asked Todd, tipping the last few drops of beer into his open mouth.

"Absolutely. Bring whoever you want. I can get us some weed. It's gonna be epic, a real end-of-the-summer blowout."

Kurt had never been much of a partygoer. His parents frowned on drinking, though they probably knew he did it.

"I'll be there," said Sam, grinning as he crushed his empty beer can against his forehead.

After their third beers were gone, the group began to break up. Jim took off first. Todd walked up the stairs after him, carrying a sack with all the empty cans. Kurt stayed where he was and watched Sam to see what he'd do. Nothing was said. Eventually, Sam got up. Halfway up the steps, with only his feet visible to Kurt, he turned and came back down.

"You're gonna be there, right?" he asked.

"Yeah," said Kurt.

Sam waited a second, an unreadable look on his face, then pressed a finger to his lips and gave a slow wink.

11

Monday morning dawned in a cold drizzle. On his way to his father's house, Dave saw a red Hyundai Sonata pull into traffic and follow him. He knew who owned the car, so before he reached his dad's place, he stopped along a quiet side street, put his cruiser in park, and slid out.

"Come with me," said Dave as soon as Monty cracked the door. His two boys were in the backseat, each playing on their phones. As they stood together in front of the sedan, the kids out of earshot, Dave asked Monty where he was going.

"My wife picked up a shift at the hospital, so I decided to take the boys out for breakfast."

"No school today?"

"Nope, it's some teacher conference."

One of the things Dave admired about Monty was his obvious devotion to his children. "Why were you following me?"

"Because I need to know what's happening with the Romilly thing."

"Nothing's happening," said Dave, folding his arms and leaning back against the hood of the car. "I told you, I've got it handled. In fact, the more I think about it, the more it seems to me that nobody's ever going to figure out what really happened. How could they?"

"You sent the backpack to the BCA in St. Paul. Why the hell would you do that?"

"Who told you that?" snapped Dave.

"People were there, asshole. They're talking."

"Look, everything we found had to be shipped to the BCA. I had no say in it."

"What else don't you have any say in?"

"Just chill, okay? Don't I always take care of things?"

Ever since Dave could remember, Monty had been part of his life. As kids, they'd lived next door to each other and were always together. Monty's mother was a wonderful woman, and Dave's dad was great. Monty's dad was a horror show and so was Dave's mom. They often said that, between them, they had one decent set of parents.

"Nobody came forward twenty years ago," said Dave. "Nobody's going to now."

"Yeah, right." Monty unzipped his windbreaker and looked up at the sky. "Your optimism makes me want to puke."

Dave laughed. "You working today?"

Monty managed a motel on the edge of town. He'd married the owner's daughter, so the job was part of the package.

"After Sarah gets home, I'll pick up the second shift."

"How *is* everything at the Bates Motel?"

"Shut up, man. Don't call it that. Too many people in this town repeat the same stupid joke. It's the Avalon Motor Inn."

People began calling it the Bates Motel long before Monty took over as manager, mostly because it was so run-down. As soon as Monty was put in charge, he went to his father-in-law and made a deal: If the father-in-law would buy the paint, Monty would paint the place himself. Actually, he'd made it look pretty good. Still, the joke persisted.

"Sorry," said Dave. "Didn't mean to offend."

"Yeah, well. Call me with any news."

"Will do. Hey, we still on for beers tomorrow night?" They usually got together at least once a week to play pool and have a brew or two. If Sarah happened to be working, they'd split the cost of a babysitter.

"For sure," said Monty.

A while later, as Dave headed up the sidewalk to his dad's place, he saw Lydia Mickler, Monty's mom, standing inside her front door, reaching into the mailbox. "Hey, Mrs. Mickler," he called, walking across the lawn to talk to her.

"Hi, Dave. How are you?"

She'd become so frail in the last few years. Her health wasn't good, and she needed a lot of help just to stay in her home. The help came mostly from her daughter, Jaxie. Monty shopped for her groceries, but that was about it. There had been some talk about moving her to an assisted living facility, though Dave wasn't sure if a final decision had been made. He still felt close to Lydia. She'd been a better mother to him than his own mother ever had. "Can I help with anything?"

"No, but thanks for the offer. You're welcome to come in for a cup of coffee. The pot's still on."

"Oh, I'd love that," said Dave, "but I'm on duty. And I need to talk to my dad."

"You give him a hug from me," said Mrs. Mickler. "Tell him to come over when he has a minute. I've still got that bottle of Scotch."

The bottle she was referring to had been given to her on her fiftieth birthday. "I'll do that." After saying goodbye, he entered his dad's house, finding him in the living room, sitting on the couch and eating a bowl of Cap'n Crunch. It was his usual breakfast, along with a mug of coffee. "Hey."

"Hey, David," he said between mouthfuls.

Dave jingled the keys in his pocket. "I called Mom."

"She still alive?"

"I asked her if she knew where your old field notebooks were, that you thought she put them in a box."

"And?"

"She has no memory of it."

"Figures." He set the empty bowl down on the end table and picked up his mug. "How come you're so interested in them?"

"The Romilly investigation, remember?"

"Oh, sure. Right."

"So, ah, I thought I'd go down in the basement and look around. I know you wrote official reports, but sometimes things don't get included that might turn out to be important."

"True. When you're done, why don't we take a drive? Maybe head up to Elbow Lake. We could do a little fishing."

"I can't, Pop. I'm on duty."

His father gazed at him with a confused look. "Oh, sure. Forgot. Maybe tomorrow." He picked up the remote and rested his legs on a footstool. "Think I'll watch Judge Judy. If you get lost in the basement, holler and I'll send out a search party."

On his way down the hall to the basement door, Dave paused a moment, sticking his head into his dad's study. His desk had always been a model of organization, but today it was covered with unopened envelopes, as if they'd simply been tossed there and forgotten. He picked a couple up and saw they were bills. Digging through the mess, he concluded that it had been several months since his father had paid the mortgage, the electric and gas bills, and the water bill. What the hell was going on?

"Pop?" he called. When his father didn't respond, he went looking for him, and found him with his head in the refrigerator. "You haven't paid any of your bills."

"No?" It felt like his father was talking to the mayonnaise. "Don't worry, I'll get to them."

"But some are two months old."

His dad straightened up and turned around. "I usually pay them in the afternoon, but lately I get busy with stuff and just don't seem to find the time. But no worries. They give you a grace period."

Dave wasn't so sure. "I can help, if you want."

"You've got enough to do. No, I'll pay them. Don't nag."

There wasn't much more he could say. "I'll be down in the basement."

"Sweep the furnace room while you're at it." He laughed.

After half an hour of digging through every box on every shelf, Dave came up empty. If he couldn't find the notebooks, that meant nobody else could, either. Chances were they'd been tossed long ago. His dad tended to hang on to stuff, thinking he might need it somewhere down the line. His mother had the opposite approach—always throwing things away to get rid of clutter. These days, his dad could be as much of a pack rat as he wanted, and his mother could live in organized nirvana. Maybe there were happy endings after all.

Admitting defeat, Dave returned upstairs, only to find his dad out on the back porch eating a second bowl of Cap'n Crunch. "Still hungry?"

His dad looked up. "Huh?"

"Never mind. I gotta shove off. Hey, did you get that AC installed in your bedroom?"

"Sure."

"Not that you need it right now. But next summer, it will come in handy."

"Absolutely." He wiped a dribble of milk off his chin.

Dave's cell phone rang. "Give me a minute." He walked out of the room and said hello.

"Tamborsky? It's Grady. I need you to get back to the station ASAP."

"Why? Did something happen?" Oh God, now what, he thought.

"Just get here." The line disconnected.

After lunch at the White Star Cafe, Jane and Cordelia parted company. Cordelia had a date with Emma and the rest of the arts board over at the old Timberline Theater on Elm, where the Firefly Community Players performed. Jane's plan was to meet with one of Sam Romilly's friends, a real estate agent named Jim Hughes. Not wanting to walk all the way to the theater, Cordelia had asked to borrow Jane's truck. Jane didn't mind hoofing it, as long as Cordelia picked her up on the way back to the lake house.

The morning drizzle had been replaced by a light fog, softening the look of the storefronts along Main. As Jane crossed the street, she saw a group of people streaming out of the town hall, an old three-story brownstone. The last person out was the mayor, Leslie Harrow, the woman Jane had met last night. Harrow stood on the street, checking her phone. When she looked up and saw Jane, she smiled and called her over.

"Nice to see you again," she said, clicking the phone off.

"I wanted to tell you how sorry I was to hear about the fire last night. I hear the house belonged to a friend of yours."

"Walk with me," said Harrow, linking her arm through Jane's. Once they were away from the knot of people, Harrow said, "Thanks. I was out there early this morning. The house is a total loss."

"Did they find her car in the garage?"

"No," said Harrow.

"Then maybe she's safe somewhere."

"I wish it were that simple. Carli and her husband, Aaron, split up a few months ago. To get him to move out, she had to give him their truck. Carli bought herself a beater, but it always seemed to be in for repairs."

"Has anyone heard from her?"

"No, and we're all pretty upset. She does, on occasion, spend the night with a girlfriend over in Clarksville, but when she didn't show up for work at the bank today and I learned that nobody's heard from her . . . I guess I'm not holding out a lot of hope."

"You don't think the husband—"

"I hate to go there. We'll have to wait and see what the fire inspector has to say. If it turns out to be arson, the police will question him. Aaron always seemed nice enough to me. In fact, he's just the kind of guy I would have dated way back when."

"Before you got married."

"I'm not married. What gave you that idea?"

"Well, I mean, that man who came up to you last night—"

"Don? He's just a friend."

"So you don't date anymore?"

"I do make an exception on occasion." She glanced at Jane but kept on walking.

As they passed a series of cars parked along the street, Harrow stopped to pull a yellow flyer out from under one of the windshield wipers. She removed her reading glasses from the pocket of her blazer and stopped to take a look. "Damn. This is just what we need."

"What?" asked Jane, watching Harrow's anger flare.

"The Klan's back."

"In Minnesota? Are you kidding me?"

"Oh, there used to be a big Klan presence in the state back in the twenties and thirties. Even today, there's still a chapter in Minneapolis. And last year, they put up Klan recruitment posters all over the Iron Range, with a KKK phone number for people to call. Hate is alive and well all over this country, and Castle Lake isn't immune."

As they passed Kepler's Grocery, Harrow scooped up a stack of the flyers from an outside rack and, once again, kept walking, more quickly this time.

"What are you going to do with those?" asked Jane, straining to keep up.

"Watch," said Harrow, walking over to a sidewalk trash can and dumping the entire stack inside. "This garbage won't appeal to very many, but there's always a few who keep it going. Makes me sick." She slowed her pace. "I need to get some lunch before my next meeting. Have you eaten?"

"Just finished," said Jane.

"Well, that's okay, I don't have much time anyway. But since I can't invite you to have lunch with me, what about dinner? We can eat our way through an antipasto platter. It's a specialty of mine, something I learned to love when I was living in Naples."

"You lived in Italy?"

"I've lived all over."

"Well, sure," said Jane, brightening at the prospect. "I'd love to come. What can I bring?"

"A nice bottle of wine. Don't spend an arm and a leg." She handed Jane a business card. "That's my number. Send me yours and I'll text you the address. How does seven sound?"

"Seven's perfect."

They stood smiling at each other until Harrow roused herself and said, "Well, I guess I'll see you tonight."

12

Dave nodded to the dispatcher behind the plexiglass wall as he made his way to Grady Larson's office. It was the largest of three offices on the first floor of the Public Safety Building.

The CLPD had nine sworn officers: a chief, one patrol sergeant, two detective/sergeants, and five patrol officers. The detectives were also considered patrol officers, but with added duties. Grady's door was open, so Dave walked in, finding his boss poring over a stack of papers. "I made it as fast as I could. What's up?" He held his breath, hoping it wasn't bad news.

"Sit down." Grady nodded to a chair as he scrutinized Dave's shirt. "Where's your badge?"

"My . . . what?" He looked down. "Oh, shit." He'd been racing out of his place this morning and instead of taking the time to pin it on, he'd pocketed it, thinking he'd do it once he was in the car. But he'd forgotten. "I——" He removed it from his pocket.

"Jeez, Tamborsky. Wake the hell up."

"I'm sorry."

"I don't want excuses. Are you tired or something? Not getting enough sleep? Where were you last night?"

Dave's head snapped up. "Excuse me?"

Leaning closer to the desk, Grady spoke out of the side of his mouth. "Look, son, I know you've been sleeping with that woman up in Clarksville. Paula something-or-other. She's pretty, and she has a good job. Why don't you put me out of my misery and marry her?"

"Put *you* out of misery?"

"If I had a nickel for every time someone said to me, 'Hey, Grady, why don't you help poor Dave Tamborsky find himself a wife and settle down—'"

"People actually say that to you? *Poor* Dave?"

"Enough said." Shifting back in his chair, he continued, "I'm taking you off the Romilly investigation."

"What?"

"I was at a party last night. One of the guests pointed out that you were a friend of Sam Romilly's. That you were in the same class. That might be a conflict."

"Are you serious?"

"The case is sensitive, son. It has nothing to do with your job performance. You know I think you're a good officer. You work hard, you're fair, and you care about the people you serve." Narrowing one eye, he asked, "Ever heard of a true crime podcast?"

"Yeah."

"Well I hadn't. Checked it out online this morning. It's some kind of internet radio show that deals with Minnesota cold cases. The same woman who mentioned that you and Romilly were friends told me she works for one. She plans on looking into Sam's death. She's pushy, so we may have some problems with her."

"What's her name?"

"Jane Lawless. She's up for the art center festival, staying out at the Granholm place. But forget about her. She's not your problem. Reopening the Romilly case is going to be a huge headache for this department. I need to avoid any appearance of impropriety. So you're done. I'm putting Bobby Saltus on it."

"Saltus? But he doesn't have my experience."

"No, but I'm planning to work with him as needed, so no worries."

Dave thrashed around inside his mind for a way to make the chief reverse his decision, but since he'd never anticipated being removed, he had no idea how to argue against it. Saltus had only been on the force a few years. He was a pretty boy. He'd grown up in the Cities, so he didn't know people in town the way Dave did. How Grady could see that as a plus was beyond him.

"I'm putting you in charge of the fire at the Gilbert house."

"Okay, but—"

"We'll get the official word on whether it was or wasn't arson once the fire investigator finishes his examination. Between you and me, it would surprise the hell out of me if it wasn't."

As if on cue, Bobby Saltus appeared in the doorway. "You wanted to see me, Chief?"

"Sit down." Grady tossed his pen on the desk.

Saltus sat on a folding chair and looked quizzically from face to face.

"I'm putting you in charge of the Romilly investigation," said Grady.

"Me?" A slow smile spread across his face.

Dave tried to hide his loathing. Saltus was a Justin Bieber look-alike with air for brains. He spent the majority of his working hours chatting up girls.

"Look, Chief," said Dave. "Okay, so I might not be able to help in the field, but I could for sure help on background. I knew Romilly. I knew his friends. That's worth something."

Grady tapped a finger against his double chin. "You have a point. Let me think on it."

Dave turned to offer Saltus a smile of his own, but instead nearly laughed out loud when he saw the pout forming.

Grady pushed the stack of papers aside and picked up an envelope. "Next. I'm gonna give you both a chance to weigh in on this." He opened the envelope, removed a piece of white typing paper, and waved it around. "This was shoved under the outer door sometime before I arrived this morning. It's typed. Short and to the point. I'll read it to you.

"To whom it may concern. I have information on the Romilly murder, but I can't come forward because I fear for my safety. Check into these four people. I know they have information they've never talked about.

Jim Hughes
Kurt Steiner
Scott Romilly
Darius Pollard

"I'll help more if I can. Sincerely, A Friend." Looking up, Grady said, "So what do you make of that?"

"I'll check into it," said Saltus.

"Hughes was a friend of Sam's," said Dave. "So was Steiner. They were on the high school swim team. Don't know much about Pollard, but Scott's Sam's younger brother, works at Lakeside Community Bank. Never done anything wrong, far as I know. None of them have."

Grady nodded, as if settling something in his mind. "Well, I think we have some work to do. Bobby, I want you to call each of these people down to the station for an interview."

"I'm on it," said Saltus.

"Dave, go check out the house fire."

He hesitated. Couldn't the chief see what a bad idea it was to take him off the Romilly case? He knew so much more about the people in Sam's life than Saltus. Then again, Grady hadn't totally cut him out, at least that's what Dave hoped his comment, "You have a point," had meant. And he figured he could push Saltus around if he needed to. No way on earth was he going to back away from the investigation.

13

The real estate company where Jim Hughes worked as an agent was on the second floor of a three-story wood-frame building, directly above Baker Drug and across from the Liquor Mart. When Jane arrived upstairs, a receptionist showed her to his office.

Hughes was a balding man with large ears and a paunch. He stood as she walked in and shook her hand. She'd already explained on the phone why she was in town and the reason she wanted to meet with him in person. Nodding to a chair, he took his seat behind his desk.

"So," he said, leaning back and folding his hands over his stomach. "You have some questions about Sam Romilly."

"Do you mind if I record our conversation?"

"For your podcast?"

"If we decided to use any of it, we'd need your written permission."

"Not a problem," he said, watching her remove the recorder from a canvas messenger bag. "This is all sort of fascinating to me."

Jane used a Sony 4GB recorder with a USB connector she would plug into her laptop when she got back to the lake house. She also attached a small lavalier microphone with dual microphones to assure good sound quality. She clipped one mic onto her shirt, then got up and clipped the other to one of the lapels on Hughes's suit coat. He seemed to be thinking hard about something, perhaps weighing what he might or might not say.

"Sam's been on my mind a lot since his remains were discovered in the cemetery at Holy Trinity. That's my church, by the way, so it seemed doubly awful. I can't imagine why he was put there."

Jane sat back down, switched on the recorder, and asked her opening question. "When Sam went missing, what did you think happened?"

"I guess I assumed he'd taken off for greener pastures. He always said he hated small towns. He was kind of a daredevil, you know, liked to take risks, so leaving all the comforts of home wouldn't have stopped him. He worked at a hardware store the summer between his junior and senior year. I suppose I figured he'd saved his money to bankroll his getaway."

"Both his mother and Emma Granholm mentioned that he didn't take his motorcycle. They thought it was strange."

"Yeah, I thought so, too, but then it would have been a lot cheaper for him to hitchhike. Instead of spending money on gas, he could've spent it on food. But now we know none of that happened."

"Did Sam ever talk about his father with you?"

"So you've heard the rumors. No, not much. Everybody knew he hated his dad, but I never remember him giving any reasons." Pausing a moment, he added, "We didn't really have that kind of friendship—where you open up about something painful. We were mostly social friends. I don't recall a deep conversation with any of the guys on the swim team. Maybe we were all shallow, but my guess is most guys are like that." He removed a large, black Moleskine notebook from his top desk drawer. On the front was a label that said 1999. "I've kept a journal since I was in junior high. When my sister died, my mom said I should write about how I felt, that it would help me. It really did, so I just kept doing it. I

92

didn't write every day, but I did record a lot of what was happening. So when Sam was found, I dug it out. I found the rumor about his dad, and I highlighted it. In reading over what I wrote about the early months of my senior year, I was struck by how many other rumors were going around—not about Sam, but in general, so I highlighted those, too. I suppose it's all part of being in high school, but I've always been kind of sensitive to rumors."

"Any particular reason?"

"Yeah, an important one. When I was in Cub Scouts, a rumor went around that one of the assistant cub masters secretly worshiped the devil. I actually believed it, mainly because he seemed so creepy. Years later, when I was in junior high, the same guy was arrested and charged with molesting boys. I know rumors aren't always true, but sometimes where there's smoke—"

Jane took his point. "I'd love to know what some of the rumors were."

"Well," he said, opening the notebook and flipping through the first few pages. "Okay, here's one. Believe it or not, it was a very big deal at the time. People were saying that on January 1, 2000, the middle of our senior year, our school would blow up. It was all part of the Y2K scare. The principal even called a school assembly to address it." He continued to page through his notes, stopping here and there to read before moving on. "Another rumor was that one of the teachers had seduced a student. We figured it was Mr. Hoffman, the football coach. He was always off in some dark corner, whispering to one of the cheerleaders. A couple guys said he kept porno magazines in his desk, but nothing ever happened to him." He turned another half dozen pages. "Oh, and this one was big for a while. People were saying that two guys, Dave Tamborsky and Monty Mickler, weren't just friends."

"Meaning?"

"That they were gay and getting it on with each other. I will say, they did seem unusually tight."

"Any truth in it?"

"Mickler's married now, so probably not, but who knows?" He continued to search the pages of the journal. "Okay, the last one I recorded was about some girl in our class getting into a car with a stranger and being attacked. Apparently it happened sometime during the summer. Never heard any other details, but that one was whispered about for months." He closed the book. "That's all I recorded. Make of them what you will."

"I'm curious," said Jane. "What about drugs? Was that a big deal back in high school?"

"Not the hard stuff, at least not in my crowd. We all drank, illegally, of course, and it was pretty easy to get weed. But that's it."

Jane glanced down at her list of questions. "Did you ever see Sam get into any fights? Anybody have a grudge against him?"

"The only fight I remember was with his brother."

"Scott? Do you know what it was about?"

"No idea. Actually, as I think about it, it was a few days before he went missing. I was on my way to meet my girlfriend at Boogaloo's, a burger joint that used to be across from the Rialto theater. As I was walking through Liberty Park, I saw them. At first, I thought they were wrestling. You know, just having fun. But it became apparent pretty quickly that they were trying to beat the crap out of each other. I ran over and did my best to break them up. After Scott took off, Sam said he thought his brother was about to ruin his life. Someone had to knock some sense into him."

"What did he mean by that?"

"No idea. And he didn't elaborate."

"How well did you know Scott?"

"He was a year younger than me, so not well. He was quiet, more studious than Sam, though that's not saying much. He was definitely entrepreneurial. He'd started a lawn service that summer. Used to cut grass and do gardening work around town. Other than that, he's more or less of a blank."

"Is there anything else you remember from that time, something that might shed light on who might have had it in for Sam?"

He hesitated. "Well, I'm not sure it's related, but there was this all-night party at the beginning of our senior year. It was at the Lang farm. Corey Lang's parents had left for the weekend, so he invited everyone he knew to come have an end-of-the-summer blowout. Something happened that night. I never found out what it was, but Sam was part of it. I asked around, but nobody knew anything, which couldn't have been true. Probably people were just being careful, or they wanted to forget about it. I'm afraid that's all I know."

Jane underlined it in her mind. "Can you give the names of his close friends?"

"Um, well, there was me, of course, and Kurt Steiner—we're both still in town. Then Todd Ott—he moved away. Lives out east, I think. And oh—" He snapped his fingers. "There is one other guy. Kind of an outlier, not someone any of us knew very well. I'm ashamed to say it was probably because he was black. At the time, there were only a few black families in town. His name is Darius Pollard. He works at Pollard Automotive Repair. His family owns it."

"In town?"

"Yeah. Over on Fourth and Brick Town Road."

The receptionist popped her head into the room and said, "Jim, your three-thirty is here early. What do you want to do?"

"I should let you get back to business," said Jane, rising from her chair. She switched off the recorder and then unhooked their mics, placing everything back in the canvas bag. "This has been helpful."

Hughes stood and shook her hand. "I hope someone can make some sense of what happened. I have to say, I don't have much faith in our police department. But who knows? Maybe they'll surprise all of us."

"Maybe," Jane agreed, though like Hughes, she wasn't about to bet money on it.

Jane waited in a coffee shop for Cordelia to pick her up. When she finally arrived, she bought herself a double macchiato. Jane asked if she really wanted that much caffeine so late in the day.

"I think I'll risk it," Cordelia said as they made their way back to the truck. Climbing into the passenger's seat, she added. "I'm not sleeping all that well anyway. That mattress is lumpy."

"You want to switch?" asked Jane. "You could take my room for a night and see if it's any better."

"Let me think about it."

As they drove east through town on their way back to the house, Jane decided to take a quick detour.

"How did the interview with Jim Hughes go?" asked Cordelia, digging through her large sack purse.

"It was good. You can listen to it if you want."

"I should have been there. We could have done good cop/bad cop and really put the screws to him."

"That wasn't necessary."

"You never know," said Cordelia. "You were probably hampered by the lack of my awesome intuition."

"Can't be helped. You were busy."

"True. And I can't be two places at once. Once again, Janey, all I can say is, I wish they'd figure out this quantum physics thing so I could be."

"Two places at once?"

"Or exist simultaneously in different universes at the same time."

"Spreading joy and enlightenment."

"And oodles of pixie dust." She pushed her hair away from her face and examined herself in the visor mirror. "By the way, Emma wanted me to tell you that she's inviting us—and a bunch of her friends—to the restaurant at Dellmann's Resort up on Chipping Lake."

"Tonight?"

"Yup. The owner is an old buddy. I hear the food is fabulous."

Turning onto Eleventh Street, Jane said, "That's too bad. I have a prior engagement."

"You do?"

"Leslie Harrow, the mayor, invited me to dinner at her house."

Cordelia's eyes darted to the bottle of wine in the backseat of the cab. "I see," she said. The wheels inside her mind appeared to be grinding furiously. "You must have met her at the party last night. She's very attractive. Good for you, Janey."

"Come on. What makes you think she's a lesbian?"

Cordelia tapped her head. "My gaydar, Janey. More accurate than Doppler. Then again, there was this guy following her around all evening. He was clearly smitten."

"You were watching her?"

"Well, she's an attractive woman, and I'm not dead."

"But you already found the love of your life."

Berengeria Reynolds was a vintner who lived in California. Cordelia had been together with her for several years. It was a long-distance romance, and an exclusive one.

"I can still look."

"Of course you can," said Jane. "I just want to underscore that I'm merely having dinner with her. I'm not looking for a relationship."

"Julia's malign influence lives on." She held up her hand. "I know. One should never speak ill of the dead—"

"But you're about to."

"She was an evil, narcissistic gorgon. A wolf in wolf's clothing. And you loved her, to my utter amazement, to her dying breath."

It was time she had a conversation with Cordelia about what had happened. It would have to wait though, because they were reaching their destination.

"Hey, where are we going?" asked Cordelia as they pulled into the parking lot behind Holy Trinity.

"I want to see the graveyard where they found Sam Romilly's remains."

"Ooh, yippie skippy. Graveyard research. My favorite."

"It will only take a few minutes. You can stay in the truck if you want to."

"And be ravaged by the undead? Thank you, no."

A stiff wind blew leaves across the cemetery grounds as they made their way across the grass. The grave was easy to find because it was enclosed with yellow crime-scene tape. The large granite marker that had once presided over Ida Beddemeyer's grave sat to the side. Next to it was the coffin, covered by a tarp that had partially blown off.

"So," said Cordelia, wrapping her shawl more tightly around her shoulders, "what's to see?"

Jane was already down on her hands and knees, crawling under the tape so she could get a closer look. While she'd been waiting for Cordelia, she'd checked the online archive of obituary notices from the Fergus Falls newspaper and found details of Ida's funeral. Ida had been interred the same day Sam had gone missing. The funeral was at eleven in the morning. The only way Sam's body could have been under the coffin was for him to have been placed there before the burial. Nobody knew what time Sam had died, but it had to have been before eleven that morning.

The pit was the width of two graves. One side, the one that had held Mrs. Beddemeyer's casket, looked a good two feet deeper than the other. The question was, had the grave been altered before or after Sam died? If it had been done before his death, then the homicide had been premeditated. It seemed far less likely that someone would be messing with a grave in broad daylight, so Jane felt that it was reasonable to conclude that the grave had been altered the night before, which meant Sam's death was a homicide. Jane looked up when she heard Cordelia say, "Do you work here?"

"Yes, I do," said a gray-haired workman in dark blue coveralls. He was standing next to Cordelia with a square-tipped shovel over his shoulder. "I'm the head caretaker."

Cordelia squinted at the name on his coveralls. "Mr. Judge, is it?"

"Judge is my first name."

"Really? Do you do a lot of judging?" She tittered.

"Jokes like that get pretty old, ma'am."

"Yes, well." She tutted, looking around and sending Jane an SOS with her eyes.

"How long have you worked here?" asked Jane, getting up and brushing dirt off her jeans.

"Started in 1989. This will be my thirty-first year caring for the cemetery."

"What's it like burying people for a living?" asked Cordelia.

He eyed her warily, finally saying, "Everybody's got to die."

Jane walked up, shook his hand, and introduced herself.

"Judge Peterson," he said in response.

"Do you have a minute?"

"For what?"

"A couple of questions."

"About that grave?" he asked, repositioning the shovel.

"Do you know who prepared it for Mrs. Beddemeyer?"

"I did."

"By hand?"

"No, we use a backhoe. The only things we dig by hand are baby graves and cremations."

Cordelia pressed a hand to her stomach.

"How much notice do you need to dig a grave?"

"Usually twenty-four hours."

"How long does it take to dig one?"

"Oh, maybe an hour—in the summer. Winter, depending on the state of the ground, can take longer."

"Do you come and fill in the gravesite after the burial?"

"That's right. And then we tamp down the soil and plant grass seed."

"What about Ida? Did you notice anything out of the ordinary when you were digging her grave? Maybe . . . someone who was hanging around that shouldn't have been?"

He shook his head. "Well, now, as I think about it, maybe I should take that back. See, I was in a car accident in August of '99, hurt my shoulder and back pretty bad. I got permission to ask a kid who'd worked for me the summer before to help with some of the digging. He was in high school at the time and liked the extra cash."

"So he was the one who dug the grave?"

"With the backhoe, yeah. I was the straw boss."

"Do you remember anything about that day—anything that stands out?"

He dropped the shovel in the grass, took out a pack of cigarettes, and lit up. "Well, now, there was this one thing." He sucked in a lungful of smoke and blew it out the side of his mouth. "I don't know if this comes under the heading of unusual, but while Darius and I were having lunch—"

"Darius Pollard?" asked Jane.

"That's right. You know him?"

"Pollard Automotive?"

"His father is a buddy of mine. Anyway, we were eating our sandwiches when these two kids came past. One of them stopped and said something kind of nasty—racist, you know—to Darius. I didn't catch it all, but Darius shot to his feet, fists clenched, and told both of them to get the hell away from him. I thought we were in for an all-out brawl. The only reason I remember it is because I knew one of the kids. Well, I mean I knew his dad—Mitch Tamborsky, one of the local cops. The kid was his son. The father was an okay guy, but the son—he always struck me as an arrogant SOB. I wasn't happy to see such bad blood between Darius and the cop's kid."

"You're saying this happened the day before Ida was buried?"

"It had to have been. It was the only time Darius dug a grave for me."

At the very least, it meant that Dave Tamborsky knew there was an open grave in Holy Trinity cemetery. "What did the other kid look like? The one with Dave."

"Jeez, hard to remember. Nothing special stands out."

Jane wondered if it was the friend Jim Hughes told her about—Monty Mickler. "You've been very helpful," she said, thanking him.

He took one last drag off the cigarette, then pressed his fingers around the tip to extinguish it, and slipped it into his upper pocket.

After he'd walked off, Cordelia moved closer to Jane and said, "You know what true-crime writers like to say."

"What?" asked Jane.

"When you need a new lead, find the gravedigger." She furrowed her eyebrows and offered Jane a conspiratorial wink.

14

Emma had known Patsy Dellmann since grade school. Dell-mann's Resort had one of the best restaurants in the area, so she hoped the evening would be fun for everyone. She was sorry that Jane couldn't make it, but Cordelia was the real draw. All Emma's friends wanted to meet the renowned theater director, and Cordelia, as Emma suspected, would not disappoint.

The two of them had arrived late, around six-twenty, and were shown to a long table already filled with friends enjoying cocktails and appetizers. While Emma made apologies, Cordelia, wearing a black-and-gold metallic print gown with strappy gold sandals and a gold lamé turban, moved slowly down each side of the table, greeting everyone individually, taking each person's hand in hers and squeezing it, favoring one and all with her high-beam smile. She could have been running for office, thought Emma, or about to win a prestigious award. Then again, she always managed to look that way.

As the conversation turned to Cordelia's wealth of entertaining exploits in the theater biz, Emma took a few minutes to silently survey the room. She was curious to see if any of her classmates had arrived early for the reunion. Seeing Kurt, she ordered a dirty martini and then excused herself.

He was seated at a table next to the window overlooking the lake. She wanted to check in, make sure he was okay after the state he'd been in last night. As she approached, she recognized the man he was sitting with.

"Ted?" she said. "Wow. If it isn't our infamous class president."

He rose to give her a hug. "Great to see you, Emma."

Ted Hammond had always been on the short side, but husky. In the years since she'd last seen him, he'd put on weight, all of it muscle. His red hair remained thick and wavy, and he looked tanned and healthy. The only difference in his appearance was a nicely trimmed beard. She'd had a crush on him in junior high, but that was ancient history. "I didn't think you'd be here until tomorrow."

"I drove up Saturday night. I don't know if you've heard, but my dad died last year, so I usually try to come up one weekend a month to spend time with my mom. This gave me a reason to spend a few extra nights. It's been a hard time for her."

"I didn't know," said Emma. "I'm so sorry."

"Thanks. My sister still lives here—she's married with a couple of kids, so that helps."

"Do you want to sit down?" asked Kurt.

"No, I can't. I'm with friends. But I wanted to come over, mainly to tell you that—"

He interrupted her. "I'm sorry about last night. Really. I was in pretty bad shape."

"No worries," she said, touching his arm. "Honestly, I'm just glad Danny was able to take me home."

"Sounds like there's a story there," said Ted, grinning at her.

"Not much of one," said Kurt.

"You heard about the party I'm throwing on Friday night for the entire class, right? After the homecoming game. If the weather holds, I thought we'd do a bonfire on the beach, maybe get a keg."

"I'll be there," said Ted.

"Is your wife with you?" She was fishing, but didn't think he noticed.

"I'm not married. Came close a couple of times, but no cigar."

She laughed. "Well, I should let you two get back to your dinner. You're both coming to the final reunion meeting on Thursday night, right? We need to get the VFW hall set up on Saturday morning. So much to do. You know, Ted, maybe you should come to the meeting for the committee chairs tomorrow night."

"I'm available for anything you need."

Emma was genuinely starting to get excited about the reunion. "We're meeting in the basement of the hall at seven."

"I'll be there."

She'd no sooner made it back to the table, where Cordelia continued to hold court, than she noticed someone else she knew— the last person she expected to run into tonight.

Scott stood at the entrance to the bar, beckoning her over. He'd been calling and texting her all day. She'd never found him annoying before, but she did now.

Carrying her martini, she crossed the room to where he stood. "Did you follow me here?"

"God, it's good to see you." His eyes were bloodshot. "You look amazing."

"You look hung over. Answer my question."

The muscles along his jaw tightened. "I'm not proud of it. Yeah, I followed you."

"That's stalking, Scott."

"You wouldn't respond to any of my texts. I had to see you, had to apologize."

"Men and their apologies."

"What's that mean?"

"Nothing."

"Look, Emma, I was desperate to see you last night, but I didn't think you'd come by, so I started drinking—too much, as it turns out. My brother's death had really hit me hard."

It hadn't seemed that way last night, but then in the shape he was in, there was probably no way to tell. Standing here now, he seemed so sad that it gave her heart a hard twist. In spite of herself, she felt sorry for him. "I wanted to talk about Sam last night."

"Did you? I don't remember much about our conversation."

"You scared me."

"Oh, Emma, I never intended to. Please, let me cook you dinner tomorrow night. I know you're leaving soon. Can't we have one last normal night together?"

She wasn't sure what he meant by normal.

"Please? I'll do something nice. I know you like my beef stroganoff. How about that?"

"I'm not sure it's a good idea."

"Come on. It might be our last chance."

He seemed so dejected. "If I agree, there won't be any drinking, right?"

He held up his hand. "Scout's honor."

She could feel her resolve crumbling. She didn't love him, not the way he wanted, but she had grown to care about him. "Okay. Seven o'clock."

"Thank you." He hesitated. "Can I kiss you?"

"Of course not," she said, appalled. Had he never listened to her? "I can't be open about our relationship. You know that."

"Just this once?"

"No," she said, taking a sustaining sip of her martini. "Now I have to get back to my party."

"Okay, sure. Tomorrow night, then. I'll be waiting, Emma."

15

Jane stood in front of Leslie Harrow's front door and rang the bell. An hour before, she'd been standing in front of a mirror back at the lake house, wondering if wearing a pair of gold hoop earrings was too much. She didn't usually dither over things like that and was more than a little embarrassed by the way she was fussing over what to wear. Much of her clothing was wrinkled from being in a suitcase. With no time to iron, and no desire to iron to begin with, she'd decided on a pair of tan cargo pants and a black turtleneck. Before leaving, she'd gone back to add a bit of lipstick to her look.

When Leslie answered the door, she seemed more relaxed than she had earlier in the day, a kitchen towel tossed over her shoulder. She had on ripped jeans and a navy-blue sweatshirt with the word Hoyas written on the front of it in big block letters. "Did you have any problems with my directions?"

"Nope," said Jane. "I just did what you said. I turned onto the road marked Dead End."

"As long as you don't have problems with metaphors, this is a great place to live."

The main room was a combination of living room/dining room, with high, vaulted ceilings and modern furniture.

"Do you ever feel color challenged?" asked Leslie as she stood next to a leather sectional. "That's how I felt when I bought the house three years ago. I couldn't decide on anything, so I just painted everything white. It's kind of stark."

"No, I like it," said Jane, handing Leslie the bottle of wine she'd brought and then removing her jacket. "It's like a gallery space. You have some fascinating art." She deposited the jacket on a chair as she stopped to examine a swirling metal sculpture.

"It's supposed to look like wind," said Leslie, perching on the arm of the couch. "Bought it in Budapest."

"That's right, you're the world traveler."

"Sort of. Do you like Campari and soda?"

"Sure."

They moved through the kitchen and out onto a deck. A table had already been prepared with the Campari, soda, and several platters and small bowls containing Leslie's promised antipasto.

"This looks lovely," said Jane.

"It's one of my favorite quick dinners. We can graze our way through it, and then I have something special for dessert."

"Is that soppressata?"

"And mortadella, Genoa salami, and cotechino—which you have to try with mustard."

"Where do you buy all that in town?"

"Actually, Kurt Steiner stocks a good assortment of deli meats. The rest I buy here and there online."

Jane saw Peppadew peppers, kalamata and Manzanilla olives, sliced heirloom tomatoes, marinated mushrooms, and artichoke hearts. "What are the cheeses?"

"The first one's a Comté from Fort St. Antoine, my current favorite. The next is a Marieke Gouda from Wisconsin. I think it's better than the Netherlands Goudas. The final one is a piece of Gorgonzola Dolce, another Wisconsin cheese, this one from Green Bay. And that"—she pointed to a small bowl—"is a date-and-fig chutney. I make it myself. The bread's an old-world farm loaf that I buy from a local bakery."

"Looks amazing."

"A spread like this makes people think I went to a lot of trouble when all I did was buy and assemble. I'm not fooling you, though, am I?"

Jane glanced around to see if there might be a dog or cat lurking somewhere, scouting out the food on offer. "No pets?"

"No, never really been a fan."

"I have a couple of dogs. A brown lab and a little black poodle."

"And you adore them."

"Beyond measure. When I'm out of town, they stay with a neighbor. She loves them almost as much as I do."

As Leslie mixed the drinks, Jane surveyed the scenery. The deck overlooked the Bullhead River and, beyond that, a wooded area. She already knew that this was the tonier section of town.

Sunset in mid-September was around seven-thirty, so Leslie switched on several strings of orange and red mini-lanterns before she sat down. The little lanterns didn't offer much in the way of illumination, but they were pretty, and as the sun dipped lower over the trees, made the deck seem cozy.

"So what brings a world traveler to Castle Lake?" asked Jane.

Leslie looked over the cheese and finally selected one, carving off a chunk. "My grandparents on my mother's side owned a farm just west of town. It's where my mom grew up. When I was a kid, I'd beg to spend the summers here. I came every year from the time I was eight until the summer before my senior year. I'd follow my grandfather around the property, initially just to spend time with him. Later on, I began to help with chores. My grandmother taught me how to cook and knit, and she was the fisherman in the family, so we'd go fishing together. I made friends, too, and honestly, there were times when I didn't want to go home."

"Where was home?"

"Buffalo, New York. My father owned a bar there, and my mother worked for the Buffalo Bills, the NFL team. She's a physician, specialized in sports medicine."

"You didn't like Buffalo?"

"It wasn't that. My family was kind of, how do I put this . . . chaotic. Anyway, Mom wanted me to pursue a medical career, like my older brother. I wasn't interested. I ended up going to Georgetown and graduated with a degree in American history with a minor in public policy. My parents paid for my schooling and assumed I'd continue on for a masters, but, again, I had other ideas."

"Such as?" asked Jane, spreading some of the Gorgonzola on a piece of bread.

"To travel. I had a friend who'd been hired by TWA. She somehow wrangled an interview for me and, amazingly, I was offered a job as a flight attendant. I moved on to Qantas six years later, and then to British Airways. I never made any money, but I did get to see the world."

"Why did you stop?"

She took a sip of her drink, gazing toward the river. "For many years, I was with someone who meant a great deal to me. Another flight attendant, Chris Boncamper. We'd just about decided to split when there was a plane crash in France and . . . Chris was badly injured."

"I'm so sorry." Jane had no idea if Chris was a woman or a man.

"Yeah, it was pretty awful. I took a leave of absence to help with the rehab. It didn't feel right to just pick up and leave. As it turned out, I never went back to work. I couldn't. Even the idea of getting on a plane to fly back home gave me panic attacks. Several months later, with the help of booze and Xanax, I landed in Buffalo, where I spent the next few weeks with my parents. My grandparents had both died while I was living in Sydney. They left me money and the farm. Initially, I was concerned about the one-sided bequests, but my father assured me that my older brother had no interest in the money or the farm, and my younger brother—he'd been in prison for eight years before he was released—was nowhere to be found. Dad suggested we continue to rent the property and offered to invest the money. Prior to owning the bar, he'd worked in finance, so I was happy to just leave it in his hands. When I got back, I had a nice little nest egg."

"Good for you," said Jane. "Do you still own the farm?"

"I came back to take a look at it and make some decisions. I eventually sold it. Couldn't believe how much it was worth. By then, I'd pretty much decided to stay for a while. I had nowhere else to go, and I felt at home in Castle Lake. After I'd been here for a year or so, I decided to get involved in town government. Initially I did a two-year stint on the town council. During my second term, I bought this place. And then I ran for mayor."

"You like being mayor?"

"I like government, especially local government, because it's where you can really make things happen. I'm a registered Democrat, but having lived with two deeply conservative parents for eighteen years, I realize that they often made some good points. They were huge Reagan supporters."

"Were you?"

"Kind of. But while I was in college, my thinking changed. Ronald Reagan was the one who popularized the idea that government wasn't the solution, it was the problem. It still makes me furious when I hear someone repeat that meretricious garbage."

"Is Castle Lake pretty conservative?"

"Yes . . . and no. People surprise you. Humans are a lot more complex than the common wisdom might allow."

"Is the town a safe place to live?"

"Again, yes, generally, but we do have crime, the same sorts of crime you find in urban areas—drugs, aggravated assault, sexual assault, domestics, property crime, car thefts."

"And murder."

"More suicides by gun than murder, but yeah, it happens. Come on, now. That's enough on my side of the ledger. I want to know something about you. For instance, Cordelia said you lost your partner last year. That must have been hard."

It was the last thing Jane wanted to talk about.

"How long were you and—"

"Julia."

"Yes, Julia."

"It's kind of a long story."

She grinned. "Isn't everything?"

The doorbell rang. "Now what?" Leslie muttered, rising from the table.

Feeling a little chilly, Jane decided to go inside to get her jacket. As she came into the living room, she saw that the man following Leslie around last night was standing just inside the doorway.

"Oh," he said, seeing Jane come in. "I didn't realize—"

"This isn't a good time, Don. Perhaps we can talk about it tomorrow."

"Sure. Right." He shifted his stance. "I was in the area and figured maybe I could get your thoughts before the meeting." He nodded to Jane. "I don't suppose you've heard anything more about that fire, specifically about Carli?"

"Nothing," she said, continuing to hold the door open.

"Well, you'll let me know if you do, yes?"

"Of course I will."

Jane had the sense that he was casting around, trying to come up with a reason that would allow him to stay.

Snapping his fingers, he said, "You know, that reminds me—"

"Have a good evening," said Leslie. "We'll talk tomorrow."

"Oh, okay. Sure." He nodded to Jane. "Good to see you again."

Once he was gone, Jane said, "Maybe I'm wrong, but I think he likes you."

"I think you're right," said Leslie, locking the door. "He's a nice man, but he's not my type."

"You have a type?"

"Doesn't everyone? For instance, if I said you were my type, what would you say?"

"Me?"

Hands on her hips, Leslie stepped closer. "I must be losing my touch."

"Excuse me?"

"I've seen you twice in twenty-four hours. Both times I flirted with abandon, but you didn't seem to notice. Or maybe you're not interested. If so—"

Jane cleared her throat and looked down at her shoes. "Cordelia tells me I not only don't know how to flirt, I don't recognize it when someone flirts with me."

"You're flirt challenged. That's hilarious." She eyed Jane a moment, then said, "Oh, screw it." Moving close, she gave Jane a kiss. "I suppose I should have asked permission, but you know what they say: It's easier to ask forgiveness."

Jane blinked a couple of times. "None required."

"Do you have any idea how many women I've met in the last few years who gave me any reason to flirt?"

"How many?"

"Two. One was married—to a guy—and the other was about to be deployed to Afghanistan. There are, maybe, a dozen out lesbians in Castle Lake. Most of them are friends. They're all either paired up or I'm not interested. In any event, I have to be somewhat circumspect."

"People don't know you're gay?"

"If they do, they don't talk about it in front of me, and I haven't made it an issue. I will, of course, somewhere down the line. I'd like to run for the statehouse next time around. But that's off the topic."

"What's the topic?"

"You. We got the first kiss out of the way. Sometimes that can take forever, you know what I mean? I realize I sound kind of clinical. I'm really very romantic given the opportunity, but I don't have a lot of time here. You're leaving next weekend, and I'm not sure when I'll see you again."

Jane opened her mouth, but couldn't quite figure out what to say.

"I like you. I think you like me. Nod if you agree."

She nodded.

Taking Jane's hand, Leslie said, "Then stay the night. Maybe we'll just have some fun. I'm fine with fun. Or maybe we'll be soulmates forever. That seems less likely, but you never know. Say something. I feel like I'm making a fool of myself here."

"You're not. But—"

"But?"

"Can we still have that special dessert you promised?"

"Before or after?"

"After."

She squeezed Jane's hand. "I think you just may turn out to be the woman of my dreams."

16

The Avalon Motor Inn was full up on Monday evening. Even room 1 had a car parked in front of it. Monty normally didn't book it because it was smaller than the other rooms. Since Dave couldn't find a parking spot in front of the building, he drove around to the back and parked next to Monty's Hyundai.

Two newspaper racks outside the office door were both empty, waiting for tomorrow's editions of the Minneapolis *Star Tribune* and the Fergus Falls *Daily Journal*. Dave pushed inside, only to find no one at the reception desk. Stepping around it, he pushed the door to the back room open, finding Monty's tall, lanky frame slouched in a recliner, watching TV.

As much as Monty hated the comparison, Dave felt the place really was the spitting image of the Bates Motel. It was about the same age, built in the fifties, with a long one-story row of guest rooms, all with knotty pine interiors. The only significant missing element was the creepy house on a hill looming over the motel grounds.

Dave cleared his throat.

"Oh, hey," said Monty, lifting a green soda can in greeting. "Come on in."

"I thought you only drank Red Bull," said Dave, making himself comfortable on the only other chair in the room.

Monty turned the sound down. "This is Red Bull."

"The can's green."

"It's the kiwi-apple flavor. I can't get enough of it."

"I've never seen it in a store anywhere around here."

"I buy it on Amazon, get it shipped for free."

Dave groaned. "I don't know how you can drink that stuff at this time of night and think you're going to get to sleep."

"It's mother's milk, man. I can drink it anytime and sleep like a baby."

The painting that Norman Bates took down so he could peer through the hole he'd drilled in the wall was, in this incarnation, a large framed photo of Monty's wife and two kids. They were a handsome family. Sarah was blond, though both kids had inherited Monty's dark brown hair and eyes. Dave secretly envied his old buddy, though he wouldn't say it out loud.

"What's up?" asked Monty, stretching his legs.

"I've got news. None of it good."

"Yeah? Like what?"

"Well, first, I was taken off the Romilly case. Larson gave it to Bobby Saltus."

"What?" He lowered the footrest and sat up straight. "Why?"

"Some woman in town for the art festival mentioned to him that it might be a conflict for me to be in charge since I was a friend of Sam's."

"Bullshit. You weren't his friend. Who's the woman? Why the hell would she weigh in on a police matter?"

"Her name's Jane Lawless." He went on to explain about the podcast she worked for, that it covered unsolved crimes in Minnesota.

"Just freakin' great. Someone should stick a sock in that bitch's mouth, or a whole hell of a lot worse."

"I'm keeping an on eye on it. Grady hasn't been feeling well lately, so he's gone more than he's at work. Saltus is a lightweight. The only thing is—"

"What?"

"The chief got a note this morning. It wasn't signed, but it included the names of four people who are supposed to know something about Sam's death. Bobby intends to call them all in."

"Who are they?"

"Jim Hughes. Darius Pollard. Scott Romilly. And Kurt Steiner."

Monty bounced his leg, thinking it over. "At least Ty Niska's name wasn't included. You have any idea if he's coming to the reunion?"

"I was curious, too. I bumped into the chair of the organizing committee this morning, so I asked about him. She said they'd sent him a snail-mail invitation when the email they had for him bounced back."

"Where's he living?"

"Milwaukee, according to her. She said he never wrote back or called for tickets, so she doubted he'd show."

Monty appeared to give it some thought. "Maybe I'll try to find his phone number and give him a call, just in case."

It drove Dave crazy that he had no idea who'd written the note. Whoever he—or she—turned out to be, they were a wild card. Dave was allergic to wild cards. He was used to being in control. "Any ideas on who the author of that note might be?"

"What about Emma Granholm? It always seemed to me that she must know more than she let on."

It was a reasonable guess, though Dave found it kind of far-fetched. He liked Emma well enough, was pretty sure she'd had a crush on him back in high school. "Other ideas?"

"What if . . ." whispered Monty, his expression darkening.

"What?"

"What if it was Becca?"

Dave's heart skipped a beat. "No way. She left town right after graduation. Far as I know, nobody even knows where she went."

"Maybe," said Monty. "But wouldn't it be damn freaky if it was her."

Dave didn't like the way this was spooling out. Too many loose ends.

"What else?" asked Monty. He took a last gulp of Red Bull.

"Grady assigned me the Gilbert fire to investigate."

"Man, I wouldn't want your job if it paid twice as much as I make." He got up and stepped over to a small refrigerator tucked in the corner of the room. "Sure you don't want one?" he asked, opening the door to reveal nothing but green cans.

"That stuff's gonna kill you one day. Do you know Carli Gilbert?"

"Not well. She's a friend of my wife's."

"So you heard about the breakup with her husband?"

"All I know is Sarah said it was super nasty. Aaron started attending our church after they split. The pastor asked me to show him around, introduce him to other members. He seems like an okay guy to me."

Dave would need to interview him, and while he was at it, he should probably interview Monty's wife.

"Is that it?" asked Monty. "No more news?"

"For the moment. Anyway, I should probably head home."

"Time for me to shove off, too." He moved over to the desk and began to set up the phone system for the night.

Monty always left his home number on the answering machine, in case a guest had an emergency. As he walked out to the front office to switch off lights and turn the OPEN sign on the door to CLOSED, Dave did something he'd wanted to do for years. He took a quick peek behind the photograph of Monty's family. Pulling the frame away from the wall, he squinted to see if there really was a voyeuristic peephole drilled into the knotty pine. Instead of a hole, he found a yellow Post-it note that read, "This is NOT the Bates Motel."

"Come on, Davey boy," called Monty. "I wanna get out of here before I'm an old man."

Smiling to himself, Dave released the frame and flipped off the overhead light.

KURT

September 2, 1999

Kurt sat with his back against one of the gravestones and waited for Sam to do the same. Instead, Sam straddled Kurt's legs, cupped his hands around Kurt's face, and kissed him.

"I've wanted to do that all week," he said. He seemed to want to go further, but stopped and rolled over, sitting down cross-legged in the grass.

Kurt was afraid of the feelings roiling around inside him. It was clear what his body wanted, and he almost didn't care what it meant. The operative word was *almost*. He was embarrassed by his sweaty palms and the shaking inside him. He'd never felt this way with Vicki or anyone else. But . . . no, one thing he knew for sure: He wasn't gay.

Kurt hadn't been thrilled by the idea of meeting Sam in the cemetery behind Holy Trinity but agreed that it was unlikely anyone would be out wandering through the graves at this time of night. They did need privacy so they could talk. A nearly full moon cast its weak light across the grass, giving the cemetery a kind of silvery, unearthly quality. He could easily imagine ghosts rising and drifting past them.

"Are you scared of the undead?" asked Sam, firing up a joint.

"No, of course not."

Sam laughed. "Sure you are. No worries. I'll protect you." He sucked in a lungful of smoke and held it. "Good stuff," he said, giving his head a shake. He handed the joint to Kurt. Settling himself against the gravestone, he pointed at the sky. "Look at that moon."

"Moon is good," muttered Kurt, trying to sound like the priest character in the movie *Young Frankenstein*.

"Moon is good. The moon is our friend."

They were on the same page.

They sat quietly for a few minutes, passing the joint between them.

"So," said Sam finally, tipping his head back. "We should talk. You start."

"How about this: Should we be sitting on some dead guy's grave?"

Sam snuffed out the joint's burning tip. "You know what I mean."

"Look, I know this isn't what you want to hear, but I'm not gay." It was true, and Kurt needed Sam to hear it.

"You seem pretty gay to me."

"I'm not. Come on, man, I have a girlfriend."

"So do I."

"Does that mean you think you're gay?"

"No," said Sam. "I don't think it, I know it. So do you."

Kurt gave his head a firm shake.

"You don't feel a thing when I kiss you?"

"Doesn't mean I'm . . . that way."

"Let me ask you this: Have you ever found yourself watching some guy, you know, just kind of enjoying it, the way he looks, the way he moves? You study him, his hair, his mouth. You wonder what it would be like to touch his skin. What I'm saying is, the guy you think of as good old heterosexual Kurt may not want to admit it, but I'll bet your body understands what your brain refuses to admit. You can't hide that, man. That moment I'm talking about is probably when you pulled your eyes away."

"No. Never happened."

"You've never stared at a guy's crown jewels just a little too long? You've never felt a jolt of guilt and looked away, only to find yourself looking at him again?"

"You're describing yourself, not me."

"I don't believe you."

"What do you want from me?" asked Kurt. He was beginning to squirm. He had experienced those things, every one of them, but he'd never given them a name, a significance.

"Listen," said Sam, his voice more gentle this time. "It's not an easy subject, although once you admit the truth of who you are— it's hard to explain, but you feel better. You feel more honest, at least with yourself. I mean, it's not 1899, Kurt. It's 1999. Stonewall happened. Things have changed."

"I don't know what Stonewall is, and as for things changing, they haven't around here. You know I'm right."

Sam turned to face him. "I took a huge chance with you on that beach a few weeks ago. Why come with me tonight if you didn't want more?"

"I don't know," said Kurt, trying to deal with his nervous embarrassment by bouncing his knee.

"I'd be willing to bet that coming here tonight wasn't just about sex. You have feelings for me, don't you? Just like I do for you. Tell me I'm wrong, and I'll never bother you again."

There was a swarm of angry bees inside Kurt's chest. If he admitted to liking Sam as more than just a friend, what did that mean, not just for now, but for the future? He hated the word "gay," hated the very idea, and yet as hard as he'd tried to ignore his body's own clear signals and come to a different conclusion, Sam was right. "Okay, I give."

"You *give*?"

"Don't make me say it out loud."

"No," said Sam. "But one day, you'll have to. Come on." He scrambled to his feet, reaching down for Kurt's hand.

"What's happening now?"

"Just stay low and follow me."

They ran across a grassy area between the graves and the woods beyond. Once they were hidden in the trees, Sam took a flashlight out of his back pocket and switched it on. "It isn't far," he said, taking the lead.

They eventually came to a small clearing within earshot of the river. Kurt couldn't see it, but he could hear the water flowing. The moon was high above them. Off to one side, Kurt saw a fallen tree, its gnarled trunk resting on the ground. Sam had already run over to it and was crouched down, removing an electric lantern and something else—something bulky. "What's that?" whispered Kurt.

Sam unfolded the blanket and spread it out on the ground, and then sat he down on it, fiddling with the lantern until it gave off a soft, yellow glow. "I want to see you," he said, motioning for Kurt to join him.

"Have you done this before?" asked Kurt, not sure what he wanted to hear.

"Had sex? Sure. Made love? No." He pulled Kurt down on top of him. "We'll take it slow."

"What if I don't want it slow?"

Sam smiled. "You read my mind."

All Kurt could think of as they took off their shirts was that he wanted this more than he'd ever wanted anything in his life. He felt like a man newly born. Newly born in a midnight wood.

17

When Jane returned to the lake house the following morning, she found Cordelia sitting at the kitchen table, dragging a spoon lethargically through a bowl of cereal.

"The prodigal returns," said Cordelia, lifting the spoon to her lips.

Jane had sent Cordelia a text last night, telling her she wouldn't be back until morning. "Stick a sock in it, okay? I don't want to hear any of your jokes. And I'm hardly the prodigal."

"If you haven't been a tiny bit prodigal, I'd be supremely disappointed."

Jane rolled her eyes. "You're up early."

"I'm having my midnight snack."

"It's just after nine."

"So? I didn't get to bed until four. And then the blasted pea inside my mattress kept me awake until well past five."

"Why were you up so late?" Jane removed her jacket before stepping over to the coffee pot to pour herself a cup. The Granholms' kitchen hadn't been updated all that much over the years, but with lots of counter space, it was a comfortable spot in which to work. The only problem this morning was that the screaming yellow walls were almost too bright for Jane's tired eyes.

"Major dinner party, remember? Everyone who met at the resort came back here afterward. I suggested we play charades, and before I knew it, it was after two and everyone was leaving. I dazzle at charades, Janey."

"I know. We play them every Christmas."

"We decided to do movie titles, so I went upstairs, found a couple feather boas, a few period hats, and various and sundry other props to help with my performance."

"You brought all that with you?" No wonder Cordelia's suitcases were so heavy.

"You never know when you're going to need something to help establish a character. I may never have been a Boy Scout, but I do believe in being prepared."

"Okay, but then why were you up until four?"

She gave a weary sigh. "After everyone took off, Emma got out the peppermint schnapps. You know me and peppermint schnapps. About four shots in, she started to open up about her marriage—and about the local guy she's been dating all summer. I, of course, in my often-called-upon role as earth mother and romantic-advice columnist, felt I should stay and listen, just in case she needed my sage advice."

Jane pulled out a kitchen chair and sat down. "Who's she been seeing?"

"Scott Romilly."

"Sam's brother?"

"The very same."

"Boy, that must feel weird, after dating Sam in high school and then finding out he was murdered. Is she serious about him?"

"Oh, it's the usual tangle," said Cordelia, pushing her bowl away. "If I'm to believe what she says, she's still got a few stray feelings for her husband. Philip is apparently a cad, but lovable. I see them as Rock Hudson and Doris Day, but it's probably more like Michael Douglas and Kathleen Turner in *The War of the Roses*.

Emma was talking to her daughter yesterday afternoon and found out that Philip's trophy girlfriend hasn't been around in weeks. Trouble, it would seem, in paradise."

"So Scott was just a summer thing."

"That's what she thought. He apparently saw it differently. When it came up that she would be leaving soon, he was aghast. He thought they were serious and that she planned to stay so they could make a life together. She said he'd been drinking and that he got pretty insistent about them staying together. So insistent, it turns out, that he frightened her."

"Not good."

"There's more. While we were at the restaurant last night, Scott appeared and floated somewhere near the bar until Emma saw him. He motioned her over so he could tell her how sorry he was about the way he'd behaved. He said he'd been drinking too much because he was distraught over his brother's death."

"How did he know she'd be at the resort?"

"Leave it to you to zero in on the problem. He followed her, Janey. That's stalking behavior."

"Has he done it before?"

"Emma didn't think he had, but as we were talking, it occurred to her that she'd seen him a couple of times when she'd been out with a friend. He didn't try to talk to her, but still, he was there."

"Creepy."

"I suggested that she stay away from him."

"And?"

"She said she'd already promised to have dinner with him tonight at his place."

"Call it off."

"She thinks she's overreacting."

"Women can be so dumb." Jane included herself in that critique. When she looked back at Cordelia, she saw that she was being examined. "What?"

"I can read you like the proverbial book, Janey. There's something you're not telling me. I've felt it for months. I assumed you would, eventually, but you haven't. Come on, what is it? Don't you trust me?"

"Of course I trust you. I'd trust you with my life."

"Then what?"

Jane had already concluded that it was time to tell Cordelia the full story about Julia. But the whole thing was embarrassing, and anyway, it wasn't something she needed to do right this minute. In an effort to put off the inevitable, she changed the subject. "I have some news about that house fire."

"You're deflecting, dearheart. I'll let you get away with it for now, but not forever. I do want to hear about the fire. And if I'm going to listen to something like that, I need real sustenance."

"Brussels sprouts? Kale? Quinoa?"

Opening the refrigerator, Cordelia removed a quart of chocolate milk and held it up as if she'd just won an award. She gave a small bow, then sat back down, opened the top, and drank straight from the carton. "You may continue."

"Leslie happened to have my favorite tea, Yorkshire Gold, so while I was making us a pot, Sgt. Tamborsky of the CLPD showed up at the front door. From what Emma had said about him, I expected a titan of the gridiron going to seed."

"Dragging his knuckles and grunting all the way."

"He was actually very nice. He wasn't terribly tall, but he was big, with a heavy, square face and a rather florid complexion. He was very respectful."

"He was talking to the mayor, Janey."

"Well, yes, I'm sure he was on his best behavior. When Leslie introduced me, he seemed to know who I was."

"Ah, the poster in the window of the art center again; the gift that keeps on giving."

"I suppose. Anyway, we all sat down in the living room while he explained that human remains had been found in the basement of the Gilbert house. They'll have to do forensic testing, but he was pretty sure it would turn out to be Carli. He said it was arson and speculated, with no evidence, that someone might have used the fire as a cover for murder. I got the impression that he watches a lot of cop shows."

"How ghastly. Does he have any suspects?"

"The investigation is just getting started, so no. Leslie asked him if he had any new information on Sam Romilly. He said he'd been taken off the case and put on the Gilbert case instead. Sgt. Bobby Saltus is now in charge. Tamborsky pretty much said that the older case had to take a backseat to the arson/murder, which is why the switch was made. Tamborsky has seniority over Saltus."

Cordelia tried to stifle a yawn. Taking a last swig of milk, she folded the top closed. "This is all terribly fascinating, but I've got to get some shut-eye."

"To be continued," said Jane.

"What will you be up to while I'm getting my beauty sleep?"

"Not sure. Finding Sam's remains has produced more leads than I anticipated."

"Don't do anything important without me."

"I wouldn't dream of it."

On her way out of the room, Cordelia paused and turned around. "By the way, I'm free for dinner. I suppose you're spending the evening with the mayor."

"Nope. She has a planning-commission meeting tonight. Why don't we find a good place to eat? My treat."

"No, Janey, it should be mine. You carried in all the luggage. You cleaned up the kitchen the other night. And you're going to put the chocolate milk away, right?"

It was easier to buy dinner than it was to schlep and scrub, but Jane didn't mind. "Deal."

"Night night. I promise, I shall be better company anon."

18

After changing into a clean pair of jeans and a red flannel shirt, Jane grabbed her messenger bag and drove back into town in search of breakfast. She found a place on Second Street, the Flame Diner, and parked a few doors down. Before she went in, she sat in her truck and called the senior podcast producer again, spending a few minutes updating him on the Romilly case. She'd already sent him the raw interview she'd done yesterday with Jim Hughes. He hadn't had a chance to listen to it yet, but told her to keep digging. He said he'd met with the board and they all green-lighted her investigation.

There was no way Jane could explore all of the leads she'd found before she and Cordelia needed to head back to Minneapolis, so she asked Will to see if one of the production interns would be willing to come back up with her later in the month to help with interviews. He said he'd check into it. Before they said goodbye, he told her to relax a little and enjoy her stay.

Jane had never been very good at relaxing. When she walked into the cafe she found that it was packed, with nowhere to sit. She surveyed the room one last time just to be sure, and was surprised when a hand rose above the crowd and waved at her.

It was Wilburn Lowry, the grizzled "prospector" she'd met on

Sunday morning at the White Star Cafe. She'd been hoping for some time alone to make a few notes about the case, so whatever he wanted to say, she intended to make it short.

"Please," he said, nodding to the empty chair across from him. He wiped his mouth on a napkin and then tossed it over his empty plate. "I was just leaving. You might as well take the table."

"Thanks."

"Since you're here, I should tell you that I listened to more of your podcast. I think it's really good."

"I'm glad."

"You're legit."

A server stopped by with a menu and asked if Jane wanted coffee.

"Please."

"So here's the deal," continued Lowry, scratching one of his fleecy, gray muttonchops. "I have something for you."

"You do?"

"I do indeed. I mean, I don't have it with me, but maybe we could meet up. How about tomorrow, same time, same place. I don't live far from here, so it's an easy walk."

"What is it?"

"Something that might help you with the Romilly investigation."

"If you could be a little more specific—"

"Nope, I like surprises, don't you? Well," he said, pressing his hands to the table and standing, "good to see you again, Ms. Lawless." He pulled a ten-dollar bill out of his billfold and dropped it on the table next to the receipt. "See you tomorrow."

At least she wouldn't have to sit through breakfast with him.

When the waitress returned, Jane ordered corned beef hash and a couple of eggs. She was hungry and figured this would hold her until dinner. She loved the sound of a crowded restaurant. It was pure white noise, just what she needed to help her concentrate.

Opening a notebook, Jane read through the bullet points she'd sent to Will, along with the taped interview. These were the leads she'd found and wanted to follow up on.

- Sam and brother fighting before Sam disappeared.
- Graveyard manager said Dave Tamborsky walked by grave where Beddemeyer would be buried the day before her burial and the day before Sam went missing. Dave with unidentified friend.
- Carli Gilbert possibly murdered and body burned in house fire the day after Sam's remains found. May not be connected, but Carli worked at same bank where Scott and father, Wendell, employed.
- Rumor around town that Wendell Romilly murdered son.
- Darius Pollard may have info about Sam, according to Hughes.
- He was friend of Sam's.
- Something happened at a party before the beginning of their senior year. Sam involved. Not sure what it means, but may be important.
- Hughes said many rumors going around school just before Sam disappeared.
- The school would blow up on January 1.
- A teacher had seduced a student.
- Dave T. and Monty Mickler, rumored to be a gay couple.
- A girl got in car with stranger and was assaulted.

Jane tapped her pen against the page. The school blowing up was obviously one of those ridiculous rumors circulating before the turn of the century. But what about the others? There might be some truth in one of them. But which one? Or perhaps there was a nugget of truth in all of them? Not that they had anything to do with Sam's murder, but what if one or all of them did? At the very least, they provided her with more questions to ask.

Energized by how much she had to do, Jane dug in to her food.

Later, when the waitress came by to ask how everything was, she asked for the bill. She was getting somewhere, she could just feel it. She needed to keep going.

Next stop, Lakeside Community Bank.

The bank was located in an old brick building along Main Street, not far from the town hall. There was a free parking lot next to the building. As Jane walked into the lobby, she found teller windows to her right and a large open space filled with desks to her left. The interior walls were covered in wood paneling with lovely old millwork details. Jane counted eight desks for the personal bankers, with glass-enclosed private offices along the front and back walls. In the center was a round kiosk where a woman sat on a stool, ready to answer questions. Jane walked up and asked if she could speak with Wendell Romilly.

"Your name?" asked the woman.

"Jane Lawless."

"Lawless? That's unusual."

"It's not a comment on my morals."

"Sounds like a standard line, one you use often."

"More than I'd like."

"Can I ask why you want to see Mr. Romilly?"

Jane explained about the podcast, handing the woman her card.

"Just a sec." She punched in a number, made the request, waited, and then thanked whoever was on the other end of the line. "I'm sorry, he's not available."

"I could wait."

"I think it's more like he's . . . not interested."

"What about Scott Romilly? Is he here?"

"I can check." Another phone call elicited a different response. "Yes, he'd be happy to see you. If you'd like to wait here, he'll be right out."

"I was sorry to hear about one of your coworkers, Carli Gilbert," said Jane. Since she was here, she might as well do a little fishing.

"Oh, my, yes. *Such* a shame."

"Did you know her?"

"Oh, sure. We'd go out for lunch together every few weeks. She was a great listener. In my experience, people like that are rare."

"Did she have other friends here at the bank?"

"Carli was friendly with everyone."

"But special or close friends?"

The woman shrugged. "She seemed to get along especially well with Scott. They were always kidding around, laughing about, you know, whatnot. I think they played golf together sometimes. Now that's a game I don't get. Hitting a little ball around. Makes no sense to me. And it costs money, you know? It's not a cheap hobby."

Jane talked with the woman until a dark-haired man in a three-piece suit appeared and extended his hand. Jane had never met Sam Romilly, but this guy looked nothing like the pictures of Sam she'd seen.

Scott invited her back to his office. Once seated in front of his desk, Jane offered condolences on the death of his brother and then explained, once again, about the podcast.

"But aren't you in town for something else? You're staying at the Granholm place, right? You're a friend of Emma's."

"I'm taking part in the silent auction for the art center. I own a restaurant in Minneapolis, so I'm donating a gourmet dinner to the highest bidder."

"That was it. I knew Emma mentioned something about it."

He didn't look like a stalker, but then, what did a stalker look like? "Are you two friends? I know she dated your brother back in high school."

"Yeah, she did. And sure, we're friends. Good friends, in fact."

"Would you be willing to answer a couple of questions about Sam?"

He eased back in his chair. "I'm afraid I can't give you much time this morning."

No use taking out her recorder. Still, maybe she could get something from him. "Perhaps we could schedule another time to talk."

"You mean like an actual interview? Something you'd record?"

"If you'd be willing."

"Let me think about it." He kept shifting around in his chair, which caused Jane to conclude that her presence made him uneasy.

"I've interviewed a number of Sam's friends, trying to get a feel for what was happening in his life right around the time he disappeared. I was told that there was some animosity between you two, that you were wresting each other in Victory Park a few days before he disappeared."

"Jim Hughes tell you that?"

She nodded.

"Figures. He's a busybody, just like everybody else in this town. It had nothing to do with Sam's death. It was personal. Between him and me and nobody else."

"Okay." She waited, hoping her silence would cause him to fill the void.

"He, ah . . . thought I was making a mistake. I disagreed."

"A mistake about what?"

He removed a package of cigarettes from the top drawer of his desk. "What does it matter now? It's all water under the bridge."

"Hughes said that Sam thought you were about to do something that would ruin your life. That seems pretty significant."

He laughed. "Sam loved drama. Obviously, he was wrong. My life is just fine, thank you very much. That's all I've got to say on the matter."

"Do you have any idea who might have wanted to hurt your brother?"

"No, none. Honestly, we weren't that close. I knew very little about what was happening in his life. He only knew what was going on in mine because he felt that, as my big brother, he had the right to stick his nose into my private business. We were fourteen months apart, hardly an age difference that conferred superior wisdom. That time in the park? He was the aggressor, not me. I was just trying to protect myself."

"But it must have made you pretty angry."

"You bet it did. He thought he knew better than me. About everything. He crossed a line. He had absolutely no right."

Even now, the anger in his voice came through loud and clear.

Perhaps sensing that he'd said too much, Scott stood. "I have an appointment in a few minutes. Why don't I walk you out?"

"I think I can find my way."

"I need a cigarette," he said, motioning her to the door.

On the sidewalk in front of the building, Jane thanked him again and began walking toward the parking lot. Scott, for whatever reason, followed.

"Hey, nice wheels," he said, glancing at her truck as he cupped his hand around the tip of a cigarette and lit up. "I've been thinking about buying a truck, but I don't want one of those mammoth Fords or Rams. What's this?"

"A Honda Ridgeline." She unlocked the door.

"It's smaller. I like that. How does it drive?"

"It rides more like a car."

"Huh." When a man in chinos and a quilted blue jacket walked past them, Scott stuck out his hand. "Mr. Mickler," he said, smiling. "Nice to see you."

So, this was Dave Tamborsky's friend—and possible lover. He wasn't bad looking. Regular features and straight, dark hair parted on the side. Nothing much about him stood out.

Mickler offered Scott a friendly nod.

"I have to tell you how much I enjoyed having your son, Max, on the soccer team this summer. He's got a ton of talent."

"I've worked with him a lot," said Mickler, pausing. "I hoped he'd do well. And next year, Jordy, my younger son, is going to try out for the team."

"How old is Jordy?"

"He'll be eight."

"If he's anywhere near as athletic as his brother, I'll be happy to have him."

"If anything, Jordy's even more athletic."

"Good to know," said Scott, tapping some ash onto the pavement. "Say, where are my manners? Monty Mickler, this is Jane Lawless. She's in town for the art festival."

"Nice to meet you." She shook his hand.

He examined her briefly. "You're the podcaster."

"How'd you hear about that?"

"It's a small town. Word gets around."

He switched his gaze back to Scott. "Well, better get my banking done. I don't like to be late for work."

"Give my best to Max," said Scott, taking a last drag off his cigarette before dropping it and grinding it out with his tip of his loafer. Turning back to Jane, he said, "Better get back myself. I hope you find what you're looking for. I don't hold out a lot of hope that Sam's murder will ever be solved, but who knows." With that, he walked back into the bank.

19

Frustration often drove Dave to eat. After he'd left his house this morning, his frustration had begun building when his plans for the day were derailed by a welfare check. The dispatcher informed him that an elderly man up near Chipping Lake hadn't answered his phone in days. He found the guy sunning himself in a hammock. When Dave asked him why he didn't answer his calls, the man told him he'd unplugged the phone. Nobody he actually wanted to talk to ever called him, so what was the point? Dave ordered him to plug the damn phone back in and answer his damn calls.

His next stop was Sarah Mickler. Since Monty had said Sarah was a friend of Carli Gilbert's, Dave wanted to get her take on what had happened in Carli's marriage. The theory he was working was that her husband had probably done it, either out of jealousy, rage, or something related to money. He'd have to check on any insurance policies issued on Carli's life. It still galled him that the chief had taken him off the Romilly case. Instead of chasing the arson/murder, he should be working on—or more accurately, squelching—the Romilly investigation.

When Dave entered Mickler's rambler, he offered Sarah his condolences. She immediately teared up, and then sniffed into a tissue as she led him back to the kitchen. She was understandably sad, but, as it turned out, she was also suffering from a cold. Dave sat at the kitchen table drinking coffee while Sarah sneezed her way over to the counter to burn him a piece of toast. The only information he came away with that might prove useful was the name of Carli's closest girlfriend, Mandy Bowden, who lived in Clarksville.

Stopping at a convenience store to buy himself a couple of Klondike bars to entertain himself on the ride up there, he made the trip in record time, calling ahead to make sure she was home. Through her tears, Mandy explained that Carli was a saintly woman, patient, kind, loving, deeply patriotic, and the best friend any woman could ever have. Dave figured she was laying it on a bit thick, but understood the impulse to speak well of the dead.

"What about the rumors I hear?" asked Dave, sitting on a plaid couch, balancing a coffee cup on his knee. "That she was having an affair."

"Oh, my," said Mandy, adjusting her glasses. "I can't believe you'd ask me that."

"I need the truth," he said. "You want to find out what happened to her, don't you?"

"Well, yes," she offered.

"So?"

"I don't want you to think ill of her."

"I promise," said Dave. "I won't."

She pressed her lips together and nodded. "I guess . . . yes, she did stray."

"What's the guy's name?"

"She never told me."

"Oh, come on, Mandy. You can do better than that."

"I do *not* lie."

"Uh-huh. So this mystery man, what *did* she tell you about him?"

"Very little," said Mandy, clearly annoyed. She tugged on her cardigan and sat up a bit straighter.

137

Dave had made a tactical mistake, but he didn't care. "Look, ma'am, if you know something and you don't tell me, that's a crime."

"I don't know his name," she insisted. Then, relenting a little, she added, "All she ever said was that he was good in . . . that he was, unlike her husband, a generous and gentle soul."

Dave's eyes rose to the ceiling. "What else?"

"He liked to give her little gifts. Mostly jewelry."

"So he was rich?"

"I suppose."

"How long had the affair been going on?"

"A while."

"What's that mean? A week? A month?"

"Years, I believe." Mandy cast her eyes down.

"Were they in love?"

"I think Carli loved him, yes."

"Did he love her back?"

"Look, Sgt. Tamborsky, may I be blunt?"

Finally. "Please."

"It was a sex thing. Carli liked sex, okay? That dolt of a husband—she called him Mr. Hockey Puck—wasn't interested. Maybe he was getting it somewhere else, too, who knows, but it seemed like he preferred drinking beer with his buddies and watching sports to her. She had tender feelings, Sergeant, and Mr. Hockey Puck stomped all over them."

"Did he know about the affair?"

"I doubt it."

"But you don't know for sure?"

She gave her head a tiny shake. "I don't want you to think ill of Carli. She was a lovely woman. She deserved much better."

They talked for a few more minutes. Dave ended the interview when he realized she'd given him all she could. Before he left, he asked if Carli had any relatives in the area.

"Just her cousin. Suzy Engel. That's her married name."

"Know where she lives?"

"In Castle Lake, over by the marina."

"Were they close?"

"Sort of. But . . . you know, they had their issues."

Just what Dave was looking for. Someone who knew Carli and wouldn't need to muck up the waters with a lot of glowing trivia.

An hour later, he was seated on the back porch of Suzy's house, another cup of coffee in hand. What he really wanted was a plate of chicken enchiladas smothered in green sauce with guacamole and sour cream on the side.

"I'm sorry about your cousin," he began.

"Boy," said Suzy. "I was totally blindsided. You're never prepared for stuff like that."

"I understand you two were pretty tight."

"Well, I mean, we didn't, like, talk every day or nothing. But she and Aaron would come by for dinner every now and then. And we'd sometimes get a drink together over at the Lazy Dog."

"I was told she'd been seeing someone on the side."

"Oh, yeah. Had been for years." Suzy ran a hand through her curly hair. "Don't know who he was, but she'd talk about him on occasion. Aaron was a dolt. Hardworking, but dull. I never understood why she married him. Maybe she was looking for stability after all the crap she pulled when she was younger."

"Such as?"

"Oh, she was into drugs for a while. A lot of sex with a lot of different guys. She tried really hard when she decided to straighten up and fly right."

"And she succeeded?"

"Yeah, pretty much. Of course, to cut Aaron a little slack, I sure as hell wouldn't have wanted to live with her. She had a wicked tongue. She could come across as sweetness and light, but underneath, she was, like, always calculating her advantage. Ever know anybody like that? Someone you think you can trust but you really can't?"

"Who do you think had it in for her?"

"Oh hell, no idea."

"Aaron?"

"I don't know. Maybe. But he always seemed kind of, like, passive to me."

"He have a temper? Did he ever knock Carli around?"

"Not that I ever knew about."

It was as if Mandy and Suzy had known two different women. "Was she seeing more than one guy on the side?

"It's possible, but I never heard about anyone except Mr. Smooth. That's what she called him."

"I was told she called her husband Mr. Hockey Puck."

Suzy laughed. "Yeah, she liked to give people nicknames."

"She have one for her friend, Mandy?"

"Yeah. Miss Bible Belt."

"What was yours?"

Her smile evaporated. "The Bitch."

"You have one for her?"

"Not something I can say out loud."

Dave's cell phone rang. "Give me a second, will you?" he said, getting up and walking out into the yard. "Tamborsky."

"It's Mason. You need to get back to the station ASAP."

Mason was a patrol cop, one of Dave's buddies on the force. "Why?"

"It's new info on the Romilly case. Just get back here."

Dave clicked off the phone. Ducking his head into the porch, he thanked Suzy for her time. He didn't wait for a response.

20

Jane stopped by city hall after receiving a text from Leslie. A receptionist directed her to an office at the end of a carpeted hallway, where the mayor sat behind an L-shaped desk talking on the phone, a pair of reading glasses perched on the end of her nose. Motioning Jane to a chair, she continued the conversation.

Jane welcomed the chance to just sit and observe. She'd already come to certain conclusions about their budding relationship, if that's what it was. While Jane was attracted to the mayor, she truly wasn't in the market for another romantic attachment, especially one that would need to be conducted long distance. Cordelia might have the stamina for it with Berengaria, but Jane saw no reason to tie herself to something with so many potential problems. Beyond that, with the exception of books on politics and government, Leslie wasn't a reader. She had no interest in poetry or novels—both things Jane felt were as necessary to life as food and water. Leslie didn't much care for dogs, either, and she was, she admitted, a workaholic. Jane had spent most of her life with her nose to the grindstone, too, and understood that two workaholics in the same relationship was a recipe for disaster. The final nail in the proverbial coffin was that, for all practical purposes, Leslie Harrow lived in the closet, a place Jane wanted no part of.

She'd spent too much of her young life hiding and avoiding leading questions to want to go back to it.

She was scrolling through messages on her phone when Leslie finally ended the call.

"I've got a potential mutiny on my hands," she said, folding her arms. "We're considering a new strategic plan for the city and tonight we're supposed to talk about land use, always a contentious issue. But you didn't come here to listen to me kvetch." She rearranged her face into a smile. "I'm hoping we can get together again for another dinner. I promise this time I'll do something more creative."

"Or we could go out."

"Only if you promise to come back for . . . a nightcap."

Jane returned her smile. "I think I could manage that."

"Thursday night? Wish I could do it tomorrow night, but I have a speaking gig over in Fergus."

"Thursday's good."

Removing her reading glasses, Leslie continued, "So what are you up to today?"

"Doing some preliminary interviews for the Romilly investigation."

Leslie wore a black blazer over a red turtleneck and looked not only professional, but beautiful—at least to Jane's eyes. "You think your podcast will do an episode on it?"

"I talked to the senior producer. Depends on what I can dig up."

"Does that mean you'll stay beyond next Sunday?"

"More likely I'll return later in the month."

"Well, you've pretty much made my day. Oh, goodness, look at the time. I'm so sorry, but I have a meeting—"

"I'll get out of your hair. Is there a restroom I could use before I go?"

"Here," said Leslie, getting up. She stepped into an empty conference room connected to her office and flipped on the light. "In the back." She pointed to a door. "If I'm in that meeting when you're done, you can get out to the hall through there." She pointed to another door. "I'll be in touch," she said, giving Jane's hand a squeeze.

Jane had forgotten to take her medication this morning before leaving the lake house. High blood pressure ran in her family, so last spring, her doctor had put her on something to help with it. Glad to see that there was a paper-cup dispenser next to the sink, she downed the pill along with two ibuprofen. After so little sleep, she was starting to drag. She took a moment to check her look in the mirror. In the past year, she'd let her chestnut hair grow out. It was long enough now to put up in a bun, so that's what she did, mainly to get it out of her face. When she returned to the conference room, she could hear voices in Leslie's office. Peeking inside, she saw a police officer standing in front of the desk, reading from a notebook. Hearing the name Romilly, she inched closer to the door.

"This report, Sgt. Saltus," said Leslie—she was out of Jane's view, but not out of earshot—"you say it just came in from the BCA?"

"That's correct, ma'am. It's preliminary. The DNA has been sent for testing, but that will take a while. The chief said I should keep you informed."

"Continue."

He cleared his throat. "In the remains that we sent to St. Paul, the lab techs found a skull. It was broken, pierced by a single gunshot. That's most likely how Romilly died."

"Assuming that it was Sam who was buried there."

"There's no reason to believe otherwise, ma'am. We found his watch, his billfold, his backpack. Through photos, his father was able to identify a piece of sweatshirt as well as a pair of hiking boots."

"Yes, I see your point. Go on."

"Two handguns, both thirty-eight caliber revolvers, both made by Taurus, were also found, along with the remains of six black plastic garbage bags, all heavy duty. The bags were wrapped around the remains. We've concluded that after the murder, the body was likely placed in them and transported to the gravesite." He paused.

"Is that it?"

"Actually—we don't understand this yet—the techs found two cartridges in each handgun. All blanks. In each gun, one of the blanks was spent, the other wasn't."

"So . . . let me get this straight," said Leslie. "A blank can't kill a man, right?"

"Well, not usually. I mean, it's not like you're firing a cap gun. If you hold the pistol too close to your body and fire, sure, you could get hurt. You could even die, but it's rare."

"So neither gun was used in Sam Romilly's murder."

"We can't be sure, but we don't think so."

"If they weren't used in the murder, what purpose did they serve?"

"As I said, we haven't determined that yet. Also, a ring was found behind the flap in Romilly's billfold."

"Can you describe it?"

"I haven't seen it, but I'd be happy to get back to you on that."

"Good work, Sergeant. Now, if you can just explain what it all means, we'll actually be making some progress."

"I think this is progress, ma'am."

"Of course. You're right."

"Do you have any other questions I could answer?"

"Not at the moment. Please thank Chief Larson for keeping me informed."

"Yes ma'am, I'll do that."

There was a knock on the mayor's door.

"Come in, Mr. Bradly," called the mayor.

The police officer turned to look. "Well, I need to get going." He nodded to Bradly and the mayor and made a quick exit.

Not wanting to run into Saltus, Jane waited a few seconds before she crossed to the door leading to the hallway. When she looked out, he was nowhere in sight. She might have been able to get the information some other way, but this kind of serendipity was what she always prayed for. Waiting another few seconds, she stepped out into the corridor and made her way back outside.

The town of Castle Lake was bordered by the Bullhead River on the northwest, Ice Lake on the east, and Castle Lake on the southwest. Castle Lake was the largest, with the best swimming beaches and a marina that offered both slips and moorings, along with a charter service and a sightseeing boat for tourists. The area around the lake was where the town had begun its life, though it had grown rundown by the late sixties.

With a vacation destination push by the town council, organized in the early 2000s, the area had revived, and so had the marina. Jane spent a few minutes strolling along Fisherman's Lakewalk, looking at the menus posted outside a couple of restaurants. She wasn't sure where Cordelia wanted to have dinner tonight, but at least now she had several good ideas to offer. Since it was a beautiful day, she sat by the water for a few minutes, enjoying a strawberry ice cream cone and trying not to overthink the situation with Leslie.

Pollard Automotive Repair was located about three blocks east of the marina. Leaving her car in the parking lot, Jane decided to walk. She was sad to see that Brick Town Road still reflected some of the town's blighted past. As she approached the building, she saw that it was a one-story stucco structure, mainly two garage bays with an attached office. If she stood on the street in front of it and looked east, she could see the VFW hall a block away, where the reunion would take place on Saturday night. Next to the auto repair shop was a storefront, Crawford Clock Works, where dozens of old clocks were displayed behind the picture window. She made a mental note to come back and check it out.

Entering the office, Jane found a young man sitting behind the counter, a crumpled brown paper sack open in front of him. He was eating what looked like a cheese and pickle sandwich. "I'm looking for Darius Pollard."

"Hey, D," shouted the young man. "You got a visitor." Nodding to the door across from the counter, he said, "He's in there."

Rolling out from under a car, Darius climbed to his feet, wiping his dirty hands on an equally dirty rag. "Can I help you?" he asked, stuffing the rag into the pocket of his gray coverall.

Jane explained who she was and asked him if he had a minute to talk

"A podcast, huh?" he said, looking her over. His head was shaved, and he had a goatee that included a few gray hairs. "My wife listens to one of those. Something about gardening. But yours is—"

"Minnesota cold cases," said Jane. "Criminal cases."

"Sam's isn't so cold anymore, now that they found his body."

"Have you been contacted by the police? I assume they're interviewing all Sam's friends."

"Nope, haven't heard a word."

He stepped away from the car and walked outside to where several empty wooden spools rested near a patch of scrubby grass. He invited her to sit on one as he pulled a package of butter rum Life Savers out of his upper pocket. He offered her the pack.

"No, thanks," she said. "Would you be willing to let me record this?"

"I don't know," he said, popping a Life Saver into his mouth.

"If we end up wanting to air any of it for a podcast about Sam's death, I would need your written permission to use anything you say today."

"Yeah?" he said, studying her a moment more. "Hell, why not," he said finally. She got everything set up and then switched on the recorder.

After an awkward start, Darius seemed to settle in. "Sam was a good guy. We were in the same high school class. Most of the white kids didn't mix with the black kids. There were only three of us, so we stuck together. I got to know Sam because he'd heard I repaired motorcycles. He had this sweet Kawasaki Kz1000. He'd tried to repair it himself, but it still ran rough, so he came up to me in the hall one afternoon and asked if I'd look at it. He brought it over to the shop later that day. He said he'd had it for a couple of months. I could see right away that there was a lot of garage rot, which was why he got it so cheap."

"Garage rot?"

"Worst thing you can do to a cycle is not ride it. Anyway, we sat down together on the pavement and I took a look. It was a fairly intense repair, but that's what I like. So while I worked, we talked. I knew right away I liked him. Once we got the bike up and purring like a kitten, we started riding together on weekends. We'd find a straight patch of highway and go WFO until we hit a curve. He took crazy-ass risks, and I did, too. He was a super cool guy."

"What did you think happened to him?"

He sucked on his candy. "Oh, I don't know, but I knew it wasn't good. He wasn't the kind of guy to hang his friends out to dry, never telling them what was going on."

"Did he have enemies?"

"Not that I knew about."

"So you had no idea what happened."

"None. I did save his bike, just in case he came home. His father put it up for sale right after he disappeared, so I bought it. My oldest son rides it now."

"What did you think of Sam's dad?"

He grunted. "A real bastard."

"Why would he sell his son's bike when there was a chance he'd come back?"

"You tell me." He crunched his Life Saver and gazed toward the street. "I figure it was just another way to stick it to Sam."

"There are rumors that he murdered him."

"Wouldn't surprise me. That man is cold as freakin' ice."

Jane made a few notes. "Do you know Dave Tamborsky or Monty Mickler?"

"Not well, but yeah, I know them."

"I was talking to the man who's in charge of the grounds at Holy Trinity cemetery. He said you'd worked for him when you were in high school."

"Haven't thought about that in years. Sure, I worked for him one summer."

"He said you'd helped him dig Ida Beddemeyer's grave."

"Crap, did I? He could be right."

"And that while you were taking a break, Dave Tamborsky walked by and said something that angered you."

"Honestly, I have no memory of it, but it wouldn't surprise me. Dave was a real pig, always calling me things like jungle bunny, coon—you get the picture."

"But you have no memory of him walking past the grave that day."

"Sorry."

She was disappointed, but moved on. "I talked to Jim Hughes yesterday, one of Sam's old buddies. He said there were a bunch of rumors flying around the school before Sam went missing."

"Like what?"

"That Tamborsky and Mickler were gay, that they were a couple."

Darius threw his head back and roared with laughter. "What a hoot. Maybe we should restart that rumor."

148

"Is there any truth in it?"

"I doubt it. What else?"

"That Sam and his brother were angry at each other."

"Don't know about that."

"What about a teacher seducing a student?"

He shrugged. "There were always rumors about stuff like that."

"A girl got into a car with a stranger and was assaulted."

He scowled. "Not very specific."

"What about this?" said Jane. "I was told there was a party at a farm near town at the beginning of your senior year. Something bad happened and Sam was part of it. I don't suppose you were there?"

He hesitated. "I may have been."

"Do you know what the rumor is about?"

More hesitation. "It's hard to remember that far back."

He'd been so open at the beginning of the conversation, but after she mentioned the party, his tone changed. He seemed more wary. "I'm committed to finding out what happened to him," said Jane. "I think he deserves that."

"Yeah," he said under his breath. "He sure as hell does."

"Hey, D," shouted a voice from inside the garage. "That car you're working on's not gonna fix itself."

"I'm almost done, Dad," Darius shouted back. To Jane, he added, "Sorry, but I gotta get back to work."

Jane unhooked his mic and then hers. As he was about to head back inside, she handed him one of her cards. "If you remember anything that might be of help to our investigation, please give me a call."

"Will do," he said. As he walked away, his shoulders relaxed. Jane read it as relief that the conversation was over.

21

People often asked Kurt when his next book of poetry would be published. It was a question he loathed. Was he supposed to tell the truth, that he'd never wanted his work published in the first place? It was ultimately his choice, he supposed, but the journey that got him there hadn't been.

Without ever mentioning it to Kurt, a friend had sent a cobbled-together manuscript of some of his poems to a small press. An acceptance letter was delivered to this friend several months later. Assuming that Kurt would be thrilled, the friend had stopped by to deliver the good news.

At first, Kurt was nonplussed. The man had no right to do it, but now that a press was on board, how could he say no? He was ashamed to admit that he'd been swayed by the stardust his new editor blew his way. And thus, the volume came out a year later.

Initially, Kurt enjoyed doing readings, meeting people to talk about the beauty of language, the importance of image and introspection. But over time, he found that the whole experience left him feeling exposed. He stopped writing. Stopped doing readings. He eventually moved beyond this "oversensitivity," as he began to think of it, but his writing never fully recovered. The book hadn't sold well. Even so, people continued to view him as a man with a certain status, a published writer, as if the two hundred lost souls who'd actually shelled out good money for the book meant anything at all. Why would someone want to know when the next book would be out if they hadn't read the first? It all began to feel not only meaningless, but squalid, which was why he wished he'd turned his back on the contract and walked away.

Kurt sat at the table in his dining room, a glass of iced tea next to him, and tapped a pencil against an empty page in a wire-bound notebook. Emma had asked him to write a few lines about Sam for the reunion memorial, which was easier asked for than accomplished. Words still felt slippery to him, as if meaning itself was an unreliable concept.

So, instead of concentrating on the task at hand, Kurt kept stealing glances at an envelope addressed to his son which had come in the mail that day. He was dying to know what was in it. Danny wouldn't be home from work for a while, and even when he did come home, there was no guarantee that he'd tell Kurt what it was about. It was probably nothing, but because Kurt was already worried about so much else, he figured he might as well add the letter to the list. He wasn't in a good mood and didn't see that changing anytime soon.

Hearing the doorbell, he pushed away from the table and padded in his stocking feet to the door. Emma was outside, looking windblown and lovely. "Hey, come in," he said, brightening just a little.

"What are you cooking out there on your porch?" she asked, sniffing the air. "Is that a roaster oven?"

"It's actually a smoker," said Kurt, inviting her into the dining room. "Can I get you something to drink? I'm having iced tea."

"No," she said. "I can't stay."

"To answer your question, I'm smoking a pork shoulder. Brought one home from the shop at lunchtime and got it going. That Oster is ridiculously easy to use. It doesn't turn out the same kind of smoked meat as a real smoker, but it's pretty close. Danny and I both love it. You're welcome to come for dinner. We'll pull a section of the roast, add some barbecue sauce, and pile it on some buns. There's plenty to go around."

"That sounds so tempting, but I'm afraid I've already got an engagement."

"With Mr. X? The guy who has no name?"

She laughed. "Yeah, with him."

"When am I going to meet this dude?"

"Probably never. It's nothing serious. I'll be leaving next week to go back home. I really miss my daughter."

The thought of her leaving filled him with sadness. "I knew that was coming. I'll miss you."

"Not as much as I'll miss you."

The comment warmed him more than he could say. They remained silent for a few seconds.

"What are you working on?" she asked, nodding at the notebook.

"My comments for Sam's memorial."

She fidgeted with the clasp on her purse before finally opening it, removing a folded piece of paper. "Here's mine. I thought you should read it, tell me what you think." She waited while he scanned the page. "I'm hoping Ted will read the class memorials. There are only three. I'm afraid if I tried, I'd start crying."

Kurt felt the same way. "This is beautiful."

"You think so?"

"It's perfect." His phone rang. Removing it from his back pocket, he saw that it was Dave Tamborsky. "Oh, jeez. I need to take this. Can you stay just a little while longer? This should only take a second."

"Sure," she said, sitting down on his chair. "No worries."

Walking into the kitchen, Kurt said hello.

"I need to give you a heads-up," came Dave's voice. "Some idiot sent a note to the police department saying he had information about Sam's death but couldn't come forward because he feared for his safety. He listed four names, people who might know something."

"Like who?"

"You, Jim Hughes, Darius Pollard, and Scott Romilly. Here's the deal: None of them know squat. The only one who does is you. Just stick to the story and we're home free, okay? There's zero way anybody can know what happened unless someone who was there talks. So be careful, man. You hear me?"

"Yeah," said Kurt.

"Text me when you get the call to come down to the station."

"Won't you be doing the interview?"

"Bobby Saltus will."

"Never heard of him."

"Looks like Justin Bieber?"

"Oh," said Kurt, groaning. "Him."

"Just be your usual, casual, earnest self. You'll be fine. Peace, man."

"Peace," repeated Kurt, feeling like a speeding train was headed straight for him.

"What's wrong?" asked Emma as Kurt dragged himself back into the dining room.

"Nothing."

She studied him. "I don't believe you."

"Emma, I can't get into it right now. But don't you ever feel overwhelmed?"

"Frequently." She sat for a moment more. "I'm here for you, Kurt."

She wouldn't be if she knew the truth.

"If you ever need to talk—"

"Thanks."

"Well," she said, rising from the chair, "I'll catch you later. Oh, don't forget the reunion meeting on Thursday night."

"I'll be there." If I'm not in jail, he thought grimly.

"If you talk to Ted, remind him about the meeting tonight. He said he'd come. And enjoy your pulled pork sandwiches."

"Oh, we will."

As she crossed to the front door, Danny breezed in.

"Hey, Emma."

She gave him a quick hug on her way out.

Danny dropped his backpack next to the couch. "There's a guy outside hiding behind a tree on the other side of the street."

"Really? A cop?"

"No, a guy in a three-piece suit. Should I go chase him away?"

Kurt glanced at the envelope with his son's name on it. "You got something in the mail today."

"I did?" He took it and studied the return address. "Cool. I gotta call Tanya."

"But . . ." said Kurt, watching his son charge up the stairs to his bedroom. How was he ever going to initiate a conversation with Danny about the elephant in the room—or, as he'd begun to think of it, the herd assembling near the couch.

22

Emma had a couple of hours to kill before leaving to have dinner with Scott. She wasn't looking forward it and intended to make the evening a short one.

Sitting on the patio with a Coke and her cell phone, she decided to give Verity a call. She kept in touch with her daughter daily, mostly through texts, but also calls and FaceTime.

She tapped in the number.

A male voice answered. "Philip?" said Emma, confused that he'd answered Verity's phone.

"Emma? Hi. This is a surprise."

"Why are you answering our daughter's phone?"

"Huh?" A pause. "Oh. Yeah, it is hers. I thought it was mine. She left it on the kitchen counter."

That wasn't like Verity. If there was a way she could have the phone physically implanted into her body, she would. "Where is she?"

"Let me check."

Emma took a few sips of the soda, looking up at the puffy white clouds scudding by overhead.

"She's in the pool," said Philip when he returned to the line. "She usually takes the phone with her. Must have forgot."

"Okay, well, will you tell her I called?"

"Sure."

"Hey, since I have your attention, I'm flying home next week. Haven't bought a ticket yet, but, you know, just an FYI. Your trophy girlfriend should move her clothes out of my closet before then."

"She has a name, Emma. It's Sly."

"Good description."

"You flying in to San Jose?"

"That's the plan."

"Text me the info and I'll pick you up."

That was strange. He never offered to pick her up before. "If you decide to come, tell Sly to stay home."

"Won't be a problem. I haven't seen her in a couple of weeks."

So Verity had been right. He'd probably moved on to a younger version, which meant he was dating someone in high school. "Did she dump you or did you dump her."

"You're always so freakin' binary, Emma. If you have to know, it was mutual."

Sly had dumped him.

"Have you had enough of the outback?" he asked, his voice dripping sarcasm.

"Now who's being binary? There's civilization and there's the hinterland."

"Amazing as it may sound, I miss our sparring. Don't you?"

"No." Nothing binary there.

"Have you found some handsome hunk in Castle Swamp to replace me?"

"Would you care if I had?"

Silence. "Maybe a little."

"Look, I'm keeping to our agreement. I'll play the part of the dutiful wife for a while longer, but only in public."

"Right. But . . . don't you miss me just a little?"

156

"You're frustrated because you don't have a bimbo in your life at the moment, someone who makes you feel young and strong and virile."

"I am young and strong and virile."

"You know what they say about bimbos and buses."

"How did we get here? When did you become so bitter?"

"When I realized you'd been cheating on me with every woman who happens to have a pulse."

"You made your point, Emma. You can stop."

"Just tell Verity I called. I'll try again later." She ended the call. The idea that her wayward husband might be inching his way toward some kind of rapprochement might have, under other circumstances, made her feel hopeful, but at the moment all she felt was annoyance. He was bored, and when he was bored he liked to play games. She finished her Coke, tapping her nails on the arm of the chair and seething. Castle Swamp, my ass. Screw him.

Soft jazz was once again playing when she entered Scott's condo shortly after seven. He took her coat and hung it up in the closet, then reached for her hand and pulled her into his arms. "Just for old time's sake," he said, kissing her.

He was a good kisser, so she didn't object.

"Are you hungry?"

"Famished."

"I was hoping you'd say you were hungry for something else."

"Did anyone ever tell you that you have a one-track mind?"

He smiled, released her, and went into the kitchen.

An old farmhouse table ran along the center of the kitchen, one that could comfortably seat six, eight if people snuggled up to make room for the extra chairs. Tonight, it was set for two. Wine glasses rested on the counter next to a bottle of old vine zinfandel.

"I thought we said no booze."

"Wine with dinner? That hardly leads to an all-night drunk."

She wondered if he'd already had something. Alcoholism was in his family DNA. If his mother had died of anything other than a broken heart, it was that. Sam had managed to steer clear of it. She'd never seen him drink more than a couple beers at any one time. He liked weed—but then, back in high school, who didn't?

Perching on a stool by the counter, she watched him cook. She liked the practiced way he used a knife, cutting up the mushrooms and shallots, chopping the dill. He turned to the refrigerator and removed a bowl of sliced beef tenderloin. As he heated the oil and began to brown the slices, he removed the cover on a pot of water to see if it was boiling. "Almost there," he said, covering it back up. "How's everything going with the reunion plans?"

"Good, I think. We have the final meeting on Thursday night. We'll decorate the VFW hall on Saturday morning. I may not have mentioned this, but I wrote a short piece about Sam. We'll have a memorial wall, and our class president will read short pieces about the three people who've died."

"I suppose a lot of Sam's old friends will be there." Removing the slices of beef, he melted a couple of pats of butter and tossed in the mushrooms and the shallots. As they sautéed, he removed a small container of sour cream from the refrigerator, one of Dijon mustard, and reached over to get the bottle of cognac he'd set on the other end of the counter.

Emma's stomach began to growl.

"I understand you're throwing a party at your house after the homecoming game on Friday night. A kegger, yes? And a bonfire on the beach?"

She hadn't invited him. She should have known he'd hear about it. Not that he seemed upset. He'd merely chucked it into the conversation.

"That's right. It will be the first reunion event."

"Official event?" He opened a package of egg noodles and tossed them into the boiling water, stirring to make sure nothing stuck.

"Well, no. The only official event is on Saturday night. But there are some brunches planned for Saturday and Sunday. You know, stuff like that."

He added the cognac to the mushrooms, let it evaporate a little, then tossed in the dill, a large pinch of paprika, more salt, and a few grinds of pepper. "The bonfire sounds fun."

"I hope so. We'll have grilled hot dogs, potato chips, easy stuff like that. And, yeah, a keg. Seemed appropriate."

"You need someone to man the grill?"

She knew where this was headed. "You're not part of our class, Scott."

"So? Nobody would care."

"I've got it covered."

"Okay. Just asking. Why don't you open the wine?" He handed her a corkscrew.

She was having trouble reading him. He didn't seem angry. He didn't seem anything, really, just focused on preparing dinner.

When the noodles were done, he dumped them into a colander and then into a bowl, adding a couple pats of butter to coat them. Returning to the sauté pan, he added the beef slices, the sour cream, and a spoonful of the mustard, waiting until everything heated through. Giving it one last taste, he pronounced it perfect. "Go sit at the table."

Emma carried the glasses and the wine bottle over. She watched him dish up their plates.

"Thank you," she said as he set a plate in front of her.

They ate in silence for the next few minutes.

"I had a visitor at the bank today," Scott said finally, pouring them each more wine. "The woman who's staying at your house. I believe her name is Lawless."

"Oh? What did she want?"

"To talk about Sam. And me. She asked if we were fighting before he went missing. Hard to miss her point. She thinks I'm the one who murdered him."

"Come on, Scott, I'm sure she wasn't saying that."

"Sam apparently told Jim Hughes that I was about to ruin my life and that he was the only one who could save me."

"Is that true?"

"Jeez, no. My brother could be so freakin' self-important. Who the hell did he think he was, telling me how to live my life?"

Just like two nights ago, the mention of the fight had darkened his mood. "If you want to talk about it—"

"Just stop, okay? You're not my therapist. You're not my mother. I'm not even sure you're my girlfriend." He shoved his plate away.

"Listen, Scott—"

"No," he said, running his hands over his face and then through his hair. "I'm sorry. We need to change the subject." He pulled his wineglass in front of him. "So, um, you still planning on heading back home next week?"

"Philip said he'll pick me up at the airport. I'm not sure why he's being so nice."

"Probably wants to get back with you."

"I doubt it. His girlfriend dumped him, so he's got some free time on his hands."

"If you were my wife, Emma, I'd never treat you like that."

"I'm never getting married again."

"You don't mean that." He took a sip of wine. Then another. "You're going to miss a lot of people here when you leave."

"I suppose."

"Especially Kurt Steiner."

"Like you said, I'll miss a lot of people."

"But Kurt—you two seem especially close."

"He's a good friend." She didn't like where this was headed.

"Just a friend?"

"Yes, Scott."

"A friend with benefits?"

She fought the urge to stab him with her fork. "No." And then something occurred to her. "How do you know Kurt and I are good friends?"

He shrugged. "I've seen you with him. You don't hide your relationship, like you do with me."

"There's nothing to hide. We're on the same reunion committee. That's all."

"Oh, I see. And you had these committee meetings while you were fishing on Chipping Lake?"

"How do you know we went fishing there? Were you following us? Scott? Tell me."

"You cheated on me, Emma. Just like Philip cheated on you. Just say it. You'll feel better if you do."

She pushed back from the table and stood. "I'm done, Scott. I'm not having a conversation with a man who's been stalking me."

He toasted her with his wineglass, then drank it dry. Picking up the bottle, he followed her to the door. "If you leave, you'll never know how much I love you."

"Stalking isn't love."

"I wish you wouldn't use such a charged word." He stepped around her, blocking her exit.

"Move, Scott."

"Or what?"

She was getting that feeling again, the one that warned her that he might not let her leave. Only this time, it was more than just a feeling. "I'll scream."

He held her eyes. "Now why would you do that? I would never hurt you."

"I'm counting to three. I'm a loud screamer, Scott."

He waited a millisecond too long, enough to make her start

161

looking around for a weapon. Then he smiled. "See you soon, Emma."

"I hope not," she said, lurching out into the hallway. He stood by the door, watching her as she rushed for the stairs. She wasn't about to wait for the elevator. Not this time.

23

The Brick Town Tavern, a place with a blue-collar, dive-bar vibe, wasn't exactly what Jane had in mind when she'd agreed to have dinner with Cordelia. Not that she had anything against a good dive bar, but when it came to food, she'd been hoping for something a little more upscale.

"Oh, come on," said Cordelia, breezing her way to a table. "You'd rather have a burger than a steak any day. Am I right?"

"I suppose," said Jane. Steaks generally bored her. Still, she wasn't sure why there were only two choices for dinner.

"I asked around and this place supposedly has, by far, the best burgers in the known universe."

When the server arrived, they both ordered Grain Belts. "And we need menus."

The young waitress looked at them with unconcealed annoyance. "We don't do menus. We serve burgers and fries. That's it. No turkey burgers or vegan stuff. Just the real thing. We got pretty much any toppings you can think of." Jutting out a hip, she added, "Just an FYI. The fries are cooked in lard and the burgers are fried with butter, so if you're going to have a meltdown, better leave now. And we only serve white buns. The soft kind. If you're looking for sprouts and tofu, this ain't gonna be a good fit."

"Good to know," said Jane.

"So, you stayin'?" she asked.

"We wouldn't think of leaving," said Cordelia with a grin.

"Then I'll get your beers and be right back."

"Do you like my new purchases?" asked Cordelia, touching her necklace and then folding her hands this way and that under her chin.

"More costume jewelry?"

"Sparkly things make me happy. Emma took me to a couple antique stores yesterday. The stuff here is so cheap, I feel like I've landed in Oz."

"Was Oz known for cheap bling?"

"And look at this." She pushed her hair back, revealing a pair of appallingly gaudy earrings. "It is my hope that one day, I will be compared to a Fabergé egg. With the all of my luscious curves, I'm already the approximate shape."

Jane surveyed the room. She had to admit, the food smelled great. At the U-shaped bar, she noticed a familiar face. It shouldn't have surprised her to find Darius Pollard nursing a beer at this local watering hole. His business wasn't more than a couple blocks away. She wasn't sure if he'd noticed her, not that it mattered. She doubted he wanted to talk to her again.

When their Grain Belts arrived, Jane asked the server what kind of burger she recommended.

"A cheeseburger," she said. "You can't improve on perfection."

"The pinnacle of burger-dom," agreed Cordelia.

Jane ordered the cheeseburger, pickles, shredded head lettuce, raw onion, and a side of fries.

Cordelia dithered, finally settling on a plain burger, with sautéed mushrooms, barbecue sauce, avocado, a slice of tomato, bacon, extra pickles, and a fried egg. "Oh, and give me a side of mayo. And fries."

As the server wrote down the order, she oozed disdain. Jane

had to agree: Cordelia's burger was a travesty of nature—but then, to each her own.

"So fill me in on what's new," said Cordelia, giving the beer a taste.

Jane spent the next few minutes detailing her visit to the bank, her talk with Scott Romilly, her brief encounter with Monty Mickler, her feeling that Sam's father probably wouldn't talk to her, and her conversation with Darius Pollard. She saved the best for last: the information she'd overheard in the mayor's office from the officer who was now in charge of the investigation.

"That makes no sense," said Cordelia. "Two bullets in each revolver, one spent, one intact, all blanks. You said they determined Sam's skull was shattered by a bullet. So what went on? Why did those revolvers end up in his grave when they had nothing to do with his murder?"

It was the same question Jane had been asking. "I'm also curious about a ring they found under the back flap of Sam's billfold. The officer didn't have any information on it."

"We should ask Emma," said Cordelia, leaning back as the burgers appeared.

"Ketchup and mustard are against the wall next to the napkins," said the server. "Either of you want another beer?"

"I do," said Cordelia. "What else do you have? Any Surly?"

"Yeah, we got Furious."

"Perfect," said Cordelia, closing her eyes in ecstasy as she bit into a fry. "These are wondrous. Magical. Beyond fabulous."

"She has a gift for understatement," said Jane. "Make it two beers."

"Two breathlessly, insanely awesome Surlys coming right up."

As the server smirked and walked away, Jane said, "Your burger is six inches tall."

"And . . ." said Cordelia, making a valiant attempt to pick it up. "Your point is?"

"Maybe you should cut it in half."

As Cordelia sawed away and then tried to leverage half the pile toward her mouth, Jane continued, "I get the feeling that something really bad may have gone down at that keg party. The problem is, nobody seems to know what it was."

"Or they don't want to talk about it."

In any investigation, there were always certain elements Jane felt might turn out to be vital, a door that would open onto the truth. Determining where to find the key to that door was the real battle.

"So, who are our primary suspects?" asked Cordelia, wiping her mouth on a napkin.

"Scott Romilly, for one."

"Emma's having dinner with him again tonight."

"You mentioned that this morning. I was hoping you could talk her out of it."

"No such luck. I sent her a text a little while ago telling her to call if she needs us."

If Scott decided to do something crazy, it would hardly be enough. "What time was she meeting him?"

"Seven, I think. Anyway, keep going. Who else?"

"Well, Sam's father. I haven't figured out how to get him to talk to me."

"Try a gun and a silk stocking."

Jane glanced over at the bar. Darius Pollard looked away quickly. So he'd been watching her. "I keep going back to Dave Tamborsky. He walked right past Ida Beddemeyer's grave the day before Sam disappeared. At the very least, he knew the grave was there and that it would be empty until later the following day."

"He had someone with him, right?"

"Mickler, I'll bet. Not that it proves anything. Anyway, as for Carli Gilbert, I haven't had much of a chance to look into her death. I'm not even sure if it's been officially ruled a homicide, but I'll find out." She wiped grease off her fingers.

"Seems like someone's headed our way," said Cordelia, picking up her beer glass. When Jane looked up, Darius was approaching the table.

"You got a minute?" he asked, placing his hands on the back of an empty chair.

"Sure?" she said.

He glanced at Cordelia, then back at her.

"This is my friend, Cordelia Thorn. She helps me with my investigations. Anything you say to me can be said in front of her."

"Yeah? This is kind of . . . sensitive."

"Not a problem," said Cordelia. "Consider me a black box."

He pulled out the chair and sat down. "Look," he began somewhat nervously, "I need to tell you a few things. Maybe I should have done it this afternoon, but it didn't feel right."

"I'm glad it does now," said Jane. She didn't have her recorder with her. Not that it mattered. The noise level in the restaurant would have precluded using it.

He repositioned his baseball cap. "Okay, so before Sam died, you should know that he was in a battle with his dad. I don't know the details, but I do know he no longer felt safe at home. I always wondered if his father was the one behind Sam's disappearance. Anyway, the next thing is, there was definitely something bad going down with his brother, but, again, it was his father he was afraid of."

Wouldn't it be ironic, thought Jane, if the one Sam really needed to be afraid of was Scott?

"See, Sam had this ability to put things in boxes inside his mind and leave them there. He could act like nothing was wrong, everything was hearts and flowers, except it wasn't. I don't think he ever told anyone the entire story, what was really going on with him, certainly not me, but I know the guy was in pain. I wish I could say more, but I can't." He pulled his cap lower over his eyes. "Okay, next. The party at the farm. I don't know if it had anything to do with Sam's death, but you should know about it. So," he said, twisting his hands together, "I got there that night around ten. I didn't want to park where all the other cars were, so I pulled off into a field about thirty, forty yards from the house.

"There were lights strung up all over the yard. People were dancing, laughing, drinking, stuffing their faces with chips. A bunch of girls were in the kitchen heating up frozen pizzas. If I recall right, the keg was inside. There were empty cups all over the place. Someone had turned on a floodlight attached to the garage and a bunch of guys were playing hoops. A few people had sparklers and were running around in the dark, waving them. Couples were making out, some had walked away from the lights and were getting it on in the trees. I was the only black person there. Even though I did get a personal invite from Corey, I didn't figure I'd stay long.

"So, like, I found a clean plastic cup and helped myself to a beer. I stood around listening to this one conversation for a while, taking it all in, and, after my third brew, I decided I'd had enough wild fun for the evening. I mean, it was a real downer for me. But that's another story. When I got back to my car, I found Sam and Kurt Steiner sitting on the ground with their backs resting against the passenger-side door. We talked for a few minutes, and then Kurt said he should go find his date. But he didn't leave. By then, my beer buzz was fading, and I was tired—I'd put in a long day at work, so I flopped on my back, just, you know, listening to them talk. Next thing I know, Sam was bending over me, telling me to get the hell up. Even though it was dark, I could see he had a young woman with him. I recognized her from school. She was crying, seemed pretty upset.

"'What the hell happened?' I asked. He said she'd been attacked. He wanted me to drive her home. Her clothes were dirty, and the front of her shirt was ripped. It seemed clear what had gone down. The only thing I didn't know was who'd done it. On the way back to town, she said she didn't want to talk. I figured I had to respect that. I dropped her off outside her house, waited to make sure she got in safely, and then went home. I assumed Sam would explain everything the next time I saw him, but he never did. I held my peace for a while, but I eventually said I hoped the girl—her name was Becca Hill—would go to the cops. The guy, whoever he was, needed to be arrested. Sam didn't disagree, but he said she refused to talk to the police. It was her decision, he said. Nothing was gonna change her mind."

"You have no idea who the attacker was?"

"None. All I know is that there were some weird vibes at the school that fall. Maybe it had something to do with Becca, maybe not. Maybe Sam's death was tied to what happened, maybe it wasn't. But I decided I owed it to Sam, after all these years of silence, to tell someone."

"What happened to Becca after the party?" asked Cordelia.

"She pretty much acted like nothing had happened. Except she missed a lot of school that fall. And she looked sick, you know? She used to be sort of bubbly, but that changed. A few weeks after graduation, she left town."

"Do her parents still live here?" asked Jane.

"No, they left, too."

"Maybe she'll show up at the reunion," offered Cordelia.

"Wouldn't that be something." He appeared to think about it for a minute and then added, "Well, I said what I had to say. I better get home."

"Thank you," said Jane.

"Yeah." He seemed like he wanted to add something more, but instead, he just said "Yeah," again, then got up and walked away.

24

Jane went to bed that night still thinking about her conversation with Darius. She tossed and turned, unable to switch off her thoughts, until the sound of shouting caused her to leap out of bed. She threw on her robe and headed for the stairs. On her way down, she met Emma, who was coming up. "What's going on?"

"Cordelia's talking to her girlfriend in California."

"Ah."

Emma offered a wan look. "They're arguing. About the color red. Do they do things like that a lot?"

"They both love drama, or, as Cordelia puts it, the parry and thrust of a well-reasoned argument."

"Uh-huh. Think I'll go hide."

"I'm sorry if we're being bad house guests."

"No, no. It's more me than her. My dinner with Scott was a disaster. We'll talk in the morning."

"But you're okay?"

"I'm fine. I'm home and I'm safe. And I'm exhausted."

Jane said a quick goodnight and then continued on down into the living room, where Cordelia was pacing in front of the fire, phone to her ear.

Seeing Jane, Cordelia mouthed, "Almost done."

While Cordelia continued to argue the fine points of "hue," Jane tossed another log on the fire and then went to find the brandy. If she couldn't sleep, she might as well enjoy the wee morning hours. When she returned, Cordelia was draped across one of the matching Chesterfield sofas, the back of her hand pressed to her forehead. Jane asked how Berengaria was.

"Captivating, as always. Intellectually rigorous. And tactless, infuriating, adorable. Shall I go on?"

"No, I get the picture." She sat down on the opposite sofa.

"Why are you up so late?"

"Couldn't sleep." Jane knew she'd never have a better moment to talk to Cordelia about Julia than this. They'd been in town for three full days. It was time she fessed up. "I've been meaning to talk to you about something." She swallowed some of the brandy, shifted her position.

"You seem a tad trepidatious, Janey."

"It's something I should have told you long before this."

Cordelia sat up. "I know that look. *Julia*."

Jane hated it when Cordelia was able to read her so easily. She needed to work harder at being inscrutable. "It was a big deal at the time, but I've made peace with it. Sort of."

Cordelia sat across from her, impassive, waiting.

"Um, well, here it is. It happened after the funeral reception at my house. After everyone had left."

"A phone call."

"No, the doorbell rang." Downing half her drink, Jane forged on. "There was a young man outside. Brown hair. Glasses. Exceptionally well-dressed. I'd noticed him at the cemetery, but had no idea who he was. Then again, I didn't know half the people who came. He introduced himself as Ben Abourgal. From Chicago. He waited for a response, but when I just stood there, he said his father was Lavi Abourgal."

Cordelia lifted her chin. "Are we talking Lavi Abourgal, the world-famous violinist?"

"Yes, exactly. He said he wasn't sure it was a good time, but he was only going to be in town for one night and he wanted to meet me."

"Because?"

"He's Julia's son."

Her mouth dropped open. "What?"

"Like you, I was completely blindsided. He was a little flustered because I think he thought I knew. As we talked, it came out that Julia was still married to his father. They had a home in Lincoln Park, and, obviously, an unorthodox relationship. Ben was raised all over the world because of his father's profession, but always went to school in Chicago. He knew about me. Knew his mother was a lesbian. But he said his father, who was very ill and couldn't come to the funeral, had always been deeply in love with Julia, though he himself identified as gay and had several longtime lovers over the years."

"Heavens," said Cordelia, a hand pressed to her chest. "Even from the grave, that witch continues to lie to you."

Jane looked down. "I know. It's why I couldn't talk about it. I was embarrassed. I still am. What's wrong with me, Cordelia? I mean, the whole thing makes me feel like I can't trust my own judgment. That's an awful way to see yourself, especially for someone who relies on her ability to parse human motives. How could I have *not* known, or guessed, that she was keeping something from me? Am I that big a sucker?"

"When it came to Julia, yes. You were."

The comment felt like a blow. Cordelia was right. Jane had wanted to be convinced. She'd allowed Julia back into her life knowing she played fast and loose with the truth, so why should she be surprised to find out that, to the very end and beyond, she continued to be a treasure trove of secrets? "I had kind of a melt-down over it. It's why I went up to the cabin on Blackberry Lake."

"I assumed it was something like that. I hate to say I told you so, but I did. Over and over. For years. But Janey, you can't be so hard on yourself. Julia had a PhD in manipulation. I think you caught on to a lot of it, but never all."

"I've worked my way through the worst of my angst. I just can't dwell on it anymore. What's done is done, and I'm moving on."

"Glad to hear it. But what about the kid?"

"He wasn't in town just for the funeral, but because he's going to take over the reins of Julia's foundation. He has a master's in public administration. He's been working for a foundation in Chicago for the last eight years."

"How old *is* this kid?"

"He's not a kid. He's thirty-one. He said he'd be moving to the Twin Cities in the next couple of months and hoped we could stay in touch."

"And you said?"

"I liked him. I said that I hoped so, too. He didn't have much time that day to talk, and I have a million questions. Oh, and there's one other thing."

Cordelia looked as if she was steeling herself for another one of Julia's whoppers.

"No, this is good. I was contacted by the trustee of Julia's estate last Friday morning. It seems she left me something. I told her I didn't want any of her money, but as it turns out, her condo is now mine."

Cordelia raised an eyebrow. "How much is it worth?"

"I asked him to find out. He texted me this morning. A million two."

Both eyebrows shot up. "My stars and garters. That woman finally did you right."

"I'm sorry I kept all this to myself for so long."

"I understand, dearheart. If I'd been as credulously idiotic as you, I wouldn't be in any hurry to announce it either."

Jane couldn't help herself. She laughed. Leave it to Cordelia to put an undiplomatic and yet bluntly accurate frame on it. "Well said. Now we should try to get some sleep."

As they made their way up the stairs, Cordelia draped an arm over Jane's shoulders. "I better get to know this Leslie Harrow while I'm here so I can tell you what to think of her."

"What a . . . wonderful idea."

"Tut. Think nothing of it."

SAM

September 11, 1999

As he made his way across the field in front of Corey Lang's house, talking with Kurt about how surprised he was at the size of the crowd, Sam heard his name shouted above the din of music blaring from a loudspeaker set in one of the windows.

"Hey Romilly," yelled Todd Ott.

Sam turned to face him, walking backward. "What?"

"I need you on my team, man," he shouted. "We're setting up a volleyball net. Corey says he's got one in the basement."

"Maybe," Sam yelled back.

"No maybes, bro. You've got five minutes and then I want you front and center."

Sam smiled and gave him the finger.

"Might be fun," said Kurt.

"This will be more fun," said Sam, offering him a sly smile.

They made their way to a lone car parked just off the county road, a good forty yards from the house. The sun had set a couple hours before, so this far away from the lights, Sam felt confident nobody could see them.

"I wonder who parked his car way out here," said Kurt, sitting down with his back against the passenger's door.

They were facing the road and not the party. Sam sat down next to him. "It belongs to Darius Pollard. It's his baby. I doubt he wanted some drunk asshole putting a dent in it." He looked up at the half moon, not enough to give too much light, which was exactly what he'd hoped for. He leaned in to give Kurt a kiss.

"You think we can chance, you know . . . more here?"

Sam looked around. He didn't see a soul. "I want to, but . . . it's not worth the risk." For the past week, they'd been meeting up in the evenings. Kurt would hop on the back of Sam's motorcycle and they'd roar out of town to find a quiet back road. He still couldn't believe he'd met Kurt. It seemed like he was walking around in a dream.

"I hate all this sneaking around," said Kurt.

"Once we get out of Castle Lake, it won't be like this. We can make a life for ourselves."

"You're set on leaving?"

"Sure. Aren't you?"

Kurt pulled his knees up to his chest. "Can I ask you something? It's nothing we've ever talked about."

"Like what?"

"You said you'd been with other guys."

"Yeah."

"Lots of guys?"

Sam picked up a rock. "No. Just three. The second and third guys were hookups. I didn't know them, and I never saw them again."

"Local guys?"

"No, both times I was in Minneapolis."

"And the first?"

Sam had been dreading this conversation. He could lie, of course, but he didn't want to. He figured it was something Kurt needed to know, even though it was still hard for him to talk about. "He was a friend of my dad's. Had a cabin on Round Lake and invited my family for the weekend. The first night, he asked me to go for a walk with him. He wanted to show me his hidden fishing hole. My dad didn't fish, but I hoped this guy would teach me."

"How old were you?"

"Thirteen. It happened so fast that—" Again, he cleared his throat. Even this long after, Sam still felt an itchy, crushed feeling inside when he thought about it. "He raped me. I should have fought him, but he was older and stronger and . . . I couldn't believe it was happening. When it was over, he acted like we'd had a little secret fun—something we should keep 'just between us guys.'"

"Oh, God," whispered Kurt. "I'm sorry. Did you tell your dad?"

"Hell, no. He already thought I was gay."

"He did?"

"Ever since I can remember, he called me a pansy ass. Light in the loafers. Crap like that. At first, I just thought he hated me on general principles. I'm not sure when I first knew I was gay. But my dad? It was like he could smell it on me, even before I'd named it myself."

"What happened to the guy who attacked you? Is he still around?"

Sam shook his head. "He worked at the bank. Left a few years later. I've often wondered where he went."

"If there is a God, he's in prison being pinned down regularly by a three-hundred-pound Nazi skinhead."

Sam laughed. "I guess, in the end, it was a lesson. I was more careful after that. It also made me more sensitive to boundaries. When I kissed you that first time, I knew I'd crossed a line."

"You didn't hurt me."

"If you'd had a different reaction, you might not think that."

"Yeah, maybe." He cupped a hand around Sam's arm, then released it when they heard boots crunching against gravel.

"Hey," said Sam, reaching up and slapping Darius's hand. "My man. What's up?"

"Got sick of the revelry." He sat down cross-legged in front of them. "I'm beat."

"Late night last night?"

"Yeah, that, and an early morning at the garage."

"I should probably go see what Vicki's up to," said Kurt.

"She's dancing out in the yard," said Darius. "Looked pretty happy to me."

"She loves to dance. Me, not so much."

"I'm a kick-ass dancer," said Darius, "but I doubt any of the girls here would dance with me."

"That's bullshit," said Sam.

"Yeah, but nothing I can do about it. Hey, if you guys don't mind, I'm gonna kick back for a few minutes and close my eyes. Keep talking, it won't bother me one bit."

Sam elbowed Kurt in the ribs and grinned. "What shall we talk about?"

Before long, Darius was snoring away, stirring only once to bat a mosquito away from his face.

They spoke quietly for a while, steering clear of the subject they had been discussing.

As Kurt was about to get up to head back, he said, "Did you hear that?"

"Hear what?"

"It sounded like an animal. Like it's in pain."

A second later, Sam heard it, too. It seemed more like muffled sobs to him, and appeared to be coming from a thicket of red pine a few dozen yards away. In a flash, he was up, running toward it. It was hard to see, but the moonlight was just enough to allow him to locate the source of the sound. Two people were lying on the ground, one on top of the other. Sam could hear the man grunting as the woman struggled to get away. Sam dove at the guy, grabbing him around his midsection and ripping him off. A moment later, he heard Kurt say, "What the hell's going on?"

The young woman was hysterical, crawling away on her hands and knees. Her skirt seemed to be tangled in brambles. The more she tugged, the louder her cries grew. "It's okay," Sam called to her. Whirling around, he squinted and realized that the attacker's pants were down around his ankles. As he tried to pull them up, Sam ran at him, knocking him back down on the ground. And then he kicked him hard in the crotch. The guy howled in pain, grabbing himself and rolling around in the pine needles and scrub. The smell of alcohol came off him in waves.

"I should kill you," shouted Sam. He positioned himself for another kick.

"Don't," called Kurt.

Sam felt strong arms pull him backward. Hearing more cries come from the girl, he broke free and rushed over, this time, getting a good look at her face. It was Becca Hill, a young woman in his class. She seemed pretty drunk. "Are you okay?" he asked.

"Keep him away from me," she cried, scooting backward across the ground.

"He's not going to hurt you anymore," said Sam. "Are you okay? Can you get up?"

She seemed pretty out of it. "Yeah," she whispered.

"Come on, let's get you out of here."

He walked her slowly out of the trees and back toward the car. When they reached Darius, Sam bent over him and shook him awake. "Hey, buddy, can you do me a favor?" He explained what he needed.

Sam helped Becca into the backseat. He spoke to her quietly, calmly, telling her that Darius would take her back to her house. He found a black marker in his pocket and wrote his number on her arm. "Call me, day or night, if you need anything. I'm here for you, Becca."

She looked up at him, her eyes only marginally less terrified. "Thank you," she whispered.

"Drive careful," he said to Darius, slapping the car's roof. He waited until they'd pulled back onto the highway, and then returned to the scene of the crime, ready to beat the living crap out of Dave Tamborsky.

25

The call came in on Wednesday morning at 7:26. After working his standard Tuesday day shift, Dave had received a call-out last night to a multiple car crash. He hadn't returned home until well after two in the morning. Since he was scheduled for the second shift today, he figured he'd be able to sleep late, but no such luck.

"Hello," he muttered groggily into his phone, noting the time on the nightstand alarm clock.

"We found Carli Gilbert's car."

Dave had assigned two patrol officers to handle the search.

"Where?" He pulled over his notebook and jotted down the info. "Call it in and get the crime scene people there ASAP."

County Road 19 ran through a heavily wooded section northeast of Castle Lake. Not many people lived in the area, though there were a few trailer homes close to the road. Dave pulled his cruiser to a stop along the shoulder behind two other patrol cars. With three cop cars, all lights flashing, nobody was going to miss seeing them.

Just as he pushed out of the front seat, a Ford Focus eased in behind him, and the driver's window came down. "What's going on?" asked an older man.

"Police business," said Dave. "Keep moving."

The guy seemed annoyed, but the window rolled back up and he drove on.

Crossing through deep grass, Dave found Steve Biggs, the senior patrolman at the scene, on the phone. He waited until the call was finished and then said, "Where's the crime-scene unit?"

"They're coming," said Biggs, brushing mosquitoes away from his face.

Dave wished he'd remembered to spray himself down with insect repellant.

Biggs led Dave through a weedy area to a section of woods. "We figure our perp drove onto a service road half a mile up. He turned off and threaded his way in until he felt the car was basically invisible. It might have been, too, if it hadn't been red."

Dave knew they'd been lucky to find it. It could have been months, or even years, before anyone noticed it rusting away in the middle of nowhere. By then, nobody would be looking for it anymore, or talking about Carli Gilbert's murder, and it would have simply been considered another piece of junk dumped in the woods.

Removing a flashlight from his belt, he approached the Cobalt cautiously. It might be morning, and the sun might be shining, but deep in the woods, the light was dim. "Is it locked?" he asked.

"I don't know. I haven't touched it."

"Don't suppose the keys are there."

"I didn't see any."

"But you've examined the interior?"

"Yes, sir. Briefly, with my flashlight."

"Any thoughts?" he asked as he pointed his flashlight into the front seat. He never understood why some people used their cars as garbage dumps. This one was a total pit, with pop cans, food wrappers, and other assorted crap tossed aside and forgotten. Switching off the light and returning it to his belt, he pulled on a pair of latex gloves. When he opened the front driver's-side door, he noticed that the seat was pushed all the way back. "Whoever drove it in here sure didn't care if he damaged the car," said Biggs. "Not much to learn from that, I suppose. There are scratches all over the paint and the front grill is broken and crammed with leaves and weeds."

Dave had already taken note of the scratches. He leaned in carefully and popped the trunk. Walking around to the rear, he removed his flashlight again to light up the interior. Nothing stood out.

"Just more junk," said Biggs.

"Did you call in the VIN number?"

"Yes, sir. Still waiting to hear back."

"Over here?" came a shout.

"The crime-scene guys must have arrived," said Biggs.

Opening the rear driver's-side door, Dave took one last look. That's when something caught his eye. "Shit," he whispered under his breath, feeling as if he'd just touched a wall socket.

"Excuse me, sir. Did you say something?"

It took him a moment to regroup. "No, nothing." His hope was that it would get lost in all the other junk. He might be in charge of the investigation, but he could hardly tamper with evidence. Or could he?

As two men, the crime-scene techs, and a woman, the other patrol officer, walked up to the car, Dave was engulfed by the heavy smell of bug spray. "I think we can do this pretty quickly. Set the perimeter and do a search of the area, just to make sure we're not missing anything."

"We know the drill, Tamborsky," said the taller of the two techs. His name was Morton. "That's why we're paid the big bucks."

Dave eyed him a moment before continuing, "We know who owns the car, or at least we will as soon as Biggs gets confirmation on the VIN number, and we know she died in a suspicious fire. My bet is that whoever tried to hide the car in the woods was the one who murdered her."

"You don't say," said Morton.

Dave shot him a nasty look. "Get busy."

"You betcha, boss," was the tech's snide reply.

Dave stayed for another half hour, watching the men work. Once the contents of the car had been bagged, he decided to shove off, knowing he would read their report later. For now, he had to figure out what his next move should be. This was a complication he didn't need and had never seen coming.

26

Jane was late to the Flame Diner for her early morning meeting. Wilburn Lowry, the man she'd bumped into yesterday at the diner, the odd guy with the gray muttonchops who said he had something for her, was already seated at a booth by the windows, waving at her as she came in the door. She slid in across from him, noticing that he had a small notebook in front of him. He was wearing a light blue coverall with the words "Junk King" emblazoned in red on a white patch.

"Junk King?" she said, looking up as a waitress approached the table. She ordered a cup of coffee, black. She was hungry, but since she'd made a date to have breakfast with Emma at the White Star Cafe at ten, she didn't want to order anything more.

"It's one of my many jobs," said Lowry, working on a stack of pancakes. "Me and my family, we do junk removal. We have an antique store just out of town on County Road 12."

"You make a living doing that?"

"Well, I mean, I'm retired. I worked for the post office as a mail carrier for most of my life. Got to know the people in the town really well. When someone mentioned moving, they often bitched about how hard it was to get rid of stuff. Not just the decisions that come with a move, but hauling away all the old junk. Seemed like

185

a business opportunity to me, so even while I was still delivering mail, I got my sons and one of my daughters involved in what we started calling 'Dad's New Gold Mine.' I love junk. Always have. It's kind of a dream come true to be allowed into people's houses to root through all the crap they don't want anymore."

"Why don't they just have a garage sale?"

"Plenty of people do. But when you're under the gun for time, it's easier to find someone to come in and do it all. We even clean the house, if they want. And we don't charge an arm and a leg. I developed this contract—they give me the rights to anything I haul away. I don't mind saying. I've found some real gems over the years."

Jane nodded her thanks as a waitress set a mug in front of her. "Is that why you call yourself a prospector?"

"Exactly. It's what I am. I'm a guy who's out there looking for gold." He shoved another forkful of pancake into his mouth.

"So," said Jane, eager to get to the point. "You said you had something that might help me with the Romilly investigation."

As he chewed, he pushed the notebook across to her.

"What is it?"

"About, oh, maybe ten years ago, I helped a woman clean out her basement. Her name was Anna Tamborsky. Ring any bells?"

"Is she related to Dave?"

"His mother. She and Dave's father were getting a divorce, and, at the time, she thought she'd stay in the house and he would move out. Turned out that she left and moved away, but during the breakup, she hired me to come in. Me and her spent most of our time in the basement. It was crammed to the gills. I guess her hubby was a pack rat. One of the boxes she told me to take had a bunch of his police notebooks in it. I would think he might have wanted to hang on to them, but I was getting my orders from her, so I took it. You gotta understand, it's just the kind of stuff that fascinates me. I guess, truth be told, I'm kind of a pack rat myself.

When I was done reading through the notebooks, I put the box on a shelf in my basement, and when Sam Romilly's body was discovered, it jogged a memory. I remembered that one of the notebooks recorded Mitch Tamborsky's investigation into his disappearance. Take a look yourself."

Jane flipped the cover back. Mitch Tamborsky's writing was light and thready, but legible.

"I read through it again this morning. There wasn't as much about the case as I remembered."

"You're giving this to me?"

He finished the last of his pancakes. "I consider it my civic duty."

"Thank you."

"It may prove to be nothing more than a time suck, as my daughter would say. But you never know when something might be important."

"Honestly," said Jane. "I really appreciate it."

Lowry downed the rest of his glass of milk. "I wish I could stay and talk, but I've got another job today. Actually, it's with the woman who lives next door to Mitch Tamborsky. Lydia Mickler. Nice old lady. She's moving to a senior facility. Both her kids have been pushing her to do it. She's not happy about it, but . . . I guess it is what it is."

As he reached for his wallet, Jane said, "The least I can do is buy you breakfast."

"Well, now." He smiled. "I won't turn that down."

She thanked him one more time as he stood to leave.

"Good luck with your investigation," he said, shaking her hand before heading for the door.

Jane had a good hour to kill before she was supposed to meet Emma. The cafe wasn't as packed as it had been when she first walked in. Even so, she felt she should order something if she was going to stay. She asked the waitress about the desserts on offer, and settled on a fresh peach pie, which the waitress brought over to the table in a white box. Emma loved peach pie, and so did Cordelia.

Centering the notebook in front of her, Jane took out her reading glasses and began to examine it. She flipped through the pages quickly at first, until she came to the night Diane Romilly called the police station to report that her son was missing. Much of what Mitch Tamborsky had written in the official police report was also detailed here: Going to the Romilly house; talking to Wendell and Diane; the fact that the younger brother, Scott, didn't want to come out of his room; Diane's firm belief that something bad had happened to her son; and Wendell Romilly's equally firm belief that Sam was just being Sam, that he'd show up eventually.

Jane sipped her coffee as she read. Nothing stood out until she got to the search of the woods, a week or so after Sam went missing. The official report, the one she'd already looked at, stated that Diane Romilly had hired a man who owned a bloodhound. The dog had alerted on a spot in a clearing. The field notes, however, added a detail that hadn't been in the official report: The spot in question was approximately thirty yards due east of the old mill ruins, specifically, the last remaining section of the east wall. Jane made a mental note to check it out.

And there was more that hadn't made it into the official report. Mitch wrote that the bloodhound, owned by a man named Judson, had somehow gotten away from him during the search. There was a comment about a broken leash, and, according to his notes, the dog, Harvey, had run off into the woods, with Judson running after him, shouting for him to heel. Mitch wrote a note sometime later saying that Judson had called him to apologize. He stated that Judson had finally located his dog in the graveyard behind Holy Trinity after one of the priests called him and reported that the animal was lying on a new grave, one, Mitch noted, without a headstone. Jane assumed it was Ida Beddemeyer's grave. The dog had found Sam after all, though nobody had recognized it at the time. That left her with a question about the spot in the woods where the dog had first alerted. Was that where Sam had died?

Jane read quickly through the rest of the comments, finding nothing that seemed of any importance. At the bottom of the last page, the word DUAL had been written in all caps and circled. Apparently, it was something Mitch had learned that had been intriguing enough to highlight, but not important enough to elaborate on. Dual. Dual what? Unless, she thought, the word had been misspelled and what he'd meant to write was DUEL. Neither, however, made any sense.

Finishing her coffee, Jane tossed some cash on the table and walked back out to her truck. After sailing down Main Street, she found a parking spot half a block away from the White Star Cafe. She made a quick stop into the art center to see if anyone had bid on her dinner. The woman behind the desk looked it up and reported that there had been forty-seven bids. She expected more before the winners were announced on Friday morning.

Feeling buoyed by the interest, Jane made her way down the street to the Lakeside Community Bank. She figured it was a waste of time, but decided that she'd ask, one more time, to talk to Wendell Romilly. She stopped at the round reception desk again to talk to the same woman she'd spoken to yesterday.

"Oh, hi," said the woman. "It's you again."

Jane smiled, glad to be recognized.

"Say, you were asking about Carli Gilbert. Did you hear that her car was found this morning? Someone hid it in the woods."

"Wow, no. Did the police make a statement?"

"Nah, I got a friend who works at the station. She called me a few minutes ago with the news."

"Pays to have friends in high places."

The woman laughed. "Yeah. I hope it will help them find Carli's murderer. Anyway, what can I do for you?"

"I was hoping you'd give Wendell Romilly's secretary another call and see if he's changed his mind about talking to me."

"I can try," said the woman, picking up her phone. "Your name again was—"

"Lawless. Jane Lawless."

"Right." She spoke into the phone and then waited, her eyes skirting the room. A few moments later she said, "Really? When? Sure, I'll tell her. Thanks, Viv." Setting the phone back in its cradle, the woman said, "Mr. Romilly says that if you make an appointment, he'll see you. Viv said he had an opening at nine tomorrow morning."

"Great," said Jane. "Should I go to his office and tell her I'll take it?"

"I can do that for you."

"Wonderful. Thanks." She still had some time before her breakfast with Emma, so she left the bank and walked over to Victory Park, where she found a bench and sat down. She checked her phone for messages. Seeing nothing from Leslie, she texted her to find out how her speech had gone the previous night. More importantly, she wanted to know if they were still on for dinner tomorrow. Jane didn't care where they ate. She refused to over-analyze the relationship. She just wanted to spend some time with Leslie before she and Cordelia had to set off for home.

27

The police station was buzzing with activity when Dave returned shortly after ten. His first move was to stick his head into Grady Larson's office and tell him the news. Grady was on the phone, so Dave waited.

"Just a minute," said Grady, shooting Dave an annoyed look. "What?"

"We found Carli Gilbert's car."

"I know. Good work." He gave him a thumbs up, then swiveled his chair away from the door and continued with the phone conversation.

Not exactly high praise, but then Dave couldn't take credit for the find, which Grady undoubtedly knew. On his way to the locker room, he bumped into one of the patrol officers.

"Hey, Tamborsky," the guy said. "Saltus has Darius Pollard in the box."

"Right now?"

"Started a few minutes ago. He had Jim Hughes in earlier."

"He learn anything?"

"Nah. Total waste of time."

Dave didn't wait to hear more. He ran down the hall and skidded to a stop outside the room right next to where the interview was being conducted. Once inside, he nodded to the officer at the monitoring station. Last year, the box itself had been completely renovated, covered in gray foam wall panels with a brown carpet underfoot. A new DVR and camera system had also been installed. Dave pulled up a chair so he could watch the computer screen and listen to the two men talk.

Saltus was seated on a rolling desk chair and Pollard was sitting a few feet away on a folding chair.

Saltus was talking:

"And you have no idea how he ended up in Holy Trinity cemetery?

"None."

"Did you spend a lot of time with him?"

"We rode together. We both owned motorcycles."

"Where'd you ride?" asked Saltus.

"Just around. We both liked being out in the country."

"He ever say anything to you about any problems he was having?"

"With his father, yeah."

"What about his father?"

"He was mean. Used to beat up on Sam."

"Did you ever see it yourself?"

"No."

"Any other problems Sam talked about? Anybody who might have had it in for him?"

"Not really. Except—" Darius hesitated. "There was this one thing that happened. It was at a party at Corey Lang's family farm early in our senior year."

"You were invited?"

"Does that surprise you?"

"Just tell me what happened."

Darius explained about leaving the party and finding Sam and Kurt Steiner sitting by his car. And then later being awakened and asked to take a girl home. "She'd been raped. It happened in a wooded area, not too far from where I'd parked my car."

Dave stopped breathing, gripping the arm of his chair.

Saltus sat up straight. "You know that for a fact?"

"I was asleep, but I know Sam caught the guy in the act."

"Who was he?"

"I don't know. Sam never told me. The girl's name was Becca Hill."

Dave was so relieved, he nearly gasped as his breath returned.

"You never asked?"

"I figured he'd explain, but he never did. All he said was that Becca refused to talk to the cops. She wanted to keep the whole thing quiet. He didn't like it, but felt like he had to respect her decision."

"You think it really happened?"

"Sure I do."

"She wasn't just crying wolf?"

Darius crossed his arms. It was his only response.

"Tell me again where you were when this thing was happening?"

"Asleep on the ground by my car."

"And the other guy? The one who was with Sam?"

"Kurt Steiner. I don't actually know what happened to him. He wasn't around when I woke up."

Saltus paused. "This girl. Becca. Was she sexy?"

"Huh?"

"Answer the question."

"Hell, man. I don't remember."

"You must have had an opinion."

Darius stared straight ahead.

"Did you ever ask her out on a date?"

"What? No."

"Were you dating someone back then?"

193

"Yeah."

"Who?"

"I'm not sure that's any of your business."

"Uh-huh." Saltus scratched his chest. "Black dudes. They like to get it on, right? Especially with white women."

The patrol tech—his name was Meyer—groaned. Glancing over at Dave, he said, "You better tell the chief about this. He's gonna hit the ceiling. Saltus is a disaster."

Dave didn't disagree.

Darius regarded Saltus with undisguised loathing. "Look, if you're suggesting I—"

"Just trying to understand, Mr. Pollard."

"Maybe I need a lawyer."

"I already explained," said Saltus a little too quickly. "There's no need for that." It was all playing out in Dave's favor. Saltus was conducting the interview so badly that none of it could be used—or even seen by the public. At the very least, Grady needed to take him off the case and give it back to Dave. At most, he should terminate his ass.

"So let me get this straight," continued Saltus, leaning back expansively in his chair. "Sam saved this girl from the clutches of some dastardly guy. Had she been drinking?"

"It was a kegger. Everyone was drinking."

"Was she underage?"

"Hell if I know."

Dave's cell phone rang. Pulling it out of his pocket, he saw that it was his dad. He let it go to voice mail. Less than a minute later, the phone rang again. Exiting the room, he stood in the hall and said hello.

"Dave? My car's been stolen. You gotta get over here right away."

"Your car?" said Dave, trying to switch gears. "Dad, you need to calm down."

"How can I? Some asshole hot-wired my Impala."

"I'll come."

"Good. I want this guy caught and put in jail——and throttled." He cut the line.

Never a dull moment in the Tamborsky family thought Dave as he headed back out to his SUV. At least he didn't need to worry about Pollard. The guy didn't know a damn thing.

"What's going on next door?" asked Dave as he walked into his father's house a while later. He could smell bacon and Dawn liquid soap, so he assumed his dad had finally gotten around to making himself a regular breakfast and done some cleaning.

"Mrs. Mickler's moving." He was seated on the couch, reading the paper.

"Oh, right. I knew that."

"She hired Will Lowry and his crew to help clean out her house."

Dave was glad to see that his father had calmed down. Dropping down on the other end of the couch, he said, "Where are your car keys?"

"In my pocket. That's why I figured the kid hot-wired it. These young punks today with nothing to do but watch video games and get up to stuff they have no business doing. Something should be done about them."

"Uh-huh," said Dave. "So when was the last time you saw the car?"

"It was right out front, parked on the street, like it always is. When I got back from downtown, I realized it was missing."

"Where'd you go?"

"Just around. I need my exercise. You and your sister tell me that all the time."

"Was it outside when you left?"

"Of course it was. Where else would it be?"

"Okay, so if it was, and it was missing when you got home, someone must have taken it while you were gone. So how long were you downtown?"

"Hell if I know. An hour?"

This was getting Dave nowhere. He wondered if someone might have been watching the house, waiting for his dad to leave. Of course, in broad daylight, they'd have to break into the car before they could hot-wire it. Unless? "Was the car locked?"

"I always lock my car. I never used to. Hell, when I was a kid, we never even locked the house. This is a different world."

The front door opened, and Dave's sister walked in.

"Well, this calls for a celebration," said Dave's dad, rising to give her a hug. "My two kids here at the same time."

Elaine carried several grocery bags. "Got everything on your list."

"Thank you, sweetie."

Dave took the bags and carried them into the kitchen. As he'd suspected, the dishes had been washed and stacked in the drying rack. Elaine came in behind him and gave his arm a squeeze. "How you doing, Davey?"

She lived forty miles away in Kilgore Township. She was married with three kids, a husband, and full-time job, so she didn't make the trip back to Castle Lake as often as she used to.

Peeking into the living room, Dave saw that his dad had turned on the TV. Wanting to talk privately to Elaine, he moved over to the kitchen counter and leaned against it. "Can I ask you something?"

"Sure," she said, making room for another box of Cap'n Crunch on the lower shelf.

"Have you noticed that Dad's become kind of forgetful?"

"Kind of? He's got a real problem. That's why I made him that doctor's appointment this afternoon. It's why I'm in town."

"I didn't know anything about a doctor's appointment. He never mentioned it."

"Doesn't surprise me. He hates doctors. I should have called you about it, but . . . it's been kind of crazy around our house."

"Have you been in Dad's study lately? I happened to walk in there the other day. He's got bills on his desk that go back a couple of months."

"That's another reason I'm here. We're going to pay them. *Today*. I won't leave until they're in my hand."

Dave felt guilty. He should have taken care of it himself. He'd always leaned on his older sister to lead in family matters, though that was no excuse. "So what do you think is wrong with him?"

"Maybe it's as simple as a vitamin deficiency, or maybe he's developing some kind of dementia. He still remembers the past pretty clearly, so mostly, it's his short-term memory that's affected."

Now came the big question. "Do you think it's safe for him to live alone?"

"That's what we need to find out. Maybe they have a pill or something that can help him. I hope so. I've thought about asking him to come live with us. I even talked to Jason about it, but it just won't work."

"I suppose, if worse comes to worst, I could move back home."

"Your call, Davey. All I know is, we may need to have a little family meeting one of these days to hash it out. None of this is going to be easy—for any of us."

The landline gave a shrill ring. Grabbing the receiver from the phone on the wall, Dave said hello.

"Mitch?" came a raspy voice.

"No, this is his son, Dave."

"Oh, David, hi. It's Stan Rankala over at the Liquor Mart. Say, your dad was in this morning. He brought back his empty case of

Leinenkugel. He asked me to carry a new case out to his car, put it in the backseat while he looked around. Which I did. He was going to come pay at the cash register when he was done. But he never did. I looked around for him just now. I mean, his car's still outside, but he's not here."

Dave put his hand over the mouthpiece and whispered, "His car's over at the Liquor Mart."

Elaine looked off toward the living room and shook her head.

"I'll be over in a few minutes to pay you and drive the car home."

"Thanks, David. Sorry for the miscommunication."

"Not a problem."

Returning to the living room, Dave told his dad about the call.

"You're saying I left the car outside the liquor store?"

"Yeah."

"Oh God," he whispered, his mouth beginning to quiver. "I don't know how. . . . I didn't—"

For the first time, it penetrated Dave's consciousness what a confused old man his father had become, and it broke his heart. "I'll take care of it."

On his way out the door, his dad offered a muted, "Thanks, David. You're a good boy."

28

As Jane sat in a booth at the White Star Cafe, sipping coffee and looking out the window, she received a phone call from Emma. There was a maintenance problem at the house she needed to deal with. She didn't offer details, but said she was going to be at least half an hour late. She apologized, asking Jane if she wanted to cancel. Since Jane was hungry, she offered to wait.

When Emma finally arrived, she ordered a bowl of the chicken wild rice soup and a grilled cheese sandwich. Since the entire menu was available all day, Jane ordered herself the meatloaf sandwich on rye.

Jane wanted to know how Emma's dinner with Scott had gone, so that was her first question.

"Not good. The only reason I went was because he promised he wouldn't drink, but I think he was already pretty well-oiled when I got there. And then, while we were eating, I got that same feeling again—like he wasn't going to let me leave. All this profession of undying love, it's ridiculous. We've only known each other a couple months."

"You need to stay away from him."

"You think? But get this: He's been following me. He even

admitted it. When I called him on it, said he was a stalker, his only response was that I was being overly dramatic."

"You're leaving soon, right?"

"Not soon enough."

"While you're here, I think you should be extra careful. Don't go out alone at night."

Her shoulders sank. "What a way to live."

"I'm sorry this is happening to you."

"Yeah, thanks. I did figure something out last night. Scott's mood seems to tank when I bring up Sam and the argument they were having before he died. It happened both nights. I mean, it wasn't immediately noticeable. More of a slow burn. Makes me wonder what really went on, you know? What if he did have something to do with Sam's death?"

"I'm meeting with his father tomorrow."

"You really are working hard at this, aren't you."

Jane was always surprised, and a little annoyed, when friends didn't see her as a serious investigator. "Since we're talking about Sam, I'd like your thoughts on one of your classmates: Becca Hill."

Emma cocked her head. "Boy, I haven't heard that name in ages."

"Did you know her?"

"We weren't close or anything, but yeah, I knew her. We both worked on the school paper. How come you're interested?"

"It's just a tip I'm chasing down. I really can't say more."

The food arrived, diverting their attention for a few minutes. Eventually, the conversation came back to Becca.

"She was funny. And super smart," said Emma. She nibbled at her grilled cheese. "She did kind of change her senior year. Became much more serious and far less social."

"Do you know why?"

"I figured she was working extra hard to pull down straight As so she could get into a good college, one with a generous scholarship."

"Did she date?"

"I think she was with Gordy Taylor her junior year. I don't re-call her with anybody her senior year, though I could be wrong."

"Did she have a good reputation?"

"Never heard anything bad about her."

Jane found her meatloaf tasteless. She added some ketchup, hoping to make the sandwich more palatable. "What about Dave Tamborsky and Monty Mickler? What are your thoughts on them?"

"You mean back in high school? Dave was a football jock, so, on principle, I didn't like him. He was built like a brick wall. *Very* muscular. Beyond that, I mean, I'm not saying the guy was stupid, but he wasn't the brightest bulb in the pack. It always seemed to me that he hero-worshiped his dad. He brought him up a lot. Kind of bragged about him. I thought it was pathetic."

"And Mickler?"

"People called him Dave's Shadow. Honestly, I don't remember that much about him. He kind of faded into the woodwork. Girls liked him, though. He was cute enough. I think he was thrown off the basketball team his junior year. That was his only claim to fame."

"Do you know why?"

"No idea. But I did see a lot of guys giving him back slaps, like he was some kind of hero bro."

Just as they were finishing their lunch, Emma's phone rang. She listened for a moment, then said she'd come right away.

"I'm sorry. It's a guy with another bid on the house repair. I have to meet him." As she dug through her purse looking for her wallet, Jane said, "This is on me."

"Really?"

"One last question before you go. Does the word 'dual' mean anything to you?"

"Like dual carburetors? Or duel as in a fight?"

"Either."

"Gosh, nothing," said Emma, sliding out of the booth. "I can't imagine what either would have to do with high school."

"Okay," said Jane. "Thanks. I'll see you tonight."

"I've got a meeting with the reunion committee heads at seven, so it will probably be late before I get home. I'm sure you and Cordelia will find something fun to do."

"I'm sure we will," said Jane pushing her half-eaten sandwich away. When the waitress showed up again, Jane was still hungry. "What do you recommend for dessert?"

"Pie," said the woman. "It's way better than the meatloaf. I saw an apple pie come out of the oven a few minutes ago. It's especially good with ice cream."

"Then I'll have apple pie à la mode. And a refill on coffee."

"Coming right up."

Jane took out her phone and was about to call Cordelia to see if she was up and around when Jim Hughes walked past the booth. He was dressed more casually today, in a red polo shirt and jeans, and appeared to be looking for an empty table. There were plenty of them when Jane had first arrived, but glancing around now, she saw that the cafe was full up. "Jim?" she called, catching his eye.

"Oh, hi," he said, smiling down at her. "Ms. Lawless. Nice to see you again."

"Why don't you join me?"

"Actually, I'm meeting my wife for lunch. I'm a little early."

"I'm about to eat dessert, but then I'll be out of here. You might as well take the booth."

"Really?" He took one last look around and then sat down. "That would be great. So," he said, folding his hands on the table and looking around, "how's your search for answers going?"

"Slow."

"Yeah, I suppose."

"Since you're here, there's a question I'd like to ask you." There was no point in setting up a recorded interview. The restaurant was too noisy, and besides, she didn't hold out hope that he'd know any more than Emma.

"This must be my day for answering questions," said Jim. "The police called me down for an interview this morning. Not sure why they wanted to talk to me, but I didn't see any reason not to do it. I don't think they learned much. Anyway, shoot. How can I help?"

Jane pulled her coffee mug in front of her. "Thinking back to your high school days, does the word 'dual' mean anything to you? Dual as in two. Or duel as in a fight."

He gave her a quizzical look. "No."

The waitress came over to take his order.

"I'm famished. My wife won't mind if I have a little something while I wait for her. How about the broccoli cheese soup? Just a cup. And coffee. If you could start a new check for me—"

The waitress nodded, writing it down and then walking back behind the counter.

"You know," he said, almost laughing, "there is one thing that comes to mind, though I doubt it's what you want."

"Please," said Jane.

"Well, in my junior year history class, we were assigned to write a short paper on something that used to be legal but had become illegal. I chose cocaine. It was really interesting doing the research. I can still remember some of it. Another guy wrote his paper on prostitution. That was a hoot. One of the girls wrote about slavery. Sam, he was in the class, too. We used to study together. Anyway, he wrote his paper on dueling. He actually said to me that he thought it should still be legal."

The waitress set a mug of coffee in front of him and the apple pie à la mode along with a clean fork in front of Jane.

"I wonder," she said out loud, picking up the fork.

"Kind of farfetched to think it had anything to do with his death," said Jim.

"You're probably right."

"Of course, if anyone was up for something risky like a duel, it would have been Sam."

As Jane dug into the pie, she realized she had another question. "You knew Monty Mickler?"

"Still do. We belong to the same church."

"Do you know why he was kicked off the basketball team?"

"Wow, you really are digging into the past." He leaned back as the server brought his soup. "Sure, I know. See, Mickler had this secret gambling operation all through high school. Mainly football games. It's how he made money. I believe it started out with guys placing bets on our high school teams, but that ended pretty quickly because we always lost. So he broadened his scope. Every Sunday during the fall and early winter, there were two NFL games on offer. The Vikings and whoever they were playing that weekend, and the Packers and whoever they were playing. I placed a couple of bets. Won once, lost once. That was enough for me. But I know lots of guys did it regularly. At the time, Monty was one of the stars on the basketball team. People always saw his buddy, Tamborsky, as the jock because he was so big, but Monty was the real athlete. He was tall and lean and fast, and his ball skills were amazing. He would have lettered for sure, but then one of the coaches found out about the gambling thing, and that was the end of Monty. I believe he was suspended from school for a while, too. When he came back, he had to act contrite, but the bets started right back up again."

Jane couldn't imagine that Monty's little gambling operation had anything to do with Sam's murder. Still, she needed to make a note of it.

"You think it's important?"

"I have no idea," said Jane, finishing her pie. "But I'm grateful for your time."

"If you have any other questions," said Jim, stirring his soup. "You know where to find me."

29

Kurt sat on a low, flat rock by the river. It was the place he always visited when he needed to sort through his feelings or come to terms with his worries. The police interview was set for tomorrow morning. It appalled him to think that he was about to lie, and lie, and lie some more, as he'd done for years. And yet, if he didn't, if he broke down and told the truth, not only would his life be ruined, but so would the life of everyone else who'd been in the woods that morning. Not that they weren't all guilty.

Picking up a bunch of stones, he chucked them, one at a time, into the water. Maybe, instead of thinking, he should try to empty his mind. Wasn't that the way to enlightenment?

Hearing a sound behind him, he turned to find a woman making her way out of the trees. It took a moment to remember who she was. He'd only met her once, at Emma's party. She was an attractive older woman, with eyes the color of lilacs. He couldn't be sure, and nothing had been said, but he had the feeling she was gay. She'd spent some time chatting up the mayor, another woman he'd always suspected might be gay, though things like that weren't talked about in Castle Lake except in whispers. Jane was the last person he expected to see out by the river. He hoped that, after a brief hello, she'd keep on walking.

"Hey," he said, offering her a smile he hoped was convincing.

"Kurt, hi."

"You out for a stroll?"

She moved to the edge of the water and looked around. "No. I wanted to do a little exploring. I've been doing research on Sam Romilly's murder for a podcast I work for in Minneapolis."

"Emma told me."

"I assumed as much. I was given some information about a spot in a clearing back there"—she motioned toward the woods—"where a bloodhound alerted. Sam's mom thought it might be where he died."

"Excuse me?"

She turned to look at him. "Since I had the approximate location, I wanted to see the area for myself."

"Where did you hear that? About the clearing?"

"It was in a police report."

He changed his mind. He wanted her to stay and talk. "Are you making progress with your research?"

"Yeah, I've learned a few things." She eased down on the ground next to him. "Since you're interested, there are a couple things I'd like to get your opinion on."

"Me?"

"Just curious what your thoughts are on Monty Mickler?"

"In high school or now?"

"Has your opinion changed?"

"No, not really. I've never liked him. He's a real wheeler-dealer. Some people find him charming, I guess, but I could never understand that."

"I was told there was a rumor going around your senior year that Monty and Dave Tamborsky were a gay couple."

He couldn't help himself. He burst out laughing.

"Yeah," said Jane. "Other people have had the same reaction."

"If you only knew how ridiculous that is." He tossed another stone into the water. "Do you think Mickler had something to do with Sam's murder?"

"I'm still working on that. But I will say, it seems like Tamborsky's and Mickler's names have both come up an awful lot as I've dug deeper into the case."

He was glad for the breeze because he was starting to sweat. "Really? For instance?"

"There was this keg party at the Lang farm right before your senior year began. Were you there?"

He had no idea what she knew, so as much as he could, he needed to tell the truth. "Yeah, I was there. Who've you talked to about it?"

"Darius Pollard."

"So you know what happened."

"A young woman was raped."

He nodded. "It was awful."

"You were there?"

"Sam and I heard this cry. I thought it was an animal, but he wasn't so sure. He ran to her first, and then I followed."

"Who did it?"

"You don't know?"

"Darius had no idea."

Kurt was caught. Talking to her had been a mistake, but there was nothing he could do about it now. "It was Dave Tamborsky."

Her eyes widened. "And nobody ever found out?"

"Sam and I both talked to Becca—she's the one who was attacked. We tried to get her to go to the police and tell them what had happened, but she refused. She said it was her decision to make."

"Where was Mickler that night?"

Kurt closed his eyes, seeing the evening replay in his mind. "He was there. I think Becca kind of liked him. I was dating a woman back then, my future wife, Vicki. I spent the early part of the evening with her. That was before the party spilled outside into the yard. It was a real madhouse.

"Initially, people were gathered around the keg in the kitchen. Some guys had brought bottles of harder stuff. Mickler spent his time in the dining room slowly getting Becca drunk, adding vodka to her Coke when she wasn't looking. I figured he was hoping for a score later that night. I should have said something. If I had, none of this would have ever happened."

"I'm not sure you can blame yourself."

"Of course I can, and I do. But, turns out, Monty was preparing her for his buddy, Dave. I didn't realize it at the time, but it wasn't hard to put together after the fact. Maybe they'd done it before, sort of a tag-team, or maybe this was the only time. Monty fancied himself a player when it came to women, and actually, a lot of girls did want to date him. Dave, not so much. I never understood why that was, because he was a jock, and girls usually went for jocks. Maybe he had bad breath or didn't shower."

"I'll make sure I put that in my report."

Kurt glanced over at her. "You do that."

"So Mickler handed her off to Dave."

"I didn't see it go down, but I figure Dave must have convinced her to leave the party with him. There was a section of trees a ways from the house, so I imagine he thought that, with the distance and the noise from the music, nobody would be likely to hear her if she cried out. That's where Sam found them. I stayed back while Sam went to see what was up. When he didn't come back, I went to see what was going on. By then, he'd pulled Dave off her. The two of them were fighting, so I broke it up." He looked over at Jane. "You may not understand this, but I wish I'd never done that."

"I hear you," she said softly.

"Dave took off. Sam walked Becca back to Darius's car and Darius drove her home. I just kind of stood there, I guess, frozen in place. That's when I realized I wasn't alone. Maybe it was a smell or the sound of rustling leaves, but whatever it was, when I turned, I saw that Monty was hiding behind a tree. He took off running, just like Dave, and I let him go. But later, I got to thinking. What the hell was he doing there? I mean, think about it. He'd prepped Becca to be raped and then he'd hidden himself to watch the show. The guy is freakin' sick."

Jane sat quietly, taking it all in. "And nobody ever found out."

"No," said Kurt. "Not a soul."

"And Becca? I understand she left after graduation. Nobody knows where she went."

He sank his hands into the pockets of his jeans. "No, not true. I got to know her pretty well that year, what with what happened to her, and then Sam. After she left town, we stayed in touch. Mostly, at least at first, I just wanted to know she was okay. We'd email each other every few weeks. She went to live with her aunt and uncle in New Jersey. Eventually, we stopped writing as much, but I always heard from her at Christmas. I know she went to college, graduated, got married, and lives somewhere out east with her husband and her daughter. She's always been very circumspect about the details of her life. I've never pressed her for more."

"I'd like to talk to her," said Jane.

"I'm not sure she'd want that."

"Could you ask? We could Skype, if she'd be willing."

He didn't see any reason not to ask. He figured there was no way Jane could tie it to Sam's murder. "I suppose I could email her."

"Thank you. Can I ask you about one other person?"

"Who?"

"Scott Romilly?"

He shook his head. "He was never a friend, although I knew him a little because of Sam. He works for a bank in town."

"What do you think of him?"

"He was an entitled little shit. If Sam was the black sheep in the family, and he definitely was, Scott was the golden boy. His father spoiled him rotten."

"Were you surprised that Emma was dating him?"

His eyes opened wide. "Are you kidding me? *He's* the guy? I knew there was someone, but she was always so tight-lipped about it."

"He's turned into a stalker. Doesn't want her to leave Castle Lake. Secretly follows her around. He assumed their relationship was serious, that she'd stay and, after getting a divorce, marry him."

"She has a fifteen-year-old daughter in California."

"He doesn't seem to think it's a problem."

"He wants what he wants, just like he always does. But . . . this stalking. Does Emma think he's dangerous?"

"She thinks he's creepy. I'm the one who thinks he's dangerous."

"I'll talk to her," said Kurt, irritated that she'd never mentioned any of it to him.

"Are you and Emma close?"

"We weren't in high school, but after spending time with her this summer, we've become friends. I think the world of her."

"One last question and then I'll leave you alone. Does the word 'duel' mean anything to you?"

His stomach tightened. "Duel?"

"The kind you do with swords or guns."

"No. Should it?"

"Were you in a history class with Sam your junior year?"

"No."

"Okay, just wanted to ask."

"Do you have a theory about what happened to him?"

"I've got a few ideas. Nothing I can back up yet." Brushing off her pants, she stood and looked toward the woods. "I'm kind of turned around. How do I get back to the cemetery?"

"Where are you parked?"

"In the lot behind Holy Trinity."

"Why don't I walk you there?"

"No, it's fine. If you'll just point me in the right direction—"

"I have to get back to the market anyway. We might as well walk together." Once again, he was torn. After talking to her for just a few minutes, he could tell she wanted justice for Sam, and also, that she was tenacious. In his current circumstance, those qualities were both good and bad. Even so, he felt the least he could do was make sure she got back to her car safely.

30

"I thought you were planning to spend some time with Leslie before you came home," said Cordelia as she rooted through the take-out sacks Jane had brought back to the lake house.

"What *are* you wearing?" asked Jane.

"Oh these?" She fluttered her eyelashes. "Chest-high duck waders. Bought them at the local Ben Franklin. They're made of mesh and nylon and are supposed to trick water fowl into thinking they aren't being covertly observed."

"Water fowl. Are you planning to go duck hunting?"

"Heavens, no."

Her hair was stuffed up under a blaze-orange boonie hat. "The hat kind of ruins the intent of the pants, unless water fowl can't tell one color from another."

"Consistency is the last refuge of the unimaginative. Oscar Wilde. Back to Leslie?"

"We both thought we'd have some time this afternoon," said Jane, getting down two plates from the cupboard. "Her meeting ran late. And tonight's that planning-commission thing, which will probably go long."

"A busy woman,"

"And then some," said Jane. "But I did talk to her. We're getting

together for dinner tomorrow night. There's a new Moroccan restaurant in town she thinks is fabulous. The Red Fez."

"You'd think the only ethnic food you'd find in this berg would
be Swedish meatballs."

Jane had given Kurt a ride back to the meat market after their
conversation by the river. Since she had a little extra time, she decided to go in and look around. Seeing the rotisserie chickens, the
potato salad, coleslaw, beans, and cornbread muffins, she knew
she had dinner nailed.

"Hey, this all looks delicious," said Cordelia, taking a taste of
the baked beans.

"How was your afternoon at the junior high school?" asked
Jane, carrying everything over to the kitchen table.

Cordelia removed a couple of beers from the refrigerator.

"Oh, you know," she said. "One tries ones best to be engaging,
even when the kids are squirming with boredom because they're
being deprived of social media for a few hours. They're not my
best audience."

"I'm sure you left a lasting impression. Years from now, they'll
all be saying, 'Oh my gosh, that woman who just won the Pulitzer
and the Indy 500 spoke at my school once."

Cordelia sighed. "*If* it gets posted on Snapchat. Otherwise, forget it."

As they ate, Jane filled Cordelia in on the information she'd
gleaned in the Romilly case, with the identity of Becca Hill's rap-
ist being the most stunning revelation.

"That man really is slime."

"So it would appear."

Spreading honey butter on her cornbread, Cordelia continued,
"So, I have to ask. After everything you've learned, what do you
think happened to Sam?"

"I may be wrong, but at the moment I believe the catalyst was
the rape. I know Becca must have had her reasons for not going to

the police, and none of this is her fault, but I think that's where it all began. The first night we were here, Emma told me that Sam believed in revenge. He called it justice, though Emma saw it as something darker. In the light of Becca's decision not to report her rape to the police, I think Sam may have decided to extract payback himself."

"How?"

"That's just it. I was confused about the two handguns found in Sam's grave. Two matching revolvers with two cartridges each still in the cylinders, one spent, the other unspent."

"And?"

"Remember, Sam had written that paper on dueling for his junior-year history class. If you take a duel as the focus of his revenge, it might account for the two handguns and the two cartridges. I spent some time this afternoon reading up on duels. They were fought to retain honor—not necessarily to kill. Each man walked an agreed-upon number of paces away. The distance meant they were less likely to do serious damage. Of course, lots of men died."

"Like Alexander Hamilton."

"Exactly. Each man had a friend with him called 'a second.' The second was there to ensure the duel was honest and aboveboard and that the weapons were equally deadly. The seconds were chosen by each man. In Tamborsky's case, I would assume he picked his best friend, Monty Mickler."

"And what about Sam?"

"Emma told me she was Sam's best friend, though her participation seems unlikely."

"Because she was female? Come on, Jane. That's not a real reason."

"Okay, maybe she was there. But if she was, she sure is a good actor because I've never once sensed that she knew anything about what happened to him. We know Sam had a lot of friends. Maybe he chose Darius. Or Kurt. Or Jim Hughes. Or it could be somebody we haven't met yet. But I'd bet money that at least four people were there that morning."

"Following your reasoning," said Cordelia, "that means Dave Tamborsky and Monty Mickler probably aren't happy you're in town digging into it." She repositioned her boonie hat. "Tell me more about duels."

"Some men used swords, others pistols. The location for the duel varied. Some were let loose in a park or wooded area, where there were plenty of places to hide. Some were the standard kind of duels we're more familiar with."

"But what would Sam get out of it?"

"I'm not sure, but both Sam and Dave must have agreed on terms—what would happen depending on who won."

Cordelia snorted. "What would winning look like? Not dying?"

"Possibly. Or maybe it depended on who was hit."

"What if neither was hit?"

"Honestly, Cordelia, I have no idea. But there must have been something in it for both of them, otherwise they wouldn't have agreed."

"If they did agree."

"I realize it's just a theory, but for the moment, it explains more about what I've learned than anything else. Then again, all of it is rendered moot because the cartridges in those revolvers were all blank. Makes no sense."

"Sam was shot in the head. That's how he died. How do you kill a man with blanks?"

"I'm obviously missing something."

Cordelia lifted the beer to her lips, but instead of taking a sip, she asked, "What about Carli Gilbert? Do you still think her death is connected to the discovery of Sam's remains?"

"I haven't followed up on any of that. I was thinking we should drive by what's left of the house tonight. Maybe talk to a few more of her neighbors. Oh, and there's a place I want to see—an antique/junk/second-hand shop out past Castle Lake."

Cordelia's ears pricked up. "Do they have costume jewelry?"

"Very likely."

"Well, what are we waiting for?"

"For you to change clothes."

"What's wrong with what I'm wearing?"

Another question Jane couldn't possibly answer.

"So many people dress in hunting clothes up here. Maybe I want to fit in."

"You never want to fit in. Your whole métier is to stand out."

"Okay, okay. How about this? Since we're going hunting tonight, I might as well dress for it." She grinned and socked Jane's arm. "Let's go bag ourselves a couple of mock ducks. They must have a few of those around these parts."

The light was fading by the time they made it to Lowry Antiques & Treasures, a one-story white clapboard building that sat about thirty feet back from the county highway. Even in the growing darkness, Jane could see that the roof sagged and the siding needed a good paint job. A brightly lit sign hung above the door, intended, no doubt, to catch the eye of potential customers as they sped past. There were also several long tables loaded down with housewares— plates, crockery, serving dishes, cups, and glassware.

What the parking area lacked in grass, it made up for in potholes. Cordelia rubbed her hands together eagerly as she exited the truck. Jane joined her as they made their way inside. The interior of the building was even more disheveled than the outside. It was also crammed to the rafters. It wasn't Jane's cup of tea, but Cordelia was in her element. Like a heat-seeking missile, she found a display case filled with gaudy costume jewelry and called a woman over to help.

After a few minutes of uninspired wandering, Jane's nose began to itch. There was no use in trying to hurry Cordelia, so she went back outside to get some fresh air. Floodlights mounted on the building lit up the exterior tables, so she began, once again with little enthusiasm, to look through the offerings. That's when her cell phone buzzed.

Taking it out of her back pocket, she saw that it was a text from Kurt.

Becca will talk to you. She has time tomorrow morning at 10 am. Will that work? If so, send me your Skype address. Hers is below. Hope you find what you want.
BHL.99w02

Jane couldn't believe Becca had responded so quickly. She was lucky that her meeting with Wendell Romilly was scheduled for nine. She doubted it would last very long.

Directly across the highway from the antique shop sat the Avalon Motor Inn, the motel Monty Mickler managed. As she poked through the dishes, she glanced up every now and then to watch the place. What she really wanted was to run over and take a closer look.

Wilburn Lowry's van pulled into the parking lot a while later. When he slid out, the pristine coveralls he'd been wearing that morning looked much the worse for wear. Seeing her, he waved and came over. "You decided to check us out," he said, smiling broadly. For the first time, his head was bare, revealing a bald head with a dwindling halo of gray hair.

"Looks like you've been busy," said Jane, matching his smile with one of her own.

"That Mickler place is proving to be a treasure trove," he said, wiping his face with a blue bandana. "Neither the owner's daughter nor her son wants much from the house, so she's giving most of it away. I said I'd help her if she wanted to have a garage sale, but she said I should just take the stuff to the garbage dump." Stuffing the bandana back into his pocket, he added, "Tomorrow we start on the basement."

A woman with curly brown hair and rimless glasses came out of the building. "I thought I heard your voice," she said, giving Lowry a kiss.

He put his arm around her. "Jane Lawless, meet my gorgeous, amazing wife, Nancy."

"Oh, go on with you," she said, though she clearly loved it.

"Nice to meet you," said Jane.

"You look tired, honey," said Nancy, wiping a smudge of dirt off his face.

"I am. Is there any of my pop in the fridge?"

"Just filled it with Dr Pepper this morning."

"Excellent," he said, giving her a peck on the cheek.

After he'd disappeared inside, Nancy and Jane were left alone. "Your husband is a very intriguing man."

"He is," said Nancy, still glowing. "He's one-in-a-million. I got lucky."

"I'm curious," continued Jane. "Do you know the man who manages the motel across the street?"

"Monty? Sure, I know him. He does a good business over there, especially on weeks like this. It's homecoming, you know. And there's an art fest and a class reunion."

"What do you think of him?"

She crossed her arms. "He's always been a good neighbor. He's got this commercial snow blower and usually comes over to help us dig out after a storm. I've met his wife and kids—he has a beautiful family. I mean, some people in town call that place the Bates Motel. Kind of looks like the one in that Hitchcock movie, doesn't it?"

Jane had to agree.

"I'm not suggesting Monty attacks women in the shower, though I will say, and this is just between us chickens, he's not exactly a model husband."

"In what way?"

"He cheats. Women come to see him all the time. I'm not trying to be nosey, you understand, but it's hard to miss what's going on. There is one woman in particular that I've noticed a lot over the years. She never parks in the lot, but I see her car here and there close to the motel. Sometimes it's in front of the rock shop down the way. Or it's at the little strip mall."

"Do you know who she is?"

"No idea."

"What does she look like?"

"Oh, blondish hair. Kind of chunky. Always wears sunglasses. Her newest car is a red Chevy Cobalt. Come to think of it, I haven't seen it for several days. But like I said, there are other women, too. He uses the room next to the office to . . . *entertain*, if you catch my drift. As far as I can tell, he rarely, if ever, rents it. Funny thing though, the women, they're never in there very long. How fun could that be?"

"So you see a woman walking up and entering the room, and then he comes out of the office and goes in—or maybe he's already in there when they arrive."

"I've never actually seen him go in or out. I guess I've always thought he must climb through a window in the back. Probably doesn't want people to catch on to his funny business. I told Wilburn that old Monty Mickler must be Castle Lake's answer to Don Juan."

"I feel sorry for his wife."

"Me, too. It's sad, you know? A human can be many things all at the same time, some of them good, some of them bad." She unfolded her arms and looked around. "Well, I better get one of my daughters out here to help me cover the tables for the night."

"You leave it all out here?"

"We've never had any problems, knock on wood. We close at nine, so I guess there's no huge rush. But, if you'll excuse me?"

"Of course," said Jane. She spent the next few minutes leaning against the front of her truck, wondering if the woman Nancy Lowry hadn't seen recently might be Carli Gilbert. That's when a crazy idea occurred to her. She went back inside and drew Cordelia away from her jewelry search long enough to explain what she needed.

"Brilliant, Janey. I love it. And don't worry, I can do it with my eyes closed and my brain tied behind my back."

"Be sure to give me enough time to get it done."

"No problem. Let's hope he takes the bait."

31

Kurt sat on the steps of the VFW hall, playing a game of solitaire on his phone and waiting for Ted to come out. It was a nice evening, with a slight breeze and the hint of fall in the air. The main meeting for the reunion committees would be tomorrow night, but tonight the woman in charge of the reunion wanted to meet with the committee chairs. Ted, as the old class president, had also been invited.

After winning two more games and losing three, Kurt looked up as classmates began drifting out. He said hi as people came past, standing to engage a few closer friends about how the meeting had gone. Finally, after it seemed as if everyone had left, Ted and Emma emerged, laughing and talking a mile a minute.

"Hey, you two," said Kurt, hands in his pockets. "Looks like you had a good time."

"Not really," said Emma. "But getting a chance to catch up with Ted was worth the price of admission." She slipped her arm through Kurt's. "I'd forgotten how funny he is."

"That's me," said Ted. "I should have been voted class stand-up comic."

"Listen," said Emma, her smile fading a little as she glanced from face to face. "I need you two big, strong hunks to walk me to my car."

"Why?" asked Ted.

"Because of Scott Romilly?" asked Kurt.

She seemed surprised. "How did you find out about that?"

"Your houseguest, Jane Lawless. She tells me you've been dating him."

"For a couple of months, yeah."

"Jane said that he's been stalking you."

"Stalking?" repeated Ted.

"Oh, I don't know," she said with a sigh. "Yeah, that may be accurate. Whatever the case, let's just say I have good reason to be a little wary of him." She tugged Kurt's arm. "I'm parked in the back lot."

Ted took her other arm and together they walked her to the darkest part of the rear lot.

"Try to find a parking place under one of the lights next time," said Ted.

"I won't be around that much longer." Opening the door, she added, "Which makes my new headache even worse. I have some electrical problems at the house. Ted offered to come by tomorrow and give me his ideas about the extent of the repair that's needed, as well as what a fair ballpark price might be. I had a couple guys out today and both said it would cost an arm, a leg, and my firstborn child to fix it."

"I think the first one really tried to gouge you with that estimate," said Ted.

Kurt took a look around to make sure Scott wasn't hiding behind a bush somewhere, and then he waited until Emma was safely in the front seat before closing the door.

"You guys are the best," she said, rolling the window down. "Don't forget the bonfire on Friday night."

"You mentioned that you had it all organized," said Kurt. "But if there's anything I can do to help—"

"Just show up and have a good time."

"We'll be there," said Ted.

"Lock your doors and roll up your window," ordered Kurt.

"I hate this," said Emma. "I hate weak women."

"You're not being weak," said Ted. "You're being smart."

"I suppose. You two enjoy the rest of your evening."

As she pulled out of the lot and disappeared down the alley, Ted said, "She's terrific. I'm really sorry her marriage didn't work out." Turning to face Kurt, he continued, "Can I walk you home?"

"I thought you'd never ask."

At the corner, they turned north. They made small talk for a few minutes, but as they approached the baseball field at the edge of Victory Park, Kurt said, "I'm glad we had a chance to talk things out last night."

"I'm glad you finally told your parents you're gay," said Ted.

"I didn't mean to give the impressions that they're fine about it."

"Oh, don't worry, you didn't." He gave Kurt a sympathetic look. "My mom isn't exactly thrilled about me either, though she's known for many years. The bottom line is, she loves me. It's one of the reasons I want to move back. She's been so lonely since Dad died. My sister and her kids are great, but I want to be around for her, too."

Ted had earned a BA in philosophy from the University of Minnesota. Exactly one week after graduation, he took a construction job to support himself and start paying off his student debt. He told Kurt that, while he would always love philosophy, he'd learned something important about himself in the four years he'd been at college: He was sick to death of living in his head and wanted to live more in his body. Swinging a hammer for a living felt right to him. After working hard for many years, he became a journeyman electrician, and later, with a friend, opened a construction company, one that proved successful as well as lucrative.

"Our clients are all over the state now," said Ted. "I can work from here, or I can go back to Minneapolis and work from there. It's only two hours away."

Kurt had to agree—he felt sure Ted could make it work.

"But that still leaves us with a problem," continued Ted. "I want to be out about our relationship. I want us to live together. No more sneaking around. You've resisted telling Danny about us, and I understand your reasons, but he's an adult now. I realize none of this will be easy. This is a small, deeply conservative town. But it's home. I'm a small-town guy at heart, just like you are."

Six years ago, right after his poetry book was published, Kurt had driven down to the cities to do a poetry reading at a library in St. Paul. Ted had been in the audience that night and they'd ended up reconnecting over a beer. A month or so later, Kurt had gone down to the Cities again for a little R&R. He'd gone to the Gay Nineties to have a few drinks with friends and, much to his surprise, had run into Ted again. Serendipity or harmonic convergence, he didn't know. After a few awkward moments, they sat down at a table and, haltingly, opened up about their lives. Kurt didn't know it then, but it was the beginning of a new life for both of them. They'd been with other men. Ted had even lived with a guy for a couple of years, but this time, he said, it felt different. As for Kurt's feelings about Sam—he had no doubt that Sam had loved him, but he also knew that their life paths would have diverged after high school.

"I've thought about it a lot since our talk the other night," said Kurt. "I'm going to tell Danny about us."

"You've said that before."

"I know. I mean it this time. But before I do, there's something I need to tell you."

Ted stopped walking and turned to face him. "That sounds ominous."

"It's something I should have come clean about a long time ago. If you still want to be with me after I'm done, then I'll talk to Danny tomorrow."

They found a bench and sat down.

Needing space, Kurt shifted away. He looked up at the stars, took a couple of deep breaths, and then began to tell Ted about the morning Sam died.

As Jane entered the motel office, a bell above the door gave a cheerful jingle. She stepped up to the counter and waited, but when nobody appeared, she hit the bell next to a small American flag on a stand. The door behind the counter opened and Mickler appeared, wiping his mouth on a napkin.

"Apologies," he said. "I was just having some dinner." Focusing on her for the first time, he blurted, "Oh, hi. I mean—"

She'd clearly caught him off guard.

"We've met before. At the bank the other morning."

"Oh, sure," said Jane. "I remember you."

"You're doing research for a podcast. How's that going?"

"Slow," said Jane. "I'm looking into Sam Romilly's death. You remember him?"

"Sure."

"Were you friends?"

"Not really. To be honest, I hardly knew him."

"Well, so many years after the fact, it's hard to find people who remember much. It's been kind of frustrating."

"Yeah, that's tough. So," he said, moving a small vase of yellow daisies to the other side of the counter, "how can I help you?"

"I'm wondering if you might have a room for a last-minute guest."

"For what night?"

"Friday and Saturday."

"I'm afraid we're booked solid. It's homecoming weekend and there's also a class reunion, which you must know about. You're staying at the Granholm place, if I'm not mistaken."

Jane tried to act disappointed. "Rats. But . . . I'm wondering. I was told you usually don't rent room number one, that it might still be free."

"Who told you that?" he asked, looking mildly curious.

"I don't recall. I've met so many new people since I arrived. Were they wrong?"

"I don't rent it very often because it's so much less comfortable than the other units. The heating and electrical plant cut into the back of it, so it's smaller. There's only enough space for one double bed. Most people want two doubles or one queen. And the air-conditioning unit sits right outside the bathroom window, which can get annoyingly loud when it comes on and off, especially during the night. People used to call me at 2 a.m. to demand their money back—pretty annoying for the guy who has to drive back here and deal with it."

"Totally understandable," said Jane. "But here's the problem: My friend can't find anywhere else in town to stay. The closest motel with an empty room is in Fergus Falls, kind of a long drive. I think that unit of yours would be more than fine, if you'd be willing to rent it."

"Is your friend coming for the homecoming game on Friday night?"

"No, for the class reunion on Saturday night."

"Oh," he said, offering a smile. "I'm part of that class. I probably know the guy."

"It's a woman," said Jane. "Becca Hill?"

His smile faded, but his mouth stayed open.

"Do you remember her?"

"Um, I think so."

"If the room isn't already promised to someone——"

"Well, now, I should probably check on that. My assistant manager sometimes books things when I'm not around." He turned to the computer screen, tapped a few keys and brought up a page. "Oh, gosh, looks like we do have someone scheduled for arrival tomorrow. It has a flag on it, so that means it's tentative. I'd have to talk to my assistant to see what it means exactly."

He was giving himself a chance to think about it. "I know Becca would be incredibly grateful to find a room here. Listen, could I take a look at it? Just, you know, to see if it's really as awful as you make it sound."

His smile was warm and utterly insincere. "I don't see any harm in that." Turning to a box that hung on the wall behind the counter, he pulled a key off one of the hooks. "If you'll follow me?"

It was rare these days to find a motel that still used actual keys, especially those with old-fashioned, triangular key tags attached. Jane stood behind him, waiting for him to unlock the door and flip on the overhead light.

"Oh," he said, stepping into the room. "I forgot. The TV in here is broken. And we had to remove a piece of carpet because of a grease stain."

The small flat-screen had a cracked glass and was resting on the floor against the wall.

"She'd only be sleeping here," said Jane, "so it wouldn't be a problem." She sat down on the bed, pretending to test it out. "This is nice."

"You think so?"

The room smelled funky. "Absolutely."

Hearing a bell jingle, Mickler walked back to the door. "Oh, gosh, I've got another customer."

"Can I stay a minute more? I want to look at a few things, especially the bathroom."

This time, the bell on the counter inside the office dinged. And dinged again. And again. Cordelia had arrived right on cue.

"Sure, that's fine," said Mickler. "Just come back to the office when you're done."

Jane gave it a moment and then rose from the bed and stepped over to the door. Cordelia had left the office door open so Jane could easily hear the conversation.

Mickler asked if he could help her.

Cordelia launched. "Yeah, I certainly hope so. My wife and I are thinking of coming back here for hunting season. I like to bag a porcupine or two every year. You know, blow them away and all that."

"A porcupine? Your *wife*?"

"Yeah. Anyway—"

With Cordelia keeping him busy, Jane began her search. First, she checked the window in the bathroom, seeing right off that it was much too small for anyone to crawl through. If Mickler spent time with his girlfriends in unit one, the only way in or out was the door. Unless there was a second door.

With only the top light on, she began to feel along the knotty pine walls. After a rushed search, she came up empty. Opening a closet that stuck out from the wall, she found that the interior was also covered in knotty pine. She ducked under the closet rod. As she pressed her hand to the back wall to steady herself, she heard a click. Pushing again, a piece of the knotty pine popped forward.

Eureka.

The door was maybe two and a half feet wide by four and a half feet tall, big enough for a person to come through with room to spare. Clicking on her phone's flashlight app, she directed the beam into the darkness and saw that there was another door directly behind the one in the closet, this one had to be connected to the room behind the office's reception area. It was all very clever. She was curious to know if Mickler had installed it, or if the original owner had.

Rushing now, she closed the inner door, then the outer one, and finally returned to the front, glad to hear that Cordelia and Mickler were still talking.

"Okay," said Cordelia, sounding impatient. "It doesn't have to be that weekend. How about the weekend after that?"

When Jane came in, Mickler glanced up.

"Sorry to interrupt," she said.

Cordelia turned in her direction. "No problemo," she offered, hooking her thumbs over the top of her waders.

"That room," continued Jane. "I think it would be perfect for Becca."

"How is it that you know her?" asked Mickler.

"I don't actually know her that well," said Jane. "Kind of a long story." She slid one of her business cards across the counter to him. "Please, if there's any way, call me."

"What time would she be coming in?"

"Her flight gets into MSP around seven on Friday night. She'll be tired after the flight and the drive up. Saturday will be a big day."

"I'm sure it will," said Monty.

"As for the time, she figured she'd make it to Castle Lake around ten, give or take."

"Nobody's at the front desk after ten."

"That's not a problem. I would be happy to pay for the room with my credit card. I could stop by and pick up a key. That way she can just go in and go to bed."

Mickler hesitated, studying her for a few seconds. "Let me see what I can do."

Jane thanked him, eyed Cordelia briefly, and then left.

Mission accomplished.

DAVE

Saturday, October 2, 1999

With Monty riding shotgun, Dave turned his dad's Ford Pinto onto a rutted dirt road a few miles east of Ice Lake. He stopped when he saw Ty Niska's weird, sci-fi, piece-of-shit Subaru XT. Niska owned it, so Dave's loathing was at least part envy.

"Hey, dawgs," called Niska, walking up to the front of the Pinto and banging on the hood. "Let's do some *bidness*."

Ty Niksa was the supreme badass at Castle Lake High School. He dealt drugs, bragged about the prostitutes he'd slept with, always carried a switchblade inside his boot, and palled around with a couple older guys who enjoyed showing off their prison tats. He also had a kind of jumpy energy that made him seem like a cork in a bottle of champagne, one that was always on the verge of exploding.

"Get in," said Dave.

Niska slid into the backseat, reeking of weed. "So what can I do for you lads?"

Dave glanced sideways at Monty. "We need a couple of handguns."

"That right."

Monty turned around to look at him. "Two revolvers. Have to

be the same make and model. And we need a box of cartridges and four blanks."

"I see. All very intriguing. It'll cost you."

"They don't have to be top of the line," said Dave, his eyes fixed straight ahead. He was nervous and didn't want Niska picking up on it. "We want something low cost."

"You gonna tell me why?"

"Can you get it?" asked Monty.

"I can get anything for a price. When do you need it?"

"A couple of days?" said Dave. "Is that doable?"

"Might cost you extra."

"How much?" asked Monty.

"Well, ballpark, a couple hundred for each handgun. How many rounds?"

"Say, fifty. Total."

"Okay, another forty, fifty bucks. And I don't know about the blanks, but I can ask around. Of course, my help don't come free of charge. But I got to say, boys, you have me real curious about what's going down."

"It's a prank," said Monty, offering Niska a mischievous grin. "Dave and Sam Romilly are going to fight a duel. Out in the woods. We'd need your help with that, too."

"Seriously, lads? Consider me *on board*. Again, for a price."

Monty explained that they wanted the ammunition so Sam could practice his shot. Dave wouldn't need to because on the day of the duel, Niska would be there to orchestrate it. He would be the one to load the revolvers with two cartridges each. Two blank cartridges. He would do the countdown and give the order to fire.

"But what's the point?" he asked, "if nobody's going to get hurt?"

"Sam will be so nervous he'll be shitting bricks," said Dave.

"I'm hoping for a good old nervous breakdown," said Monty with a laugh.

"You guys are nasty. I like the way you think."

"For the whole thing," said Monty. "How much?"

"Say, seven hundred."

"How much?" asked Dave, turning all the way around.

"It's a deal," said Monty.

"No," Dave countered. "It's too steep."

"I've got the money. It's fine."

"Your little bookie business still going strong?" asked Niska.

"Never mind where I got it. How fast can you get us the stuff?"

"Might take a couple of days."

"Two days," said Monty. "If it takes any longer, the deal's off."

"Oooh, can I really be in the presence of Dirty Harry? You're a freakin' poser, Mickler. Always have been. Anyway, when is this duel happening?"

"Next Saturday morning," said Dave. "We'll get you the details later."

"I intend to take off as soon as it's over. If there are any repercussions, I wasn't there. You hear me?"

"We hear you," said Dave. His hands were sweating as he gripped the steering wheel. He hated this almost as much as he hated what he'd done at the party. It was a nightmare, and no matter how hard he tried, he couldn't wake up. Monty had been there for him, like always. He needed Monty at his side right now, someone who never judged, just cared about him.

"Well, nice doing business with you sons of bitches," said Niska, pushing the door open with his boot. "I'll be in touch."

32

On Thursday morning, Jane arrived at the bank just before nine and was directed to Wendell Romilly's second-floor office. She found him seated behind an oak desk, wearing a three-piece suit and looking deeply wrinkled, tanned, and wizened. Oddly, the suit—even the collar of his shirt—seemed too big for him. She wondered if he might be ill.

"Ms. Lawless?" he asked, standing.

"Thank you for agreeing to meet with me."

"Have a seat." He resumed his chair. "This won't take long."

She wondered what he meant by that.

The walls were painted a cream color, the lower third covered in a beautiful oak wainscoting. What appeared to be an original oil painting, a landscape with billowing clouds, something inspired by Constable no doubt, hung on the wall behind him. A built-in bookcase covered most of the wall across from his desk. Three narrow, arched windows at the far end of the room provided some natural light. She could easily see herself happily spending her working life in a room like this.

Fixing her with a dour stare, he said, "I think we can cut to the chase."

She'd been about to ask him if he minded if she recorded their interview. "Pardon me?"

"You're here because you want to get the dirt on me and my son. I know you've been scooping up all the gossip you can find."

She wouldn't have put it that way, but of course he was right.

Tapping his fingertips together, he went on. "I didn't murder my oldest son, Ms. Lawless. We had our differences, to be sure, but nothing that would have caused such an overreaction on my part. I can't prove it one way or the other. I'm also sure you have no evidence of my guilt because none exists."

Again, she couldn't argue the point.

"Perhaps you could enlighten me about something. Why is it that you think my younger son, Scott, had something to do with Sam's death?"

"Well," she began, crossing her legs, "shortly before Sam died, he and Scott were seen fighting, wrestling each other in Victory Park. Later, Sam said that Scott was about to do something which he thought would ruin his life. Whatever it was, Sam apparently tried to talk him out of it."

He stopped his finger tapping. "I thought it might be that." Rolling his chair closer to the desk, he folded his hands and gave himself a minute to think. "People have been whispering behind my back for years. They've obviously blown what happened out of all proportion. That's why I'm going to tell you something I've never talked about before. It's nobody's business, but to end your little foray into my family's past, I think it's necessary." He squared his shoulders. "The summer before his junior year, Scott started a small business—cutting people's lawns. He earned a nice chunk of change for his efforts. One of his clients, a teacher at the high school—Nicolle Chapman—spent *her* summer trying to seduce him. She succeeded, Ms. Lawless, because Scott was young and stupid and, like most kids his age, wanted desperately to get laid.

"She was married, though for work reasons, her husband was away more than he was home. I don't know all the details, but Scott told me she was unhappy. He also said that they were in love and would be together forever—nothing I could say would ever change that. Now, this is the first I've heard that Sam knew about it. If my sons fought, it was because of Scott's relationship with Nicolle Chapman. As soon as I learned about it, I went to see her. I told her that if she didn't stop seeing Scott, I'd report her behavior to the school board. She would have been fired and she knew it. I also gave her a thousand dollars to keep her mouth shut. I didn't want there to be any repercussions for my son."

"How did Scott take that?"

Drawing a circle with his finger, he said, "Not well. But he got over it. Life went on."

"The morning Sam died—"

"Scott was home. I'd gotten up early that morning, around five. I couldn't sleep, so I went downstairs to make myself a sandwich. While I was sitting at the kitchen table, I heard footsteps coming down the stairs. A short time later, the front door opened and shut. I finished eating and went upstairs to see which one of my kids had gone AWOL. Scott was asleep in his bed. Sam was gone. I showered, shaved, and dressed, and, as I walked past Scott's bedroom a second time, I checked in on him again. He was still snoring and hadn't moved a muscle. He'd been out late the night before, drinking. His pity party lasted several more weeks until I told him that if he didn't straighten up, he'd have to find some-where else to live."

"Why are you telling me this?"

"Because," he said, barely concealing his contempt, "I know that if I tell *you* the truth, it will have the same effect as putting a full-page ad in the local paper."

"I see," she said.

"I doubt you do. Are you a parent?"

"No."

"You make my point for me. I'm finished with you, Ms. Lawless. You can leave."

It seemed pointless to thank him. He was going to say his piece no matter how nicely she'd asked. When she reached the door, she stopped and turned to face him. "You're a thoroughly unpleasant man, Mr. Romilly."

"So I'm told."

"I feel sorry for your children."

"I do too, Ms. Lawless." He waved her away and returned to the work on his desk.

Jane's sluggish brain cried out for caffeine, but she didn't want to be late for her Skype call with Becca. She found Emma in the lake house kitchen, standing at the counter eating a piece of toast. "Oh, you made coffee," she said, quickly getting down a mug and pouring herself a cup.

"Where were you?" asked Emma, licking jam off her finger.

"I had to interview someone in town."

"Someone?"

"Wendell Romilly."

"Ugh," she said, dropping another piece of bread in the toaster. "Let's not talk about that family."

Something in the tenor of her voice made Jane stop. "What? Did something happen?"

"Just another one of Scott's epic texts. His third. This one started out with a proposal of marriage. He plots out our entire life together, how great it will be. The last one was all about how we could convince Verity to come live with us. And the one before that was a rumination on how he could permanently eliminate Philip from my life."

"Did he threaten him?"

"Not in so many words. But that man is obsessed."

"I want to hear more," said Jane, "but right now, I have to run upstairs. I've got a Skype call at ten."

"Oh, just so you know, Ted Hammond's coming by to give me his thoughts on that electrical repair. I'm going to ask him to look at a few other things while he's here, so if you hear banging or whatever, that's what it is."

"Thanks," said Jane.

Once upstairs, she tiptoed past Cordelia's door and entered her own bedroom, closing the door behind her. Sitting down at a small desk next to the window, she opened her laptop. She checked her email while she waited. At exactly ten, the call came in.

Jane clicked on the Skype icon and the page opened.

"Jane?" asked Becca.

"Thanks for calling." Becca was a plump, middle-aged woman with shoulder-length straight dark hair and glasses. Her clothing, what Jane could see of it, was tailored business attire.

"Of course." Her voice was low, her affect somewhat flat.

Before Jane broached the subject of recording the conversation, she wanted to get a feel for who Becca was. From what Kurt had said, she valued her privacy. Asking up front about a possible recording might put her off, or even worse, spook her into being less forthcoming.

"Kurt emailed me yesterday," Becca began. "He'd already told me about Sam, about what the police found in the graveyard. I was surprised, of course . . . and, frankly, pretty devastated. Sam was one of the good guys in my world back in Castle Lake."

"Are you coming home for the reunion?"

"No interest in that."

"You live somewhere out east?"

"I live in DC. I have a law degree from Columbia. After I graduated, I began working for RAINN. Are you familiar with that?"

"I am," said Jane. The Rape, Abuse & Incest National Network was the nation's largest anti sexual-violence organization, which made total sense.

"I head a committee on national policy. I also do pro bono work when time allows."

"You're married?" Jane had noticed a gold band on her left hand.

"Happily married, with an amazing daughter. I'm sorry I don't have much time this morning. Before we get started, there's a question I'd like to put to you."

"Sure," said Jane. "Fire away."

She hesitated, but only for a second. "Do you think Sam's murder was somehow tied to my rape?"

Jane had changed her mind about Becca's affect. It wasn't flat, it was decisive and to the point. "Yes, I'm afraid I do."

"I've always wondered about that. Everyone said he'd run away. Now I wish he had." She looked down, straightened some papers on her desk. "Okay, what did you want to ask me?"

"I'm wondering if you'd allow me to record this."

"For your podcast."

"That's right."

"No," said Becca firmly. "Depending on what happens with the official investigation, we might be able to revisit that later."

"I entirely understand," said Jane, glancing down at her notes. "Okay, so first, I'd like to know if, after the fact, you told anyone what happened to you. I mean, I know Sam and Kurt were both there."

"To clarify. Unlike Sam, who pulled Dave off me, Kurt didn't actually see the rape occur, only the aftermath. Sam was the only witness. I told my mother about the rape the next day, but I didn't say anything to my father. A couple days later, I opened up to my closest girlfriend. In terms of documentation, which I think you're after with your question, I wrote about it contemporaneously in my diary—or, I should say, I wrote about my reasons for not going to the police. Even as a kid, I knew I wouldn't be believed. Dave's dad was a high-ranking police officer in town. And I'd been drinking. That was, in my youthful opinion, enough right there to preclude any further investigation. If I put myself through this secondary horror, as I called it in my diary, I felt it would scar me almost as badly as the rape had. I've thought long and hard about my decisions over the years. For instance, I was incredibly stupid to drink as much as I did that night. You may not believe it, but it was unusual behavior for me."

As Jane scratched a few notes, she said, "But Kurt told you about Monty Mickler, right? That he was adding vodka to your Coke back at the house?" She looked up.

All expression had died on Becca's face. "What?"

"Mickler was purposely getting you drunk."

She cleared her throat, looked off to her right. "No, he never mentioned that."

Jane was a little surprised but forged on. "Mickler was also there when Dave attacked you. Kurt thinks he wanted to watch. I would assume, since he softened you up, that he felt he deserved to see the results of his handiwork."

Becca looked back at Jane, her lower jaw quivering. "I'm trying to find some way to express myself without resorting to my usual explosion of swear words."

"Feel free," said Jane.

She pressed a fist to her lips and gave herself a few seconds. "To be fair, you should know that shortly after I returned to school that fall, I told Kurt I didn't want to talk about what happened anymore. He responded that he worried about me and needed to know I was okay. Of course, I wasn't okay, but I agreed to let him walk me home once in a while so we could talk. That's how we became friends, and that's where we left the discussion of the assault. I wish he had let me know those details, but I understand why he didn't. But, wow." She looked up. "What a——" After biting

240

her lower lip for a moment, she continued, "That explains a lot. Tell me, do you think Dave—and Monty—had anything to do with Sam's murder?"

"Since I can't prove anything, I don't want to get into specifics, but yes, that's my working theory. Removing Sam from the picture meant that there were no witnesses to what happened, except for you, the victim, and the perpetrator. I think they bet on you staying silent."

"Yes, I see that."

"I know it's years after the fact and that there's a statute of limitations on rape cases, but if you were asked to make a formal statement, would you?"

"I'm not sure how much weight it would carry, but I would. Without hesitation."

Jane was glad to hear it.

Becca turned as a voice said, "You've got a call." Returning to Jane, she said "I'm sorry. I have to take this."

"Thanks for your time," said Jane.

"Please, stay in touch," said Becca. "I like to think there's some justice in this world, even if it's delayed."

33

"We appreciate you coming down to the station," said Sgt. Bobby Saltus, his legs splayed wide as he sat on a rolling chair.

"Happy to do it." Kurt was finding it impossible not to fidget. Dave had called him last night to tell him that he'd be sitting in on the interview today. "Interview, my ass," Kurt had responded. When the cops called you in, it was an interrogation. He felt certain Dave's only reason for being in the room was to make sure he didn't slip up and reveal a piece of the truth. When Kurt asked if Scott Romilly had come in yet, Dave snorted, saying they'd received a letter from his lawyer stating that all questions regarding Mr. Romilly should to be directed to him.

"You and Sam Romilly were friends, right?" asked Saltus.

Kurt nodded.

"You gotta answer audibly, man, otherwise the recording can't pick up your answer."

"Oh, sure. Yes, I knew him."

"And Wendell Romilly?"

"I've met him. I know he and Sam fought a lot, mostly about Sam's refusal to follow rules."

"And Sam's brother, Scott?"

"He was always kind of a cipher."

"A what?" asked Saltus.

"He was hard to read."

"Oh. Okay," said Saltus, tapping a pen against his thigh. "Did Sam have any enemies?"

"Not that I knew about. Most people liked him." The questions went on like this for a while, with Saltus taking the lead and Dave remaining silent. Kurt felt thoroughly poked and prodded, though none of the questions touched on anything important. And then Saltus upended the metaphorical table.

"You're aware that Sam's remains, along with some other items, were found in Holy Trinity cemetery, right?" He didn't wait for a response. "One of the items was Sam's billfold. In the flap behind the cash compartment, we found a ring." He pulled a tiny plastic sack out of his pocket and waved it at Kurt.

"What's that?" asked Dave, grabbing for it.

Saltus held it out of reach. "A gold band," he said, looking pleased with himself.

Kurt had begun to notice some friction between the two men.

"Do you recognize it?" asked Saltus.

"No," said Kurt. "I've never seen it before."

As soon as he placed it on the table, Dave snatched it.

"There's an inscription around the inner surface," continued Saltus. "S.A.R. & K. J. S. Forever. I interpret it this way: Samuel Alan Romilly and Kurt Jacob Steiner forever. What are your thoughts about that, Kurt?"

Kurt's eyes locked on the ring. He hadn't heard Sam's voice in his head for years, but it was there now, pure and deep and clear. He was overwhelmed. "I think—"

"Were you two, like, together?" asked Saltus. "As in gay?"

"Of course they weren't gay," said Dave. "He's married, or he was. He has a kid."

Saltus didn't take his eyes off Kurt. "Well?"

Kurt had never imagined it would happen like this, but now

that the question had been raised, he refused to deny it. "Yes. We were."

Dave's expression froze. "Are you kidding me? What the hell, Steiner?"

"I loved him," said Kurt.

"And you were, like, doing the nasty?" asked Saltus.

"Whatever we were doing is none of your business."

"Goddamn," said Dave. His face flushed. "This is total bullshit."

"Did you have a lover's quarrel?" asked Saltus, inching his chair closer to Kurt.

"What? No."

"Did you find out he was sleeping with someone else? I'll bet you were, like, red hot about it, ready to get yourself some payback. I mean, he'd betrayed you. Nothing worse than that. I don't blame you, man. We all know what it's like."

"I don't know where you're getting this," said Kurt, "but that never happened."

"Come on, man. You'll feel so much better once you tell the truth."

He couldn't believe this guy actually thought he was making sense.

"And then there's the little detail about the revolvers, the ones we found in the grave. I mean, I understand why you wanted to get rid of them. But the blanks? Why load them with duds? Were you just trying to scare him? Did you hold the gun too close?"

"With . . . blanks?"

"This interview is over," said Dave, standing up.

"Yeah blanks," continued Saltus. "There were two blanks in each handgun. One spent, one whole. I need to know why."

"Cripes," said Dave, giving Saltus a shove. "You're an idiot. That's not information we give out."

"Ignore him," said Saltus, rolling his chair even closer.

Kurt didn't think it was possible to feel shocked by anything

244

that had happened in the woods that morning, but this revelation about the guns sent him reeling.

"We're done," said Dave, reaching behind Saltus to turn off the recording.

Feeling confused and utterly overwhelmed, Kurt opted to play Scott Romilly's card. "I'm leaving," he said. "If you want to talk to me from here on out, you can contact my lawyer." The fact that he didn't have one hardly mattered.

Coming in the front door of his house a while later, Kurt found his son sitting on the couch, eating a sandwich and listening to music.

"Hey," said Danny, pulling the earbuds out of his ears. "What the hell happened to you?"

He wondered what had given his emotional state away. "How come you're home? I thought you worked this afternoon."

"So," said Danny, dropping the sandwich on the plate resting in his lap, "I need to tell you about that."

Kurt was happy to listen to anything that took his mind off the police interrogation.

"Tanya and I are moving in together. Last time I was down in Minneapolis, we found ourselves an apartment. A copy of the apartment lease came in the mail yesterday. It's cheap, but really cool. It's not in very good shape, but it's bigger than here."

Kurt didn't know how to respond. He'd always felt bad that their house was so small, but it was what he could afford, and anyway a happy family life didn't depend on the size of a bedroom. But that wasn't the real issue. "I had no idea you intended to leave."

Danny moved to the edge of the couch. "I've never made a secret of not wanting to spend my life here."

"I know, but—"

"It's time, Dad. Tanya is sick of living with her aunt. She's making good money as a bartender, and I found out last night that the job I applied for in Bloomington wants to hire me."

"What job?"

"A security guard. That pay isn't a lot, but with Tanya's take it's enough to cover our expenses. We figure if we save for a couple of years, we can quit our jobs and spend some time traveling, seeing the world. You could even stay with us when you come down. I mean, you're in the Cities at least once a month. Lately, even more. Come on. Don't be upset. I know it comes out of the blue, but it's for the best."

Kurt lowered his head for a few seconds, then looked back up. "You're right. I'm happy for you. It all sounds great."

"The thing is, I'm also kind of worried."

"About what?"

"That . . . if I'm not here, you'll be lonely."

"Oh, Danny," said Kurt. If he ever needed proof that he'd raised a great kid, this was it. "You don't need to worry about me."

"But I do."

He gripped the arms of his chair. Maybe this was the opening he'd been looking for. He had so many secrets, but this one took precedence. "There's something I've been wanting to talk to you about." He paused, trying form just the right words. In the end, he simply said it. "I'm gay, son. In fact, Ted and I have been together for many years."

Danny blinked, hesitated, and then smiled. "Oh, hell, Dad, I know that."

"You do?"

"Give me *some* credit. I'm not a moron."

He wanted more. But mostly, he was relieved. "I didn't want to tell you before because I hated to think you'd feel like you needed to live in reaction to me."

"Dad, please. The world has changed, at least for my generation. You see it as this big deal, a secret to be guarded at all cost, but it's not. It's just who you are."

"God, but I love you."

246

"Since we're telling secrets, I've got one, too. You can't get mad, okay?"

"Okay." Kurt would have promised him anything.

"I smoke. Cigarettes. If you can be gay, I can smoke. In fact, I need one right now."

As he walked to the front door, he put a hand on his father's shoulder. "All good?"

"All good, son."

34

Jane made her way along the dirt path toward the clearing. She found Kurt sitting on a tree trunk, just where he said he'd be. "I got your text," she said, sitting down next to him.

"Thanks for meeting me."

"Why here?" she asked.

"I wanted someplace private. And . . . because this is where it happened. I've been such a fool, Jane. I don't even know where to start." He rose, moving a few feet away. "I was interrogated by the police this morning. During the interview, I was given a piece of information that absolutely froze my blood. What I thought happened to Sam that morning . . . it was all a lie."

Jane's heart sped up. "I don't understand."

"It was an execution, Jane. Right in front of my eyes, and I never saw it."

A shiver passed through her.

"Look," he said, squeezing the back of his neck, "I should be telling this to the police, I know, but because of Dave Tamborsky, I can't. As I see it, you're the only person who's really been looking into Sam's murder. The police investigation is a sham." He began to pace. "Dave told me that they'd received an anonymous letter telling them to talk to Jim Hughes, Darius Porter, Scott Romilly, and me. I believe it was just a way to muddy the waters, to give the cops something to do that would have absolutely no meaning."

"You've lost me," said Jane.

"Hughes knows nothing. Neither does Darius or Scott. The only one who does know what happened is me, and whoever wrote the letter—I think it was Monty Mickler—was counting on me to keep my mouth shut. I was there the morning Sam died, Jane, so I bear some of the blame. When this all comes out, and it will, I'll probably go to prison."

This wasn't a time for recordings or note taking. Jane needed Kurt to stay in the moment, with no distractions. "Why do you think it was Mickler not Dave who sent it?"

"Because Dave isn't that devious. He's not an idea guy, he's a follower. Mickler has always been the driving force in what happened. I see that now. Look, I realize you're only a podcaster, but you seem serious about getting to the truth. That's why I wanted to talk to you."

Jane couldn't believe her luck.

"This may take a few minutes."

"I'm in no hurry."

He nodded, sitting back down. "Okay, it all began with Becca's rape. You already know about that. She refused to press charges against Dave. Sam couldn't stand the idea that Dave would get away with it, so he went to him, told him that if he didn't tell the police what happened, Sam would. Mickler showed up right about then. When he caught the drift of what was being said, he laughed at Sam, said even if Becca herself talked to the cops, nothing would come of it. Dave could just say it was consensual. They were both drunk and stupid, but that's all. It was his word against hers.

"If Sam had a weakness, it was his need for justice. He'd been sexually assaulted by an older man when he was in his early teens. He knew how it felt. That guy got away with it, but if Sam had anything to do with it, Dave wouldn't. He came up with this idea of a duel. They'd find some guns and square off in the woods."

"Dave agreed?"

"Not right away, although he was as hotheaded as Sam. He and Mickler met with him the next day and brought their own spin. They'd asked this guy, Ty Niska, to get them two matching handguns and a bunch of ammunition. They'd each have a few days to practice their shots, and then they'd meet here, in this clearing, at daybreak the following Saturday morning. Ty would be here to load the guns and do the countdown." He stopped and looked up. "I can't believe anybody's that crazy."

"How were the stakes defined?"

Kurt rose and began, once again, to pace. "If Sam won, Dave would go to the police and confess. If Dave won, Sam agreed to never bring the subject up again. No talking to the cops or anyone else about it. Ever."

"What did winning look like?"

"If one of them was shot, that was a win."

"And if nobody was shot?"

"There were supposed to be two rounds in each revolver. If nothing happened with the first shot, they'd repeat it, countdown and all. If nothing happened the second time, it would be considered a draw. In that case, they'd have to agree to another duel, or some other way to settle the matter."

"Like what?"

"It was never specified, at least to me." Kurt picked up a stick and began to break it in pieces. "You're going to hear this soon enough, so I might as well tell you. Sam and I were lovers."

Her eyebrows shot up. "You're gay? I . . . I guess I have terrible gaydar."

He looked like he might say more, but left it there.

"You said you were with Sam when he died. How did you get involved?"

"Sam had been nervous as a cat the last few days before the duel. I could tell something was up, though I had no idea what. He called me at home the night before, said he had to talk to me, but he couldn't do it until the following morning. He told me to meet him just before sunup at the graveyard behind Holy Trinity. It all seemed very covert, like we were in a spy novel. He also said he had a gift for me, something special, so I better show up. He made me promise—no, not promise, *swear*—that I'd be on time. Honestly, he scared me. So I got there early and was waiting for him when he arrived. That's when he told me the whole thing. Needless to say, I was appalled. I tried to talk him out of it. I begged him to come home with me so we could figure out another way to make Dave pay. He wouldn't even consider it. He needed me to be his 'second,' to be another pair of eyes and ears, just to make sure Dave didn't try anything funny. Mickler was Dave's second. Sam seemed so desperate. He wanted me there with him. I couldn't say no. The last thing Sam said to me before we walked into the clearing was that he doubted most guys could hit the broad side of a barn when they were nervous. That I shouldn't worry."

"What was the gift?" asked Jane. She didn't want to interrupt his story, but she didn't want that detail getting lost.

"I'd completely forgotten about that part of our conversation until this morning. During my interview with Saltus . . . he showed me a gold band that was found in Sam's wallet. Sam had our initials engraved on the inside. And the word *forever*." He folded his arms and bent over, clearly in pain.

Jane started to get up, but he held out his hand. "No," he said, his other hand pressed to his eyes. It took nearly a minute before he straightened up. "I never expected to hear from Sam again. I can't begin to tell you what that felt like."

251

Watching him, Jane's heart nearly broke.

"Anyway," he said, his face turned up to the sky. "Everything happened very quickly after that. While Niska was loading the revolvers, Mickler began to clutch his stomach, like he was about to throw up. Just before Sam and Dave walked their ten paces away, he said something like, 'I'm gonna puke.' He ran into the woods. Because I felt the same way, I didn't think anything of it.

"Niska waited until they were in position, then counted, one, two—and then, when he said three, there was this loud discharge. I couldn't believe it when I saw Sam fall. We all ran over to him, but even at a distance, I could tell he was gone. His—" Kurt's voice broke. "His . . . head wasn't . . . part of it was missing. I collapsed next to him and held him, rocking him, whispering to him. Niska took off running and never came back. Mickler, at that point, was still missing. Dave stood over us, the revolver at his side. When I looked up, I saw that he was crying, too. He just kept saying stuff like, 'I didn't mean, I didn't know, I never wanted . . .' Mickler eventually appeared and more or less took charge. He said he and Dave had prepared a place in Holy Trinity cemetery, 'in case the worst happened.' His words. They'd dug under the grave of a woman scheduled for burial that morning. I remember being amazed that they'd thought so far ahead. But even in a daze, I was angry. I told Mickler we had to talk to the police. He leaned down very close to my face and said that wasn't going to happen. We were all in it together. Did I want to spend the rest of my life in prison? It was still early, maybe an hour after sunup, so Mickler insisted there was nothing to worry about. Nobody would be in the cemetery at this time of day. It was risky, I guess, but he and Dave must have felt they could get away with it.

"Mickler's idea was for the three of us to carry Sam there. But I couldn't. I couldn't let go of him. It's so long ago now, and I can't recall my exact thoughts, but I do know part of me wanted to die. Mickler had to drag me away from him. He actually had to uncoil my fingers from Sam's clothing. He told me to run, to make sure I got rid of my clothes, which were covered in blood. I remember standing up, watching Mickler and Dave carry him away. I couldn't move. I could hardly breathe. I sank to the ground, buried my hands in the dirt, and cried. And then—I have no idea how long I stayed there—I ran home. Mickler said we'd meet up later to talk about it. When we did, he had another choice threat. He said if I ever said anything about what happened, I might not get hurt, but someone I loved would. He left it hanging in the air like that, then moved on to some self-serving crap about how we all needed to stick together. We'd done something truly terrible, but we had to move on to salvage what was left of our lives. He said Sam would have wanted that. I hated him more in that moment than I'd ever hated anyone in my life—before or since."

Sitting back down on the log next to Jane, Kurt continued, "Life resumed. Classmates wondered where Sam had gone, and I did a lot of shrugging. I also spent a bunch of time that fall in the bathroom, dousing my face with water and smiling at myself in the mirror. I had to practice because it was like I'd forgotten how. Most days, my face felt like concrete."

Kurt squeezed his hands together and looked off into the woods. "This was what I thought happened. Dave shot Sam and he died. But then, this morning, I learned something that changed everything. Saltus told me that both of the revolvers had been loaded with blanks."

Jane already knew as much, but hadn't seen any point in mentioning it.

"So, for the last couple of hours, I've been asking myself, if the revolvers had no actual bullets in them, how did Sam die? There's only one answer. I didn't know Mickler all that well, but

I did know he liked guns. He brought a rifle with a big, expensive scope to a party once—a month or so before the one at the farm. He seemed so proud of the thing, he couldn't stop touching it. I always gave him a wide berth because I thought he was sort of shady, and this was just one more reason."

When Kurt looked down and stopped talking, Jane prompted him, asking him what he thought had happened.

"It was Mickler. I'm sure of it. He'd run into the woods saying he was sick, but that was only a ruse. He must have had the rifle stashed somewhere. He took up a position, sighted Sam through the scope, and on the count of three, fired. I figure he relied on the fact that I was so jumpy and otherwise crazed that I wouldn't notice. He was right. Like I said, it was just one huge, loud bang. Instead of a duel, Mickler and Dave had pulled off an assassination."

By the end of the telling, Kurt's voice had grown hoarse.

"I don't know what to say," said Jane softly. "I can't imagine living through something like that."

Wiping a hand over his eyes, he said, "The whole duel idea was idiotic from the outset, but Mickler, in his Machiavellian way, used it to put a lid on the rape. Becca wouldn't talk. Sam was dead. He knew Sam was going to ask me to be his second, so my participation in the duel effectively silenced me. With one shot from a rifle, Mickler had given Dave back his life and, in the process, provided himself with a little light entertainment."

"You really think he's that evil?"

Kurt turned to face her. He didn't need to say it out loud. The answer was in his eyes.

When Jane's cell phone rang, she jumped. She pulled it from her pocket to see who was calling, but didn't recognize the number. "I'm sorry," she said. "I should have turned this off. Would you mind if I took it?"

"Go ahead."

She said hello.

"Jane?"

"Yes?"

"Monty Mickler, the manager at the Avalon Motor Inn. Say, I've spoken with my assistant manager and apparently the man who'd requested unit one won't be able to make the trip after all. I would be happy to rent it to your friend for tomorrow night and Saturday night—as long as she understands that the room doesn't have all the standard amenities."

"That's welcome news," said Jane. "None of that will be a problem."

"Excellent. Oh, and you can pick up the key anytime. You think she'll be arriving around ten?"

"I talked to her this morning, and yes, that's the plan."

"Did you mention you'd talked to me?"

"No, should I have?"

"No, no. If I'm not here when you stop by, you can get the key from my assistant manager."

"Thanks again," said Jane.

"You're more than welcome." He cut the line.

"Sorry for the interruption," she said to Kurt.

"Sounds like good news."

"It is." Maybe for both of them. "Will you tell Emma what you just told me?"

"Yeah, after the reunion meeting tonight. Wish me luck. I'm not sure she'll ever speak to me again after she finds out what I did."

"I don't think you did anything," said Jane, "except try to help the man you loved. As you said, you couldn't change his mind."

"Seems pretty weak though, doesn't it? I should have done *something*."

They sat in silence for a few minutes, each absorbed by their own thoughts.

Finally, leaning back, Jane said, "I want you to know that I appreciate the trust you've placed in me."

255

"Just nail those two bastards."

"I'm working as hard as I can. This will help." She wanted to tell him what she had planned, but because she had no idea if it would work, she couldn't. Even so, he seemed more at peace now that he'd told someone the truth. She had to be satisfied with that.

35

Over the course of the afternoon, Dave tried to call Kurt at least five times. Each call was sent immediately to voice mail. Finding a few minutes between a traffic stop and the visit with Monty he'd been putting off, he stopped by Kurt's house. His kid answered the door and said his dad wasn't around. Six strikeouts was enough for one day. Kurt wasn't stupid. By now, he'd put together what had really happened to Sam. Dave was left with nothing to do except hope Kurt realized his silence implicated him as much as Dave and Monty. He'd left several messages to that effect.

The Avalon Motor Inn's parking lot usually emptied out at dinnertime, as guests went off in search of food and entertainment. It was just after six when Dave parked his car in front of room 1. He found Monty in the back office, his feet up on a footstool, watching Fox News. "Hey, man," he said. A stack of clean towels rested on the only other chair. Dave had to move them over to the desk before he could sit down. "I've got some news, none of it good."

"You're just full of sweetness and light these days, man."

"You said you wanted me to keep you informed."

"And I do." Monty picked up the remote and turned the TV off. "I've got some news, too, except I can't tell you about it just yet."

Dave wasn't in the mood for Monty's games. "Saltus interviewed Kurt Steiner this morning."

"I thought your chief told you to do it."

"No, he said Saltus should do it, but that I should sit in. Not that it helped. Saltus had some information I didn't know about. Get this: Sam and Kurt were homos. Kurt still is. It's mind-blowing."

In reaction, all Monty did was raise an eyebrow.

"Saltus told him about the blanks. It came out of his mouth so fast, I couldn't stop him."

"So Kurt knows?"

"I'm not positive, but he's not stupid. He probably put it together."

"But he didn't say anything to Saltus?"

"Not yet."

"If he goes to the cops, it implicates him, too," said Monty. "He won't. He's too interested in maintaining his good name. Mr. Famous Sensitive Poet and all that."

Dave wished he could be so sure. "Maybe you should talk to him. I've tried. He won't answer my calls."

"Is that all?" asked Monty, checking his watch.

"You got an appointment or something?"

"The wife took the kids to Rowdy's Hamburger Shack for dinner. When they're done, she's dropping a Triple Cheeseburger off for me."

Dave could feel his stomach growl. The fact that he could eat at times like this amazed him. "Okay, I'll make this quick. We found Carli Gilbert's car yesterday morning."

"That right. And?"

"And," said Dave, "I need to know why you did it. Why you murdered her." He could tell Monty was having a hard time figuring out how to arrange his face.

"Why on earth would you think I had anything to do with her death?"

"I found one of your green cans in the backseat."

He laughed. "You think I'm the only one who drinks that stuff?"

"I've been in every grocery and convenience store within a seventy-five-mile radius of Castle Lake and I've never seen one for sale. Don't try to bullshit me, okay? Your prints on the can will prove it."

Monty considered this. "Okay, well, so maybe I did do it. But you gotta understand, bro. I never wanted to hurt her. I loved her—or at least I did once upon a time. You remember when I told you Sarah and I were headed for divorce? I was so screwed up that I started looking at other women. I'm not proud of it, and I'm not using that as an excuse, but I was lonely and frustrated. I thought I'd lost Sarah, and I not only wanted to hurt her, but I needed someone in my life. Carli was there for me, Dave. She was such a good listener. One night, we'd been drinking tequila shots, I let it all hang out. Maybe . . . maybe I told her things I shouldn't have."

He'd figured it was something like that.

"Not everything, but enough, yeah. I didn't think it mattered because we loved each other. I figured when Sarah and I split, I'd move on to Carli. It was hard to end it with her. She was such a wonderful woman. But a few weeks ago, I had to tell her we were done. I couldn't cheat on Sarah any longer. Let's just say, she didn't take it well. And then when Sam's remains were found last Sunday, she threw it in my face, said she should go to the cops with what she knew. I mean, I couldn't let that happen, could I? My choice was to either continue the relationship with a sword hanging over my head, or . . . or Carli would have to go."

Monty was usually too smart to make such a stupid mistake, but when he drank, his good sense deserted him.

"So, what are we gonna do?" asked Monty. "Is there any way you can help me out? I'm not sure what I'd do if some DA put the screws to me. You're stronger than I am, Dave. I've always relied on your strength."

Monty's tone changed when he wanted something. His usual confidence would disappear. True, Dave owed Monty his freedom, so the stuff he'd done over the years to keep Monty out of jail seemed justified. And yet, no matter how many times Dave pleaded with him to change his ways, he never did.

"So, can you help me?" asked Monty.

"I'll do what I can."

"You're the man."

"I wish I knew what makes you tick."

"Yeah? What's that mean?"

"Sometimes, it's like . . . I don't understand you at all."

"You and me, Dave, we're closer than brothers. It's what that Bible verse says, where David talks about his friend Jonathan. He said their feelings surpassed the love of women."

"Huh?"

Hearing the bell jingle over the front door, Monty got up.

"Better shove off," said Dave. "I just wish I understood you better. Like, what makes you happy." He headed for the door.

Stopping Dave and turning him around, Monty stood with his hand on the doorknob. He kissed Dave on the cheek, letting his lips linger.

Dave backed up until he hit the wall.

"Power makes me happy, man. Simple as that. Are we *communicating* now? We love each other. You tell me that all the time. Except you love me more. Understand? Is that simple enough for you?" Opening the door, he walked out into the front office, where both of his sons raced up to wrap their arms around his legs.

Dave nodded to Sarah as he skirted around the counter and made a hasty exit. He stood outside the office for a few seconds, wondering what the hell had just happened.

His cell phone rang. Glancing at it, he saw that it was his girlfriend.

"Hey, Paula," he said, his voice sounding a tad strangled.

"Hey, yourself. I was just at the grocery store and found two beautiful rib eyes on sale. Don't suppose you're free for dinner tonight."

"Um, sure, I could be."

"I've got baked potatoes ready to go into the oven, and salad fixings. I'm sure there's still some of that thousand island dressing you like in the fridge. Are we on?"

Her home was forty-five miles away. "Give me an hour."

"Can you stay the night?"

"Don't see why not."

"Perfect, baby. See you in sixty."

As Dave slid into the front seat of his SUV, his thoughts continued to pinball around his tired brain. Monty had never spoken to him like that before. He sensed that something big had just gone down between them, but for the life of him, he wasn't sure what it was. Maybe in the next hour he could figure it out.

36

Jane and Leslie followed a young woman to a table next to a brightly painted wall in the Red Fez restaurant. As they sat down, Jane said, "Boy, I'm glad you made reservations."

Leslie glanced around. "I've never seen the place so packed. It's probably because of homecoming—and the reunion. We often have special events going on in town on weekends, especially in the summer and early fall, but this is unusual."

They had to shout to be heard.

"Must mean the word-of-mouth on this place is good," said Jane.

Leslie gazed at her a bit too long, looking a little too happy.

"Careful. People will notice."

"I don't care. You look beautiful tonight."

Jane rarely blushed, but she did now. "I'll give you my thoughts on how you look later. In private."

Leslie's smile widened. "Let's hope the food here pleases the gourmet."

"I'm easier to please than you might expect." Jane was just glad they'd finally found some time to get together.

"How's the podcast investigation going?" asked Leslie, opening the menu.

"It's picking up. I got a text right before I left the lake house. My producer is pretty pleased with what I've been digging up."

"Anything you care to share?"

"Not at the moment. But I will, when I can."

Jane was starting to feel a bit anxious about what she'd set in motion. Before arriving at the restaurant, she'd stopped by the motel to pick up the room key. Monty had been in the middle of a heated conversation with an annoyed customer, which meant she didn't have to answer any probing questions about Becca.

"Oh, they have the couscous tfaya tonight," said Leslie. "It's lamb with these sweet, spicy caramelized onions and raisins. The tagines are also good. One tagine serves two. They bring the clay pot right to the table."

Jane wished the noise level wasn't quite so loud. Shouting wasn't a good way to conduct an intimate conversation.

"You thinking what I'm thinking?" asked Leslie.

"Should we order our food to go?"

That elicited another smile.

As they decided on what to get, a large figure loomed over the table.

"Cordelia," said Jane, glancing up. "What are you doing here?"

"Oh, you know, I was in the neighborhood."

"Nice to see you again," said Leslie, smiling at her. "Listen, Jane, I need to use the restroom. On my way back, I'll put in our order."

Jane waited for Cordelia to sit down on the chair Leslie had just vacated. "You're wearing a red fez."

"When in Rome," she said, "Or in this case, Casablanca. I'd sing a few bars of 'As Time Goes By,' but you wouldn't be able to hear me."

"Where'd you get it?"

"Where else? My trunk."

"Do you always travel with a red fez?"

"Not always, but often. Why is this only a table for two?"

"Because there are only two of us having dinner."

"But what about me? You knew I was coming."

"I did?"

"You asked me to give you my official take on Leslie. I am, after all, very experienced in these matters. We wouldn't want to have another Julia situation on our hands, would we?" She pulled the menu over and began perusing it. "I had to park half a mile away. That was one long walk. I don't suppose they serve black-cherry soda."

"I doubt it."

"Blather. Have you ordered us any wine?"

"I'm sorry, Cordelia, I really didn't realize you were coming tonight."

"You asked me to. I said I would."

"Yeah, but . . . the thing is. Leslie is a wonderful person."

"Yet to be determined."

"No, I mean, I think you can trust my judgment on this one. Besides, we're not even dating—officially."

"Come on, Janey. I saw the way you were looking at each other."

It was an argument she wasn't going to win. "Look, whatever our relationship is, or turns out to be, Leslie and I have decided to order our food to go. It's too loud in here to talk."

"Well then, what did you order for me?"

"Um, well—"

Cordelia narrowed one eye. "Spit it out, Jane. You're obviously trying to communicate."

"It's just—"

"I'm not invited. Is that it? You feel you don't need my expertise?"

Jane hated to hurt her feelings, but she didn't need Cordelia tagging along. "Right."

"Proceed at your peril," she said portentously.

"I'm not going to marry her. At least not tonight. There will be plenty of time for you to get to know her."

"All right. I won't belabor the point, at least not now. I will expect a full report in the morning. Anyway, before I go, I should tell you that Wilburn Lowry called. He couldn't find the business card you gave him, but he knew we were staying with Emma, so he called the lake house."

"What did he want?"

"For you to call him first thing tomorrow morning. He said he needs to talk to you, that it's vitally important."

"Vitally? He didn't say anything else?"

"No. Now, as long as you're leaving the table unoccupied, maybe I'll stay and have dinner."

Jane hated to think of her eating alone.

"Emma has that final meeting with the reunion committees tonight. She asked me what I was doing for dinner. I think I'll call her and tell her to join me. She doesn't have to be over to the VFW hall until seven-thirty."

"Great idea," said Jane. "Are you coming to the art festival event in the morning? They're announcing the silent-auction winners."

"I suppose I'll have to be there," said Cordelia. "I don't know why they schedule these things so early."

When Leslie returned, she drew an unused chair away from another table and sat down. "It will be a few more minutes."

Cordelia backed up a few inches and stared down her nose at Leslie. "Since we have some time, why don't we get some basic details out of the way."

"Details?"

"Date of birth. Place of birth. Yearly income. Dating history. Religious and political affiliation."

Leslie looked at Jane, hoping for an explanation.

"I'm just kidding," said Cordelia.

Jane let out a breath.

"There's plenty of time for that later. But," she added, adjusting her fez, "you're a politician, my dear. In the few minutes we have remaining, perhaps you'd like to explain Brexit to me."

37

On Friday morning, Jane and Leslie drove separately to the art center. On the way there, Jane shook her head in wonderment at the night she'd just spent. She couldn't quite believe how much fun she'd had. It was a word she'd almost forgotten. Now that it was back in her life, she was more than a little intoxicated by it.

The food from the restaurant hadn't turned out to be as good as they'd hoped. Leslie hadn't liked her dinner at all, so they ended up splitting Jane's bastilla, talking nonstop the entire time. Jane was beginning to see the kind of woman Leslie was—generous, imaginative, introspective, maybe a little too idealistic—and she liked what she saw.

After dinner, they'd listened to music, mostly oldies, and eventually got up and danced their way into the bedroom, where they fell on the bed laughing. It felt strange to be with someone who was so much fun. Even in good times, Julia had never been like that. Around midnight, deciding they were hungry and deserving of a treat, Jane, brandy in hand, tossed together the makings for one huge chocolate chip cookie. They ate it while playing Scrabble using made up words. The only rule was, whatever you made up, you had to be able to define. It was an experience she wanted to repeat.

Jane arrived at the art center before Leslie. She waved to Emma and Cordelia, who were seated toward the back. The room, which was normally an exhibition space, had been set up with chairs and a lectern. She was a little surprised to see so many people in attendance. She did a quick count and realized it was close to forty. Taking a seat near the front, she offered Leslie a restrained smile when she walked in and sat down next to Cordelia.

The head of the council, Connie Johnson, a gray-haired woman in a blue linen blazer, welcomed everyone to the morning event. She thanked several dozen people for their help with the festival and then launched into a short pitch for the next day's main event: Cordelia Thorn's talk about the importance of community theater in the life of a small community, to be delivered at the Rialto theater. Cordelia stood, gratefully and skillfully acknowledging the applause. Once all that was out of the way, the names of the silent auction winners were announced. People stood as their names were called. The gourmet dinner was the last. When Leslie's name was read, Jane turned to smile at her. Standing, Leslie clasped her hands together like a winning prize fighter and beamed at the crowd. Jane couldn't help but wonder how much she'd bid. The art council was no doubt appreciative of her generosity, which was the point. Jane was grateful, too, because it meant another date with the mayor.

As everyone began leaving, Jane stood up and looked around. Leslie nodded to her as she ducked out, holding a pretend phone to her ear and grinning. Cordelia was engulfed by people wanting a moment with her, which left Emma alone—just the person Jane wanted to talk to. They walked out together. It was a beautiful day, perfect weather for that night's bonfire.

"How did your reunion meeting go last night?" asked Jane. What she really wanted to know was whether or not Kurt had talked to her about Sam.

"So-so," said Emma. "You know, don't you? Kurt said he'd already spoken to you."

They walked to a bench in the park and sat down.

"Initially, I guess, I was both shocked and confused," Emma began. "But I understand some things now, why Sam was the way he was."

"You mean about him being gay? You never wondered?"

"I did, sure, but it's not the kind of thing you ask the guy you're dating. And honestly, I figured if it turned out he was gay, I was okay with it. Even then, as much as I cared about him, I didn't think we'd be together forever. More than anything, we were friends."

"And the rest?"

"That's harder. Kurt was afraid I'd never want to see him again after I found out, but that wasn't my reaction at all. He was sucked into that ridiculous insanity pretty much against his will. He tried to talk Sam out of it. Between you and me, I think he's really scared that when this comes out, he'll go to jail. But how could he? He's every bit as much of a victim as Sam. The only reason he never spoke up about what happened was because of Monty's threat. Who knew Dave and Monty were such scum?"

"I'm glad Sam had you in his life," said Jane.

"Sam *and* Kurt," said Emma. "Oh, gosh, look at the time. I've got so much to do before tonight."

"Did you get a chance to talk to your uncle Grady?"

"Yes, he said he'd be free at eleven."

"I can't thank you enough."

"I wish you'd tell me what you have planned."

"Let's just hope it works."

Emma sighed as she rose from the bench. "I wish I weren't leaving next week. But I have to get home. Philip has been making more noises about getting back together."

"How do you feel about that?"

"It's never going to happen."

There was a finality in Emma's voice.

"And Scott? Is he still texting you nonstop?"

"That guy is bonkers. He's one person I'll be glad to put in the rearview mirror."

"You're being careful, right?"

"As careful as I can be. I really don't see him trying to hurt me. I just think he's obsessive. Once I'm gone, he'll find someone new to fixate on. Lucky her."

Wilburn Lowry was carrying a broken rocking chair down the front steps as Jane pulled up outside the Mickler house a few minutes later. She rolled down the window and called, "Where do you want to talk?"

"Give me a sec," he called back, stuffing the chair above a bunch of other junk toward the back of the van. And then he slipped into the seat next to her.

"What's up?" she asked.

"You're never gonna believe this. I found something last night I think could be important. Down in the basement, under a lot of other crap, I discovered a black plastic leaf-and-lawn bag with a varsity letterman jacket inside. When I saw the blood on it, I closed it right back up."

"Are you sure it was blood?"

"Trust me. I know what old blood looks like."

"Do you know who the jacket belonged to?"

"Dave Tamborsky. There was a patch with his name sewn on the inside, near the collar."

Jane hadn't expected that.

"What should I do with it?" asked Lowry.

"Leave it right where you found it."

"Already done that. But what do you think it means?"

Her mind was already spinning through the possibilities.

"What I wonder is, if it belonged to Dave, why did Monty have it?" Lowry said. "It looked like he tried to remove the chenille letter. He got it halfway off, but then just left it. What's all that about?"

"I'm not sure." What if it actually was Sam's blood? If so, then it was a direct link between Dave, Monty, and Sam's murder.

"Do you think Dave might have had something to do with Sam Romilly's death?" asked Lowry.

"Yeah, I do."

"So, should we turn it over to the cops?"

"I think we have to." She didn't have a lot confidence in the local police, though she did feel she had no other choice than to take a chance. Emma insisted that her uncle, the police chief, Grady Larson, was a man with a great deal of integrity. Jane was about to test that theory.

38

Classmates began to arrive at Emma's lake house around nine that night. Kurt had left the homecoming game early so he could help get the fire on the beach going. The temperature was in the low sixties, with minimal wind and clear skies; a perfect evening for a bonfire.

Earlier in the day, a few guys from the class had dug a pit in the sand and unloaded a bunch of firewood from a U-Haul, carrying it down to the beach. Some of the wood seemed green to Kurt, though other logs were excessively old and dry. With the help of fire starters, the blaze was finally going strong. Several dozen metal tiki torches had been set up around the property, all filled with citronella to ward off mosquitos. Standing on the patio and watching as more and more classmates began to congregate down by the lake, Kurt found it a lovely sight.

Emma had been flitting from person to person, welcoming everyone, explaining that the grills were almost hot and it wouldn't be long before the buffet table, set up on the patio, would be stocked with burgers, brats, buns, all the fixings, as well as potato chips and brownies.

Ted drifted in around ten, saying that the Castle Lake Knights had lost again. That explained why people had been arriving early.

He stood with Kurt near the keg for a while and talked to friends, most of whom they hadn't seen in years. Kurt judged that maybe half the guests were down on the beach. He was beginning to smell smoke from the sizzling brats, so that would change as soon as the round chafing dishes were filled.

Monty and Dave hadn't arrived yet. Kurt wondered if they'd even put in an appearance. Looking around for Emma, he excused himself and went into the house. They hadn't had a chance to talk privately since last night. If he was going to enjoy the evening at all, he needed to make sure things were still okay. Finding her alone in the living room, he partially closed the pocket doors so they could have some privacy.

Emma seemed deep in thought. She stood quietly staring up at the painting of her mother and father above the mantel.

"What are you thinking?" he asked, moving up next to her.

With her eyes still fixed on the painting, she said, "They were so happy. Don't you wonder how that happens?"

"I don't think it ever just happens. I think it takes work."

"But there has to be . . . something. A shared set of values, beliefs, whatever. I worked at my marriage, but it fell apart anyway."

"I'm not sure Philip was trying as hard as you were."

"No, you're right. We shared a lot of passion, at least early on, but clearly we had different ideas about the ground rules."

"Relationships are always difficult."

"Maybe, but my parents made it look easy." She sat down on one of the couches.

Kurt sat down on the couch across from her.

"Philip texted me a few minutes ago. He said he'd pick me up at the airport in San Jose, that he really wanted to, but now he's getting some friend to do it. I texted back that I was an adult and could find my own way home."

"How are you going to pull off living with him until Verity graduates?" asked Kurt.

She shook her head. "With my teeth gritted and my eyes averted."

"Are we okay, Emma? You and me?"

"We're fine. I think I was just in shock last night. It's a lot to take in."

"Sam never wanted to hurt you. Neither did I." She hadn't really answered the central question he'd put to her. "You never suspected Sam was gay?"

"I suppose, if I'm honest, there were a few tells. I noticed the way he looked at other guys. He was the captain of the swim team, so I guess I thought he was looking at them to judge what kind of swimmers they might be."

Kurt couldn't help himself. He laughed at the absurdity.

"Yeah, I know. Talk about naive."

"No, I'm not laughing at you. It's what we all do. We spin these stories when we don't understand something. It's so human."

Kurt turned when he heard a knock.

"Am I interrupting something important?" asked Ted, sticking his head inside the doors.

"Not at all," said Emma. "Come join us."

Removing a folded piece of typing paper from the back pocket of his jeans, he came in and handed it to her. "That's the quote I promised you on the electrical repair. You were right. The first guy you had out here probably took one look at the house and jacked the price up accordingly."

"Just what I thought," said Emma.

"But, yesterday, while I was looking around, I did find some other things you really need to address."

"Such as?"

He sat down next to Kurt. "Well, most critically, the roof. It needs to be replaced as soon as possible. You've got some water damage in a couple of the bedrooms, which you may have noticed. It's only going to get worse, and the fix will be more expensive the longer you wait. Also, I found a couple of worrying cracks in the foundation. That should be looked at by a structural engineer. I don't think it's anything that can't be repaired. Also, you have plumbing problems."

"Ugh," said Emma. "Should we just tear the place down?"

"No," said Ted, laughing. "Your parents put off the repairs and they shouldn't have, which has left you with a lot of work to do, but this house is incredible. I think that you should consider contacting the state historic-preservation office to ask that it be placed on the national historic register."

"Seriously?"

"I can get you some information if you want."

"What?" asked Kurt, seeing a look of distress on Emma's face.

"How am I going to handle all this from California? And who can I trust to do the work?" She sat back, drumming her fingers on the arm of the couch. "You know . . . an idea just occurred to me. The guy who caretakes the property when I'm gone is moving to Arizona to be closer to his daughter. I've been talking to another guy, hoping to convince him to take it over, but the truth is, I don't like him. What if—" She looked at Ted. "What if I hired you to do the repairs? You said you planned to move back to Castle Lake, that you and Kurt were thinking of buying a house together. What if you lived here, took care of the place while I'm away?"

Kurt and Ted exchanged glances.

"Let's think this through," said Emma. "As far as I'm concerned, you two could live here rent free as long as the grass gets cut regularly, the flower beds tended, and the snow shoveled in the winter. I would pay for all the repair materials if you'd chip in the work. Does that sound like something you two might be interested in?"

Kurt couldn't believe his ears. Living in a place like this would feel like a dream.

"It's tempting," said Ted.

"The other proviso would be that you'd need to keep one of the bedrooms free for me, and a second for my daughter, should I ever convince her to come here. There are five bedrooms, so that still gives you three for your own use—say, if Danny wants to come stay here, too. All I ask is that you treat the place the way you would your own. We could put this all into a contract. Spell it all out."

"I can't spend my time just working on this house," said Ted.

"No, I understand that. If what you said about the roof is correct, maybe you should start there. I don't really care how long it takes to do the repairs, as long as the house doesn't fall apart in the meantime. I guess I should ask how much you think the materials would cost?"

"It won't be cheap. Maybe twenty thousand. Likely more, depending on what I find."

"I would happily caretake the grounds," said Kurt.

"I never even took the pontoon out of the boat house this summer. You would have use of that, too."

Ted took hold of Kurt's hand. "I think we should do it."

Kurt wasn't one for snap decisions, but this was an offer he couldn't pass up. "I'm in, too."

"Fabulous." Emma clapped her hands. "We have a deal. Well," she said, pushing off the couch, "I better see to my guests."

Still holding hands, Kurt and Ted followed her out.

Kurt was talking to Jane, Cordelia, and a bunch of old classmates when Dave finally appeared. He was alone, in uniform, and looking about as stone-faced and grim as Kurt had ever seen before. Glancing around nervously, he shook a few hands, slapped a few backs. When he caught Kurt's eye, he made straight for him. They walked a few paces away from the crowd, away from the bonfire and the light from the tiki torches.

"Hey, man," said Dave, thumbs hooked over his belt. "Why didn't you answer any of my calls?"

"You know why."

"Look," he said, his eyes skirting the crowd, "about those blanks. I can explain."

"You don't need to."

He moved closer, lowering his voice to a whisper. "But we're okay, right? You're going to keep your mouth shut?"

Matching Dave's whisper, Kurt said, "If I could figure out a way to burn you and Mickler to the ground and not get caught, I would. Who knows when an idea might occur?"

Sweat began to appear on Dave's forehead. "Uh-huh. But—"

"Shove off."

"But—"

"Get the hell away from me."

A while later, Monty arrived with his wife. Kurt turned his back on them and went over to stoke the bonfire. As he stood looking down into the flames, a man in a clerical collar strolled up.

"Hey, Kurt," the man said. "Long time no see."

The guy was decidedly fat, at least two hundred and fifty, maybe three hundred pounds. His head was shaved, and he sported a beard that surrounded his lower jaws.

"You don't recognize me, do you."

"I'm afraid I don't," said Kurt.

"Ty Niska? Remember me?"

Kurt nearly dropped the poker. "Jeez, man. I can't believe you came." Ty's hands were covered in tattoos. "You're . . . a minister?"

"I am. Surprising, huh? You probably figured I'd end up dead or behind bars."

"Well—"

"No judgment. You'd have been right. I was headed in a pretty dark direction after graduation. Got heavily into drugs and ended up spending four years in lockup. As soon as I got out, I reoffended. That time I was in for six. It took a while, but I gradually turned it around, with God's help."

"Really," said Kurt. "I mean, wow."

"How you doing? I heard you married Vicki Nestor, had a kid."

"All true," said Kurt, walking over to get another log. "But I'm divorced now. I've taken over running my parents' meat market."

"Cool."

They stood next to each other in the light of the bonfire, arms folded, watching as people drifted from group to group.

"Pretty good turnout," said Ty.

"Where are you living now?"

"Chicago. Listen," he said, waving at someone across the way, "I heard Sam's bones were found. What's going on with that?"

"Tell me something. How much did you know about Dave and Monty's plan to get rid of Sam?"

"They told me it was just a prank. Nobody was supposed to get hurt. I mean, there was no way. I put blanks in those revolvers. When Sam got shot, I took off as fast as I could. Neither Monty or Dave would talk to me about it later except to tell me to keep my mouth shut. Believe me, I stayed as far away from you guys as I could for the rest of my senior year."

"I wondered if you were in on it," said Kurt.

"No way. I didn't sign up to be part of a murder, man. That's what happened, right? Mickler must have fired the kill shot from the woods?"

Stepping back into the shadows, Kurt briefly explained what he'd learned.

"Wow, that's dark," said Ty. "So what's happening with the investigation?"

"Officially, very little. Tamborsky works for the police these days. I don't know this for sure, but I suspect he's put a damper on it."

"I ran into him up on the patio. He didn't seem all that friendly. Couldn't get away from me fast enough."

"Doesn't surprise me."

They stood and gazed into the fire for several minutes, neither one speaking.

"Tell me this," said Kurt finally. "You're a minister now. How do you live with all the bad stuff you did?"

"I guess, in the end, you have to repent. I know—blah, blah, blah. What I mean is, you have to radically change the way you live. And then you ask God for forgiveness."

"You think you've been forgiven?"

"I don't think it, I know it. I mean, if redemption isn't possible, why go on living?"

As they continued to talk, Dave and Monty stomped their way through the sand toward them. If the situation weren't so serious, Kurt would have found it funny.

"Hey, Ty," said Monty, sticking out his hand. "Didn't expect to see you here."

"I got a written invitation. Seemed kind of churlish to turn that down."

"You're, like, a minister now?"

"I'm the assistant pastor at the Church of Christ's Kingdom in the Washington Park section of Chicago. I also work for an outreach program that helps guys adjust back into the community after they leave prison."

"Good man," said Monty. "You really landed on your feet."

So far Dave had remained silent, mostly looking over his shoulder, giving the impression of a guy who wanted to be anywhere but where he was.

"You heard about Sam's remains being found?" asked Monty.

Ty nodded, folding his hands in front of him.

"We're still in agreement on how to handle it, right?"

"You mean am I here to talk to the police, tell them what I know?"

"You always did get right to the point."

"No, Monty. That's not my intention."

"Excellent." All through this friendly interrogation, Monty kept smiling. In the flickering light of the bonfire, Kurt thought he looked like a ghoul.

"Nice to see you again, Niska," said Dave, breaking awkwardly into the conversation, "but, you know, I gotta bounce. I'm on duty."

"Where are you staying?" asked Monty, gripping Dave's arm and preventing him from leaving.

"At the Crown Motel."

"Good, good. Well, we'll see you tomorrow night."

"Hope so," said Ty.

After Monty and Dave escaped, Kurt whispered, "Watch your back."

"Yeah, I picked up on that. I might sleep in my car tonight."

They spoke for a few more minutes, and then, as Ty faded back into the crowd, Kurt made his way up the lawn toward the patio. He was halfway there when he heard shouting.

"Get your hands off me," came Emma's voice.

Kurt took off running, finding her behind a fir tree, where Scott Romilly was trying to wrestle her to the ground. Grabbing him around the waist, Kurt yanked him off and then swung at him, connecting a right to the side of his face.

Scott howled, staggering back.

"He's crazy," said Emma, backing up. "And he's drunk."

"Oh lordy," said Scott, touching his face and grinning. "If it isn't Miss Emma's boy toy." He leaned over and snatched a pint of booze off the grass. "Mr. Stud Muffin to the rescue."

"Shove off," said Kurt, "before I beat the living crap out of you."

"My, my. A threat from the town butcher. I'm terrified." Weaving his way once more toward Emma, he stumbled and fell. "Oops," he said, trying but failing to right himself. "Seem to have misplaced the ground."

"He can't drive in that condition," said Emma.

"What are we supposed to do with him?" asked Kurt.

"I have no idea. Maybe we could lock him in a closet until he sobers up."

"Hey folks, not nice to talk about a man like he's not there."

"Why can't you leave me alone?" demanded Emma.

"Because I adore you with all my freakin' heart. Okay, so you've been cheating on me all summer with all manner of scumbags—exhibit one is standing right next to you—but I forgive you because that's the kind of guy I am."

"Scott, listen to me," said Emma. "I think I should call your dad. He can come pick you up."

"No way," he said, scrambling to his feet. "I'm not a child. The old man always thinks he's gotta clean up after me, but I can clean up after myself." He stopped, held up a finger. "Wait, that didn't come out right."

Emma took out her phone.

"No you don't," said Scott, lunging for it.

"Get the hell away from her," said Kurt, shoving him back.

Emma spoke into her phone. "Mr. Romilly? This is Emma Granholm."

"Nope, not happening," said Scott, turning and rushing off into the darkness.

Good riddance, thought Kurt.

Emma spoke for another minute or so and then hung up. "He's coming."

"Should I go after him?" asked Kurt.

"I suppose. Maybe you could sit on him until his father gets here."

Kurt had some trouble locating Scott. By the time he found him, he was in his car, skidding his way toward Ewing Road. "Hey, man, stop," Kurt called, standing in the middle of the private drive. Taking out his own cell, he called 911. "Ah, hi. There's a guy who's just left a party at Ice Lake. The Granholm house. He's drunk and heading for town via Ewing Road. I'm afraid he's an accident waiting to happen." The operator assured him that a squad car was in the area and that they'd check up on him.

Knowing it was the best he could do to save the guy from himself, Kurt turned away and returned to the party.

39

The text came in just as Dave pulled up to the curb outside his dad's house. It was from Monty:

> u left before i could talk to u. everything
> is handled. After tonight, all will be good.
> Monty to the rescue. Fist pump!!!!

What the hell did that mean? Some new horror, no doubt. Going in the front door, Dave found the TV on but the couch empty. "Pop?" he called. "You here?"

His father stuck his head out of the kitchen. "I'm making some microwave popcorn. You want some?"

"Nah, I'm good." Dave sat down on the recliner by the front window. On the table next to him was a yellow flyer. He'd seen them in town and knew what they were. He was surprised to find one in his father's house. When his dad returned to the room with the popcorn still in the bag, Dave held it up. "What's this?"

"Nothing."

"The Klan, Pop? Get rid of it. You don't believe that crap."

"No."

"I'll throw it away for you."

"Just put it back on the table where you found it."

"Seriously?" Reluctantly, Dave did what he was told. "Look, can you turn the TV off?"

"Why? It's almost time for Hannity."

"Just for a minute? I need to talk to you."

"If it's about that doctor's appointment—"

"It's not." His sister had called to tell him it would be a few more days before the test results would be back. The doctor agreed that their dad's short-term memory was impaired, but beyond that, he wouldn't comment. Dave was glad his sister had taken the lead on this, as she always did. At least when Dave went to prison, his father would still have her in his life to care for him.

Once the TV was off and his dad was munching on the popcorn, Dave looked down at his hands and said, "Honestly, Pop, I don't know where to begin."

"Begin what?"

"I . . . I did something really bad. It was back in high school. And then, to cover it up, I did something even worse."

Shifting in his seat, his father said, "I don't want to hear it."

"What? But I need to tell you."

"Nope. Whatever it is, if it's forgiveness you're after, you got it. I'm not perfect, either, you know."

"I know, but—"

"I'd hate to be judged by the worst thing I ever did."

That stopped Dave. The comment made sense. He felt as if his dad had thrown him a life raft.

"I was in 'Nam, son. You don't think I did stuff I regret? Things I'm ashamed to even think about? A man lives with what he's done, he doesn't whine about it. He doesn't cry or second-guess himself, he just gets on with it. Whatever you did, David, be a man. You hear me?"

"Yeah," said Dave.

"Good, now can I listen to my program?"

"I suppose."

"Remember: Always be a man. Admit your guilt, but move on." He turned the sound back up.

Is that it, thought Dave? He wanted so much more from this difficult revelation—a real conversation, something deep and meaningful. A father-son moment. What he got were a few tossed off words of wisdom, and then Hannity shouting in his ear.

Grady Larson's house was on Pine Avenue, about half a mile west of the police station. Dave knocked on the front door just after eleven. Grady's wife, Alice, answered it, a bunch of curlers in her hair covered by a scarf.

"Evening," said Dave, removing his hat and holding it in both hands. "I know this is kind of late, but I need to talk to the chief."

She looked behind her.

"Who is it?" came Grady's snarl.

"Dave Tamborsky," he called.

"What the hell do you want?" He was in his bathrobe and slippers, a pipe clenched between his teeth.

"I'm sorry to bother you, sir, but this is important."

Grady seemed annoyed, but allowed Dave to come in. They settled in the study, Dave in an old wingback chair, Grady behind his desk. "Make it quick."

"Okay. Well, so . . . I'm here to . . . to—" He could feel sweat trickling down his back. This was it. The end of the line. His father had told him to be a man, and that's what he was hoping to be. He removed the Beretta from his belt and set it on the desk. Next he took off his badge and placed it next to the pistol. "I've come to tell you that I conspired to murder Sam Romilly. I did it to cover up a rape I'd committed."

Grady bit down hard on the stem of his pipe. "Dave, I'm not sure what's going on—"

"Please," he said. "I have to turn myself in. I'm guilty."

285

"Maybe you are, son," said Grady, measuring his words. "But take my advice: You need to find yourself a good lawyer. After you've done that, if you still want to come talk to me—"

"You're not listening," said Dave, his voice breaking. "I don't *want* a lawyer. I'm afraid that if I don't do this now, I'll lose my nerve."

Grady puffed on his pipe. "You're sure about this? If I arrest you, you can't take it back."

Dave thought of Monty, of what he'd think when he heard Dave had talked. But this had to stop. *He* had to end it before Monty escalated things even more. Dave had seen the gleam in Monty's eye when they were talking to Ty Niska. If Monty perceived Niska as a threat, Ty might never leave Castle Lake alive. The cover-up was turning out to be far worse than the original crime. "I'm sure," said Dave.

"All right," said Grady, removing the pipe from his teeth.

"You need to cuff me."

"I think we can dispense with that."

"No," said Dave, feeling something break inside him. "Do it. But please, you have to understand—I never wanted any of this to happen. I've tried to be a good cop, serve my community. I hoped that would be enough. But it's not. I can't keep this a secret anymore. It was either come here tonight and turn myself in or blow my brains out. As it turns out, I'm too much of a coward for that." He broke down, pressing hand over his mouth as he choked on his sobs. His tears humiliated him. He tried to get a handle on himself, on his emotions, but it was as if the protective wall he'd built inside his brain had cracked in two, allowing all the sludge and slime he'd kept behind it for so long to come pouring out.

When he was finally able to look up, all he could see were Grady's monumentally sad eyes staring back at him.

40

"You're sure you want to do this?" asked Cordelia, unwrapping a third lump of bubble gum.

With her hands draped over the truck's steering wheel, Jane gazed across the highway to the motel. The assistant manager had closed and locked the office door shortly after ten. Ever since, all appeared quiet. "You were the one who thought it was such a fabulous idea," said Jane.

"You shouldn't listen to me when I'm wearing my boonie hat and duck waders."

"I'll try to remember that."

For two days, Jane had been working through roadblock after roadblock to make sure her plan had a chance of success. The problem was, she'd been so focused on making it work that she hadn't given much thought to her part in it. She was used to accepting certain risks, but this did seem a tad foolhardy, even for her.

"What about Saltus?" asked Cordelia.

"He's out there somewhere. When he sees me go in, he'll join me."

"What if Mickler shows up with a gun?"

"Saltus didn't think that was very likely, and I agreed. Too many people around to hear the shot. If I'm right, and he does try to get at Becca, Saltus thought he'd use a knife."

"Lovely. Nothing dangerous about a knife."

Jane didn't respond.

"You trust that guy?" asked Cordelia.

"Saltus? He was my last hope, so I don't have much choice. I did talk to him at length this afternoon. He's kind of dopey and socially clueless, but he seems to understand the basics of police procedure. It was clear to me that he loathes Dave Tamborsky, feels that he's in competition with him. That's probably why he's on board."

"You explained to him that you'd met with the police chief?"

"I did."

After Lowry had found Dave's varsity jacket covered in dried blood, Jane thought she had the leverage she'd been looking for. Grady Larson was Emma's uncle. Emma had called him asking for a personal favor: that he agree to meet with Jane that day. Jane had arrived at the police station at the appointed time and spent a good hour going over the information she'd unearthed. Larson had listened quietly but impatiently, and even before she was done, cut her off, saying he needed her to turn over all the information she'd collected. He allowed that she'd made some progress, but said she didn't have enough hard, provable evidence to back up her theory. On that basis, he said the police would keep working the case—without her help, thank you very much.

Perhaps it was for the best that he hadn't given her time to explain what she had in the works for tonight. Since he hadn't officially shut anything down—and he had no power to keep her from continuing her investigation—Saltus had no hesitation in coming on board. If anything, he seemed excited to be part of it.

"I'm heading over," said Jane.

"Maybe I should go with you," said Cordelia. They were parked in the lot outside Wilburn Lowry's junk shop.

"If Mickler does sneak in through his private little door, I don't think it would be good for him to find a crowd waiting for him."

"Three's a crowd. Cute."

"Wish me luck?"

"No. I don't want you to do it. You haven't thought this through." She gripped Jane's arm. "I have a bad feeling."

Jane had a bad feeling, too, but had managed to push it away. "I'll be fine."

"I had a dream last night, Janey. You were swimming in this big, open body of water and you dove under. I thought you were looking for something and would come right back up, but you didn't. I waited. It went on too long. It was *too long*, Janey. You were never coming back up."

Jane didn't put much stock in Cordelia's dreams. "It wasn't real, Cordelia. I'm here. I'm just fine. You have to let me do this. It's important."

"I know that."

"Cordelia?"

"I need to hug you."

A hug might break her resolve. She didn't want to go there. "We'll have plenty of time to hug when it's over." She pushed out of the front seat and trotted across the highway. She was dressed all in black—black jeans, a hoodie, and boots. She'd already parked a car, one that Emma had borrowed from a friend, in the parking space outside the room.

After unlocking the door, she switched on the overhead light and immediately began to set up the bed, making it look as if someone were sleeping in it. She'd dropped off a couple pieces of luggage earlier in the day, both filled with things she'd need to set up the room properly.

As she finished, smoothing the blanket, plumping the pillow, then standing back to regard her handiwork, she heard a knock on the door. She raced to answer it, looking through the peephole to make sure it was Saltus. "Thanks for agreeing to this," she said, holding the door open for him. She was glad to see he was in uniform, which happened to be dark blue.

Silently, he began to walk around. Checking the sheets on the bed, he motioned for her to come over. "Look at that," he whispered, pulling the bottom sheet away from the mattress. "He's put a heavy-duty plastic under liner on. I'd say he's planning ahead."

It was a disturbing thought. "I should probably set the toiletries out in the bathroom."

"Good call. Where's the secret door?"

She pointed to the built-in closet. While Saltus continued his examination, she opened the hanging cosmetic bag she'd brought and began to put out a few items. All of this detail might turn out not to be necessary, but if Mickler did show, and if he walked in the bathroom, it wouldn't look right if he didn't find anything personal.

Finally, after putting out a pair of slippers and tossing a bathrobe on the end of the bed, Jane sat down under the front window, her back against the wall.

"That's some hidden door," said Saltus, flipping off the overhead light and joining her.

Jane had left the nightlight on in the bathroom, which provided them with just enough illumination to see.

Now the only thing left for them to do was wait.

"I have a friend sitting in a truck across the street," said Jane, pulling her legs up to her chest. "She'll call when she sees Mickler drive in. If, that is, he actually shows."

For the next couple of hours, they talked quietly. At exactly 12:57, according to Jane's watch, her phone rang. She'd no sooner clicked it on than she heard Cordelia's strangled voice saying, "He's here, he's here. He's just driving in. Be careful, Janey. Aw, jeez, I wish I had more bubble gum." She ended the call.

Shortly after one, Jane heard a small thud come from the office next door. She shot to her feet and went into the bathroom, where she climbed into the bathtub and drew the shower curtain. With so little room to hide, she felt she'd be safest there. Saltus planned to fit himself into the space between the wall and a tall bureau, with his weapon drawn.

The sound of a door creaking open alerted her that Mickler was now inside. She'd been hoping he'd give the bathroom a pass, but no such luck. She could hear him pick through the bottles on the shelf under the mirror. He must have opened the perfume because the scent of lily of the valley filled the air around her. She held her breath and tried to remain as still as possible, though her heart was beating so fast and loud that she began to wonder if he could hear it. Glad now that she'd remembered to wet the toothbrush, she prayed he wouldn't look behind the curtain. And then, as quickly as he'd come in, the footsteps moved away.

An anxious silence followed. Less than a minute later, Jane heard a scuffling, scraping noise, but couldn't tell what it was.

"What the—" came Mickler's voice.

"Drop the knife," ordered Saltus.

"Who the hell—"

"Drop it!"

"I don't know what's going on, but you have no right to be in here."

"Kick the knife away from you. Do it!"

More silence.

"Good, now, on the floor. Hands behind your back."

"This is *my* motel," shouted Mickler. "You're trespassing."

"Down on the floor. Now! Move!"

Jane edged out of the bathroom. She saw that Mickler was in a crouching position next to the bed.

"This is illegal trespass," Mickler grunted.

Saltus racked the slide on his 9 mm. "One last time. Flat on the ground, asshole."

Grudgingly, Monty finally complied. As he stretched forward onto to his stomach, he said, "You have no right to be here."

In an instant, Saltus was on top of him, pulling his hands all the way back and cuffing his wrists.

"He has every right to be in here," said Jane.

Mickler raised his head to look her way.

"I rented the room with my credit card, so technically, it's my room for the night. I invited Sgt. Saltus to come in, so he's here legally. You're not."

"I'm arresting you for breaking and entering, and attempted murder," said Saltus, hauling Monty to his feet.

"You set me up. I want a lawyer. This can't be legal."

"Fine," said Saltus. "I'll read you your rights on the way to the squad car. When you get to the station, you're allowed one phone call."

"You'll pay for this," said Monty, switching his furious gaze back to Jane. "I'm an innocent man. I just wanted to make sure everything was okay for Becca. Nothing wrong in that. She's an old friend."

"If that's so," said Jane, "then why did you stab that pillow with your knife?" Even in the dim light, she could easily see the damage he'd tried to inflict.

"Move," ordered Saltus, shoving him out the door.

Once they were gone, Cordelia burst into the room and smothered Jane with one of her bear hugs. Generally Jane found these shows of affection a little too bone crushing for her taste, but tonight, the strength of Cordelia's arms around her felt like safety itself.

"So what do we do now?" asked Cordelia. "Do you have to go down to the station to make a statement?"

"Saltus said I could do it in the morning." In the distance, she heard sirens. "Saltus called it in. A crime-scene unit should be here momentarily."

"Good," said Cordelia. "I need a drink."

"Black-cherry soda? Strawberry?"

"No, amazing as it may sound, I want one of those hard-boiled, mean streets, lemon drop martinis."

"Make it two," said Jane, slipping her arm around Cordelia's waist, "and you've got yourself a deal."

41

Late the following morning, feeling hungover after drinking too many martinis at a bar with Cordelia, Jane stood at the French doors inside the lake house and watched her friend pace back and forth across the patio, gesticulating with gusto as she delivered her speech to a squirrel who sat on a platform feeder about twenty feet away. She was practicing the speech she would give later in the day. Jane had already read it, but it was entirely new information for the squirrel, who looked up every now and then, perhaps when Cordelia made a particularly salient point.

Jane might have been the worse for wear after last night's drama, but she was glad she'd been able to play a small part in finding justice for Sam and Becca. She would visit the police station later to give a statement. She was dying to know what Monty Mickler had done or said after his arrest. She'd asked Bobby Saltus to give her a call, but so far he hadn't.

Hearing the doorbell chime, she hurried to the front of the house to answer it. She found Leslie standing outside.

"Oh, it's you," said Leslie. "I thought it would be Emma."

"She's not here. But I make a reasonable substitute."

Leslie didn't seem to pick up on the humor. "I should have called first, but I didn't want to get into it on the phone."

"Into what?"

She glanced around before focusing her gaze on Jane. "You look tired."

"Well, actually, last night—"

"I know all about it. The entire town is talking about little else." She didn't seem very pleased with the news. "Why don't you come in?"

"You know," said Leslie, unbuttoning her leather jacket, failing to give Jane a hug, "if you were my girlfriend, I might be kind of upset with what you did."

Not exactly the response Jane had expected. As they walked back to the living room, she said, "I thought it was a pretty great result."

"Do you often take that kind of risk?"

Jane turned to look at her. "Not often."

"But sometimes." Leslie removed her leather jacket before sitting down on one of the antique couches.

"I've taken risks over the years, sure. But only when I think the outcome justifies it."

Leslie digested the comment. Changing the subject, she asked, "Where did Emma go?"

"She left around eight to help set up the VFW hall for tonight's reunion."

"Oh, of course. I should have known that."

"Is something wrong?"

"I'm afraid so. I went by the hospital this morning to visit a friend, and I bumped into Wendell Romilly. We've served on several boards together, so I know him fairly well. He was there because of his son."

"Scott?"

"He was in a car accident last night. Apparently he'd been drinking pretty heavily. He must have come to Emma's party because it happened on Ewing Road as he was headed back to town."

"Is he okay?"

"Unfortunately, no." Leslie unspooled a silk scarf from around her neck. "The paramedics think he must have lost control of his car, or swerved to avoid a deer, or—" She looked away. "Whatever it was, the car skidded into a ditch and flipped. He was badly hurt. The worst part is the injury to his spinal cord. One of the doctors told Wendell that there was a chance Scott might never walk again. He has no feeling in his legs."

"That's just awful," said Jane. "I'm so sorry."

"Yeah, it's a real blow. Wendell mentioned that Scott had been dating Emma most of the summer. I thought she should hear about what happened from a friend."

"It wasn't a good relationship," said Jane. "One of the reasons she's glad to be leaving is to get away from him."

"Oh, I didn't know."

Cordelia chose that moment to breeze in. "Ah, if it isn't the good mayor. Are you here to talk about the romantic dinner Jane's preparing for you tonight?"

Leslie glanced at Jane with an inscrutable look. "Maybe."

Cordelia draped herself over the empty couch.

"You look winded," said Leslie.

"Just did a run-through of my speech out on the patio."

"How did the squirrel like it?" asked Jane.

"He was rather noncommittal. By the way, the caterers are back. I talked to the supervisor and he said it's the final cleanup. Just an FYI, there are still plenty of grilled hot dogs in the fridge, so if anybody gets hungry, just let me know."

Jane detected a definite chill in the air. Could Leslie really be that upset with her because of what she'd done last night? "Have you talked to Saltus this morning?" she asked.

"He came by the house to give me an update on the Romilly case."

"Did he say anything about Mickler?"

"He's lawyered up. Refuses to talk. But something else happened last night you probably haven't heard about. Dave Tamborsky went to Grady Larson's home to hand over his badge and gun. He admitted to raping a young woman in high school and then conspiring to murder Sam Romilly to cover it up."

Jane was astonished. By the looks of her, so was Cordelia. "Why would he just . . . confess?"

"From what Grady said, the situation had been weighing on him for years. After Monty Mickler murdered Carli Gilbert and then burned her body to cover it up, Dave said he'd reached his breaking point."

"Excuse me?" said Jane, moving to the edge of her seat. "*Mickler* murdered her?"

"It all came out during the interrogation down at the station after Dave was arrested and booked. Mickler apparently told Carli some of the details of Sam's murder one night when he'd been drinking. Dave was afraid another guy, Ty Niska, might suffer the same fate. Niska's in town for the reunion. He was there the morning Sam died, so if he talked to the police, it would have been curtains for all of them."

"Did Dave ask for a lawyer?"

"No, but Grady insisted," said Leslie. "The guy sat next to Dave during the entire interrogation. Grady was apparently very unhappy that Dave wasn't taking any of his advice."

"A lawyer might be able to negotiate a plea deal," said Jane.

"Dave just kept saying he wanted it over, that he deserved to be punished."

"He must have been in serious pain to do something like that."

"A conscience is a great and terrible thing," offered Cordelia.

"So what will happen next?" asked Jane.

"It's in the hands of the county attorney. I guess we'll have to wait and see."

Jane wondered about Kurt's involvement. "Do you know if Dave said anything about Kurt Steiner?"

"He made a special point to say that Kurt knew nothing about what they'd planned. Sam was the one who dragged Kurt into the woods the morning he was killed. As for Kurt's silence, Dave said that Monty had threatened him, threatened to hurt someone Kurt loved if he ever talked. Kurt did withhold evidence, but the threat should be a major mitigating factor. I doubt he'll serve any time, especially if he agrees to testify at Mickler's trial."

Jane felt her cell phone vibrate. Removing it from her back pocket, she checked to see who was calling. "Oh, it's Evelyn Bratrude. She takes care of my dogs when I'm away."

"We'll be home tomorrow," said Cordelia. "Why is she calling now?"

Jane said hello.

"Sorry to interrupt your vacation," said Evelyn's soft voice, "but Mouse wasn't feeling well last night. I took him to your vet this morning."

"What's wrong?"'

"He's been kind of lethargic for a few days. I didn't think much of it, but when he didn't eat his dinner, and then he vomited once in the night, I thought I should have him checked over. Now, Jane, I don't want you to get upset."

Jane immediately got upset.

"He has pancreatitis. He's dehydrated, so they put him on an IV. They want to keep him overnight."

"How serious is it?"

"What?" said Cordelia, sitting up straight and waving her hand. "Tell me."

Jane held up a finger.

"They think he'll be okay, but I won't lie. The vet said it was a serious illness in dogs. But again, she felt like we caught it in time. He should be right as rain in a week or two."

That sounded like sugarcoating. "I'm coming back."

"Today?"

"I'll leave right now. Which vet saw him?"

"Dr. Thompson."

Jane had taken her dogs to Dr. Thompson for years. She even had her home number. "Is Gimlet okay?"

"She's fine," said Evelyn. "She's right here next to me in the car. We're sitting in front of the veterinary office. I feel terrible that this happened while I was taking care of them."

"Please," said Jane. "You did the exact right thing."

"Goodness, I hope so."

"I'll see you this afternoon."

"All right. Drive safely, dear."

Jane put the phone away and then looked up. "Pancreatitis. I have to go back."

"But he's okay, right?" asked Cordelia.

Jane struggled to push away the crushed feeling in her chest. "He's staying the night at the clinic."

"Not an answer."

"I don't know the answer, Cordelia. I'll call you when I've talked to the vet and spent some time with Mouse."

Cordelia leaped off the couch. "I'll go pack half a dozen hot dogs for you. I know just how you like them. Ketchup, ballpark mustard, sweet relish, and onion. You'll need sustenance while you're on the road."

As Cordelia rushed off, Jane walked Leslie out to her car. "I hope you understand," she said, feeling guilty that she was leaving without making the promised dinner. She also felt more than a little uneasy about Leslie's reaction to what she'd done last night.

"You really love those dogs, don't you," said Leslie. It was a statement, not a question.

"They're my family."

"I'm beginning to understand that. Will you call me, too, let me know how Mouse is doing?"

"Of course. I'm really sorry about our dinner tonight."

"Don't give it another thought. We've got time. At least, I hope we do."

"So, does that mean you're not so angry at what I did last night that you never want to see me again?"

She laughed. "Hardly. I'm just trying to figure out who you are. I learned long ago that trying to change someone is impossible."

"So there will be a romantic dinner in our future?"

"Many, I hope, if I have anything to say about it."

As they stood between Leslie's Audi and one of the catering vans, another van drove up and parked. Three men got out, each with a cleaning caddy, and headed around the side of the house.

"There's so much I want to show you," said Leslie, reaching for Jane's hands.

"That's a question of mine: How does the world-traveling Leslie Anne Harrow spend her free time?"

"Truthfully, I walk."

Jane hadn't expected that. "As in . . . hike?"

"No, just regular old walks. And drives. I've spent the last few years visiting all the small towns in the area. So, for instance, I can take you on an architectural walk, show you the historic buildings that fascinate me. All the strange doors. I adore old doors. I have hundreds of pictures of doors from all over the world. I can take you on a local garden tour, show you all of our wonderful summer gardens. Then there are the lake walks. Oh, and we can't forget the simple town walk, just strolling around a town, visiting favorite shops. We could do the ten-best-bakeries tour. Or the best hole-in-the-wall restaurants tour. And the dive bars. So many to choose from."

Jane laughed. "I want to do all of them."

"The ordinary, the familiar, they're magical. That's what I learned on my travels. I don't have to travel to Borneo to find beauty or meaning."

Squeezing Leslie's hands, Jane said, "*You're* magical." She wanted to do more than just hold hands, but felt she needed to respect Leslie's boundaries, especially with all the catering people wandering around.'

Leslie seemed to have no such qualms. She wrapped Jane in her arms and kissed her. "Maybe we can extend that magic to us," she whispered.

Jane wanted that, too, whatever it meant, wherever it led. She wanted it more than she could say.